JUST CURIOUS

Just Curious

ARIELLA TALIX

Ringmaster Publishing

ISBN-979-8-9856766-3-1
Cover design by: CIF
Photographers: sakkmesterke, Red Umbrella and Donkey, and Viorel
Sima
Library of Congress Control Number: TXu 2-245-721

"What is beautiful is moral. That is all there is to it."

-Gustave Flaubert

Chapter One

Willa Camden squinted at the television. She was trying to figure out how she knew the woman giving her acceptance speech at the Oscars for Best Original Screenplay. Willa recognized the grating tone of the woman's voice and the fake smile with overly whitened teeth. She appeared to be in her early to mid-thirties. The woman simpered at the audience and clutched the statuette to her chest. Her angular face was covered in gaudy makeup. It was too bad, Willa thought. If she hadn't been so made-up, she might have been attractive. Unfortunately, her brassy-blond hair had a terrible case of dark roots.

"There is something so familiar about her..." Willa muttered to herself. She was certain they'd met. Her name appeared on the screen: *Deb Abbey*. It didn't ring any bells; she certainly wasn't one of the screenplay writers Willa knew.

"I'm so proud of this work," Deb enthused nasally to the audience. "It started out as a novel, but I just saw everything in my head so vividly, I changed the work over to a screenplay about a quarter of the way through. Thank you to the Academy and to the actors, director, and the entire crew who brought my words to life so wonderfully. I can't name you all, but you know who you are. And thank you to the people who inspired me." Music played, and Deb turned to head offstage.

Huh, not much of a speech—especially for a writer. Dying of curiosity, Willa grabbed her laptop and Googled the movie—

which was apparently new—to see if that would give her any clue about the writer's identity.

Within seconds, she had the trailer booted up. Her face went scarlet, and she began to shake. Like a ton of bricks, the memory of meeting "Deb Abbey" came back in a rush and settled in her chest, crushing her.

"Fucking bitch!" she hollered at her laptop as her world blew apart. Willa jumped up and thundered around her house, finally deciding she needed to get outdoors before she broke something in her rage. She went to the fireplace where they'd always kept a bowl of smooth beach stones. She loaded up her pockets and ran for the door where she kicked off her shoes. Thoughtlessly, she flicked on the backyard lights and stomped down the stairs to the beach, where she ran to the water's edge. Hot tears poured unchecked down her face. She hadn't even locked the door behind her.

Chapter Two

Jackson Mitchell was looking idly out his back window as he contemplated his next business venture. The sunset over the Pacific had long since faded to night, but he still stood there in his dark house, looking at nothing. His brain did that to him sometimes. He could be so deep in thought, he forgot about his surroundings. He'd only recently bought this house, and its location right on the La Jolla Shores beach comforted him. It was a place where he could be creative. The soothing sound of the water and the glorious sunsets sucked him in. As soon as he set foot inside, he had made an offer on the spot.

He blinked, pulled from his reverie when the neighbor's yard lights went on, illuminating their shared stairs down to the beach and much of the sand beyond. Jackson caught a glimpse of a woman running toward the water, her long blonde hair flying behind her in silky disarray. She was slender and dressed in yoga pants and a lightweight hoodie. He knew she had to be chilly on a windy night in February, even if this was southern California.

Jackson frowned at the sight of her. Her jerky movements projected the message that she was extremely upset about something, and this was made even more clear when he heard her screaming at the top of her voice.

He couldn't take it. This was someone in need of help. Jackson grabbed a jacket by the door and took off after her. When he reached the sand, he kicked off his shoes.

As he drew closer to her, he could see that she was repeatedly wrenching something out of her pockets and heaving it at the water. Each time she hurled whatever it was, she screamed profanities at the ocean. They were pretty colorful.

"Um, I'd ask if everything is okay, but clearly it isn't. Want to talk about it?"

At the sound of a voice close behind her, Willa whipped around, looking like a terrified animal. "What?" she gasped, clutching her heart. "You scared the shit out of me."

"Sorry, I don't mean to startle you. Is there anything I can do?" Jackson realized then that her eyes were pale blue but currently rimmed with red as if she'd been crying. And she was shaking like a leaf. "I'm Jackson Mitchell, your new next-door neighbor. Sorry I haven't been over to say hello yet. I was working up the courage to come ask to borrow a cup of sugar." He shot her a disarming grin, but she just stared at him. "...Now probably isn't the time, I'm guessing."

Willa surveyed him carefully. He had a charmingly crooked smile and earnest blue eyes. She had to look up to gaze at him; he was tall. His dark, wavy hair was tossed about in the wind, and his scruff gave him a distinctively masculine look.

She smiled at him ruefully, despite the fact that she was currently angrier than she'd been in years. Looking back toward the water, she answered, "I don't think anyone can help. It's a done deal, and I'm an idiot. Thanks, though."

She pulled another rock out of her pocket and heaved it into the ocean, giving a hefty grunt with her effort. Just then, a wave swept in and covered her feet and ankles with freezing ocean water. She gave a squeak and a little jump and shivered.

"That's an interesting anger management technique you have, unless there's a fish out there that's been causing you grief. Were those rocks?"

Out of ammo, Willa stuffed her freezing hands into her pockets. She turned to face Jackson and said with a sniffle,

"Yeah. It was my dad's favorite way to relieve stress and burn off anger. It's surprisingly effective. I'm Willa, by the way."

"Willa Camden, yes, I know," he replied. When she looked at him in surprise, he added, "My real estate agent is a big fan of yours. I think she kept hoping for a glimpse of you because she's showed up unannounced a few times at the house," he chuckled. "After I moved in."

Willa narrowed her eyes. "Hmm... I think maybe that has more to do with *you* than with hoping to catch me. Is she single?"

"Oh, yes. She made that very clear." He said flatly as he looked into her eyes. "Look, Willa, you're clearly freezing. Come back upstairs and let me make you a hot drink. You can tell me what's on your mind or not, but I'd lose my gentleman status if I ignored the blue lips and the shaking." At that, he whipped off his jacket and enveloped her in its instant warmth. He put a hand in the small of her back and gently propelled her toward the stairs. Once they were through, he locked the gate behind them and snatched up his discarded shoes. He liked Willa's comment about his real estate agent since it let him know she might be a teensy bit attracted too.

She was just about the prettiest thing he'd seen in ages, but she obviously had quite a temper. He couldn't help thinking as he looked at Willa that she was the quintessential, long-legged California beach girl—blonde, blue-eyed and beautiful. He bet she would rock a bikini when the weather warmed up. His real estate seemed more valuable than ever.

When they reached his door, they toweled off the sand from their feet, and he led her inside.

Chapter Three

"Wow," Willa whispered when she looked around at Jackson's house. "You've sure done a lot in a couple of weeks to make this look so... uh... perfect."

Jackson smirked. "I moved in two months ago. But thanks."

"Seriously? I must be so out of it; I've lost all sense of time lately. I was working like a dog..." She looked around at the colorful furnishings and huge paintings. "You have quite an eye for décor. This is wonderful."

Jackson burst out laughing. "You ought to have seen the dump I left in Silicon Valley that I shared with three room-mates. You'd never have suggested I cared a thing about my surroundings. I have a friend to thank for this. I assigned a bud-get, and this wonderful scheme is what Casey came up with." He looked at Willa who was still shivering. "So, what can I get you to warm up? I can make Irish coffee, hot buttered rum, tea laced with anything you'd like or just a regular hot drink with no booze if you prefer. You definitely need to warm up."

"I've never had a hot buttered rum, but that sounds amaz-ing. Thank you."

"Perfect. I'll be right back. Make yourself comfortable." He took off toward the kitchen, and she wandered through the open living area to study the paintings on the walls. He must have given his friend one heck of a budget judging by the qual-ity of the artwork. Her favorite was a magnificent seascape on the wall across from the picture window that faced the ocean.

It made her feel as if she were surrounded by water. The rest were less representational, but all were exquisite. Staring at the paintings, Willa also wondered what kind of a friend this was he trusted with his home comforts. Did he have a girlfriend? It sounded like a possibility.

Willa heard the beep of a microwave, and a minute later Jackson was back with two steaming, fragrant mugs. He led her to the couch and set down the drinks with a couple of napkins. "Let's have a seat. I turned up the heat a little bit too. It's chilly tonight."

After getting situated on his splendid couch, she gratefully picked up the warm mug and sniffed. The aroma and steam were comforting, so she took a tentative sip.

"Careful. It's still pretty hot," he warned.

She smiled at him over the lip of the mug.

"So, what were you working on?" Jackson asked. When Willa looked at him with a question in her eyes, he clarified: "You said you were working like a dog?"

"Oh, I guess you already know from your realtor that I'm a writer," Willa replied. "I was on a deadline for one book and then had to rush out of town for a multi-city book tour for another one. I'm sorry. I didn't mean to be an unfriendly neighbor, but I guess I sort of missed the part where you moved in. I just got back two days ago, and I've mostly just been trying to catch up on sleep."

"Nothing to apologize for," Jackson replied with a slow smile. "Though I'm glad we're meeting now."

Willa's heart thumped in her chest, but she wasn't sure how to respond. She really wanted to know about that girlfriend now.

"So, I don't mean to be a nosy neighbor, but obviously something set you off tonight. I'm all ears if you need to get it off your chest."

The delicious hot toddy filled Willa's senses with warmth. She was still wrapped in Jackson's big jacket that smelled of sea air and leather. She could feel her anger dissipating as she sipped her drink, enjoying its creamy texture and the lightly sweetened cinnamon and rum flavors. She knew the drink had clove in it, but there were other spices that melded together so well, she couldn't differentiate them. Finally, she gave a big sigh and said, "You'll probably think I'm the dumbest person on earth."

Jackson sat at a comfortable distance from Willa. He wasn't crowding her, but he also made her feel like he was connected to her somehow. His face was open and honest, patiently waiting for whatever she wanted to share. He was calming in the best possible way. Everything about this handsome stranger made her relax.

Willa turned away for a moment and stared at nothing and then said, "I was watching the Academy Awards a little while ago and made a terrible discovery."

"What did you see?" he asked with his dark brows furrowed.

"Let me backtrack a bit so it makes sense," she began. "I was just finishing my senior year at Stanford when I saw a flyer about a writers' meeting at the public library. I was anxious to meet other writers who were hopefully not fellow students, so I went to it. The so-called meeting was run by a woman who said her name was Deborah Abrams. She told us she was a literary agent looking for talent to represent. You can imagine how that got the attention of everyone in the room."

"Absolutely," Jackson interjected with a smile. He saw that Willa was looking sort of emotional and added, "Just a sec. I'll be right back." In no time he'd placed a box of tissues on the coffee table in front of them.

"Thanks," she said softly, reaching for a tissue. After drying her eyes and dabbing at her nose, she continued. "She'd ordered everyone to bring a two-to-three-minute sample of their writing and asked each of us to stand and read to the group. She was horrible to some of the writers and told them to leave before they'd even finished."

"Wow. A real charmer. So, then what?"

"I was so nervous." She looked right into Jackson's eyes and the depth of her frustration was obvious. "Deborah narrowed it down to three of us finally. She said she liked our styles. But then she kicked out the other two when she discovered they didn't have full novels."

"And I take it you did?" Jackson took a healthy swallow of his hot drink.

"I'd been working on mine throughout college. It wasn't anything I'd done for a class—it was just a labor of love. I had about ninety-five thousand words, but it was still rough and not edited at all." Willa let out a long sigh. "I practiced and practiced the passage I'd selected before showing up and reading it to her, and she seemed to really like it."

"Well, so far so good. What happened then?" His blue eyes bore into hers.

Willa blushed under his scrutiny. "She asked me for the full manuscript so she could supposedly shop around for a publisher for me. She was interested—she said—in representing me and she was impressed with the quality of my writing—especially from someone so young. I offered to email the entire document to her, but she preferred that I give her a thumb drive. We made arrangements to meet the next morning at Starbucks so I could turn it over to her."

Willa set down her drink and put her face in her hands. "I was so freaking stupid." She looked up at Jackson with a tortured expression. "All I had from her was her business card, and she had my *novel* that I'd spent years working on. I didn't even think about how to protect my work, or how I would prove it was mine, you know?"

"You were young," Jackson said gently. "And it sounds like you were trying to make a connection."

"Well, it was a big mistake," Willa said bitterly. "As soon as she got hold of the drive, she took off. And because it was on a thumb drive, I have no proof that I gave her anything."

"Uh oh." Jackson looked at her with an understanding expression.

"Yeah. Uh oh. It was the end of the school year, and I had projects due and finals to take—which, in retrospect, she was undoubtedly counting on. Then I had graduation, and my parents were driving up for that. I was so busy, it didn't even dawn on me for a while that Deborah hadn't contacted me. So finally, I called her and had to leave a voicemail. After that, I got a brief text from her that said something like, 'Looking for a pub.'"

Jackson watched Willa's face suddenly crumple in grief. Apparently, the tissues were a good idea.

In a shaky voice, she went on with her story. "My parents were there for graduation, and everyone was so happy and we had so much fun. Afterward, they helped me load all of my stuff into their car, and they dropped me off at the airport. I was planning to visit my friend in Boulder, Colorado for a couple of days and then fly home to La Jolla." She paused to clear her throat. "I'll never forget how they told me they were so proud of me, and I thanked them for everything and told them that I loved them both so much." Willa's voice cracked and she looked away for a moment. Her eyes were clearly tortured by a memory. "It was a good thing we all said those words to each other before they left. On their way home, they were driving down the coastal highway to enjoy the scenery. But as it got dark, a heavy fog rolled in, and a sleepy semi driver plowed right into them. I never saw them again." She bowed her head and stopped speaking.

"Oh my god, Willa. I'm so sorry. How long ago was this?" Jackson wanted to wrap her up in his arms and keep all the sadness away, but he doubted that was quite the thing to do to someone he'd just met. It was amazing enough that she'd opened up to him.

"Five and a half years." She took another deep breath. "You can imagine what it was like. I felt so alone, and the grief was positively crippling. I'm an only child, suddenly the owner of this house and the heir to my parents' entire estate. Plus, I had to deal with the trucker's insurance company. It was a nightmare that took a long time to resolve in court, though it did give me plenty of money to live on... well... forever." She sighed and shook her head, "Anyway, the manuscript I'd given Deborah was the last thing on my mind. But—once in a while, Deborah would send a short text similar to the first one, although her messages grew further and further apart. I eventually realized about a year later that I hadn't heard from her in months, so I called her number only to find it had been disconnected. All I had was a post office box and an email address, but I didn't get any response from her no matter what I did."

"So, I take it, this story has something to do with you watching the Academy Awards tonight?"

"Yes. It has everything to do with it. I finally decided to just forget about the book and Deborah. I convinced myself that the writing had to have been immature and she simply couldn't find a publisher who was interested." Willa took a fortifying gulp of her rum now that it had cooled enough and continued. "Apparently, I was wrong. Deborah Abrams now goes by the name Deb Abbey—or maybe that's her real name and Deborah Abrams was fake. Anyway, she accepted an Oscar tonight for Best Original Screenplay. She looked familiar—remember I'd only seen her once, and it was years ago. I was curious and bothered by something about her, so I looked up the trailer for the movie and discovered to my absolute horror that she stole my book, wrote a screenplay—or had someone else write one from it—and won the damn award. From *my* book! I feel like such an idiot. How could I have let this happen?"

"Oh, Willa," Jackson finally couldn't resist and scooted closer to her so he could gently take her hand. "Don't feel like you did a thing wrong. You were inexperienced and she took advantage of that. She probably recognized immediately how talented you are. You should be proud your book won the award. Isn't there anything you can do to get back at her for plagiarizing your work though? Do you know any lawyers?"

Willa scoffed at his statement at the same time she registered how nice his large hand felt wrapped around hers. "I know lots of lawyers. My dad was a lawyer. But proving plagiarism is terribly difficult, especially since the only proof I would have had that I'd written the book was in the car... with my parents. All I packed when I flew to Boulder was a few changes of clothes. I had my phone, and that was all I cared about for a few days. The laptop was destroyed. I wasn't using anything like Cloud storage back then." She shook her head in apparent disgust. "If I claimed plagiarism, it would be my word against hers, and who would believe a college kid had written something award-winning?"

"Well, it's happened before. And you have a track record of successful books after that one. That ought to count for something," he countered.

"Maybe." Willa looked down at her hands. "No wonder she wanted a thumb drive instead of an email with the file attached. That could have been all the proof I needed. The text messages she sent sounded more like someone looking for a bar or a nightclub because she never wrote out the word 'publisher.'" Sighing, Willa continued, "Ironically, one of my inspirations was Gunnar Dahl. He was a few years ahead of me at Stanford, but he dropped out—already a multimillionaire—

after his sophomore year. He said any more college was a waste of his time, and he had writing to do. I'm sure you know about all of his books and movies. I'd love to get a movie contract for one of my novels."

"Sure. I'm a fan," Jackson said with his crooked smile. "I've also read... um... one of your books. After moving in and hearing Kelly—the realtor—gush about you, I was curious." Now it was Jackson's turn to blush. "I must say, it was not exactly my normal genre of reading material, but it was certainly attention-grabbing... and... um..."

Willa laughed. "Steamy? Is that the word you're looking for?"

"That one will do." The sound of Willa's laughter made Jackson's insides feel all squiggly. *I could listen to that forever. Lord, she sure is pretty, even in my huge jacket and with a runny nose. I would love to kiss that gorgeous mouth of hers.*

Cocking her head to the side, Willa asked, "It's none of my business, but I'm curious. Which one of my books did you read?"

Looking sheepish, Jackson thought for a brief moment and then blurted out, "*The Passion of Three*. God, I can't believe I admitted that to you." He loved the book so much, he read it twice. She could definitely tell a story—that was certain. And hot? Whew!

Willa countered, "Hey, there's nothing wrong in exploring a new outlook on life." *Interesting selection, Jackson.* She tried her best to not smirk at his obvious discomfort.

Chapter Four

Jackson sat staring out the window at the floodlit property and beach, wondering how Willa got her inspiration for her MMF romance. Was it from hands-on experience? The idea gave him ideas...

"So, enough about me and my many tragedies," Willa said. "Tell me about yourself. Are you a native Californian?"

Jackson shook himself back to the moment and answered, "Yes, I grew up in Castroville on an artichoke farm that has been in my family now for three generations. I'm afraid I'm the renegade who needed to get out of farming and do something else with my life."

"You don't like artichokes?"

Chuckling, Jackson answered, "On the contrary. I love them. They taste great, they're versatile, full of fiber and protein and low in calories, and they provide more antioxidants than any other vegetable, did you know that?"

"I was shockingly unaware," she said with raised eyebrows and a grin. "You sound like a commercial, and they sound like the perfect vegetable." Her blue eyes twinkled as she looked into his, and he was glad to see her cheering up.

"They are. I love to eat them, but I just didn't want to devote my life to growing them. Since I'm a born nerd rather than farmer, I went to Berkeley where I studied computer science. I was still close enough to home that if they needed me in a crunch, I could be there. But my family respected my choice. My brother, who's four years older, adores the farming life, so they know their business is safe with him. He actually went up to UC Davis to study agriculture with hopes of being more of an asset to them."

"What happened when you left Berkeley?" She peered at him over the rim of her mug as she blew on the hot drink.

Jackson swallowed a lump in his throat. The way she did that... it could give a man ideas. "I had an offer right out of school to work for what sounded like a great startup. And it was a good experience for a while. I was living in Silicon Valley and made lots of valuable connections there. After a while, though, I got bored and needed to do something on my own. So, I tinkered around and came up with an app that did pretty well. Maybe you've heard of it. I called it Face-to-Face."

Willa's eyes widened as she gasped, "*You* created Face-to-Face? I'm impressed. You must be really smart."

Jackson barked out a laugh. "I guess. I get by, at least."

"So, why are you living here instead of Silicon Valley? Isn't that where the company is?"

Shaking his head, he explained, "I love creating things. When the product took off, I ran the company for a couple of years and then sold it to the highest bidder. I discovered that running a company is *not* my forte, and I don't enjoy it."

"I'm curious then. If you sold your app, I'm assuming— given its huge popularity—that you've done quite well for yourself. So, why aren't you living in a mansion up in Malibu or closer to home in Carmel? I mean, this house is gorgeous, but it's just a... house."

Jackson grinned. "I hardly need eight bedrooms, a tennis court, and a pool. I was ready for a change and this was just what I wanted—a beach house. Plus, I have a friend who lives near here who was quite persuasive. I love the beach access and the view, and the atmosphere is exactly what I was looking for. It's certainly not a small house, by any means, and the neighbors are great." He winked at her and enjoyed watching her cheeks turn pink.

Wondering about this "friend" of his, Willa said, "Well, you can't beat the view, that's for sure. It does get sort of crazy sometimes in the summer months though. I've had to shoo people out of my driveway when they think they can park in it and go to the beach. A few of them ended up getting towed when I couldn't get out. I hate to do that, but I hardly think it's fair to force me to take an Uber because someone wants to save themselves a walk to the beach."

"I completely agree," Jackson said in a serious voice. "In the interest of full disclosure, I also have a larger house in Aspen. It's being renovated now or I'd be there skiing, but it's not quite ready yet."

Looking excited Willa asked, "Oh! You're a skier too?"

"I can't get enough of it. I take it you also ski?"

With a big smile, Willa answered, "I love to ski. One of my best friends went to Boulder for college and stayed there, so every so often I take off for a visit and we ski all over Colorado. It's so gorgeous. I've thought of moving there myself, but I'd miss the ocean."

Jackson nodded thoughtfully. "I know just what you mean. The mountains are wonderful, and skiing is one of my favorite things in the world to do, but there is nothing as soothing as hearing the surf pound outside. It relaxes me and sort of resets my brain somehow."

"Exactly," Willa agreed. "Whew, this stuff really warms you up from the inside out, doesn't it?" She finally peeled Jackson's jacket off.

Jackson could feel his stomach rumbling and realized he had yet to have anything to eat. "Are you hungry, Willa? I'm kind of starving and was thinking of ordering some takeout. Does that appeal to you?"

Blinking, Willa assessed her own level of hunger and agreed immediately. "Yes, actually. Thank you. I'd love something to eat. What did you have in mind?"

"Just a sec." He strode toward the kitchen and returned with a stack of menus that he set down in front of them. "What do you feel like? Mexican? Chinese? Pizza? Burgers? Chateaubriand?" He winked at her and her insides fluttered.

"I could definitely do some damage to a plate of fish tacos, if Mexican food sounds okay to you. This place is excellent," she said as she indicated the menu sitting on top of the stack.

"Perfect. It's my favorite." Jackson took out his phone and placed an order that sounded large enough to feed an army. Looking at her, he announced, "They'll be here in about thirty minutes. Can I refill your drink while we wait, or would you rather switch to *cerveza* with the Mexican food?"

Willa looked down and realized her mug was empty. *That sure went down easy.* "That was delicious, but beer sounds great to go with the food."

Jackson gave her a blinding smile as he took her mug back to the kitchen. This time Willa followed him.

"This is a wonderful space. Do you ever cook?" she asked looking around.

"I do, actually. I've been trying to teach myself by watching YouTube videos," he laughed. "What about you?"

"Oh, I cook a few things, but I'm not all that great at it. A lot of times I just throw a bunch of random stuff in a bowl and call it a salad."

He chuckled at that, and they fell into a companionable silence for a moment. Willa couldn't remember the last time she felt so comfortable with someone right from the start. "So," she said finally, "what else do you do for fun besides skiing and cooking?"

"Well," he thought about his answer. "I run almost every day, and I work out in my gym. And I'm trying to explore the San Diego area. I've been to a few places like the zoo and SeaWorld—which isn't all that fun by yourself. I'd definitely like to learn more and do more. Any suggestions?"

With a serious look, Willa answered, "It doesn't happen until July, but a lot of guys enjoy the Over the Line Tournament on Fiesta Island." Her eyes twinkled as she waited for his reaction. She wasn't disappointed.

Jackson raised one sexy eyebrow, and his eyes turned a little hot. "That's the three-person baseball tournament where all the teams have crazy, provocative names, right? Names like 'My Face or Yours' or 'If You Want Twelve Inches, We Need a Fourth Guy?'"

"It is," she laughed. "It's so funny to hear the announcer call the teams to their respective courts because he has to say the names without laughing too hard. One crowd favorite is 'The Announcer is Gay' so he has to say it over and over in a straight voice. A lot of the teams are just for fun, but there are some really skilled players who take it seriously, too. I haven't been to it for years."

"Then let's plan on it for next July, alright?" He looked hopeful, so she smiled and nodded. She felt warm inside, and it had nothing to do with the rum.

They chatted more about various beaches and restaurants that Willa had always liked. Some were new to Jackson, so they said over and over again that they'd check things out together. Willa wondered if this was Jackson's way of saying he wanted to date her, or whether he just really needed a friend. Either one would have been great, but she wouldn't mind a date with the man.

Finally, there was a buzz indicating someone was at the front gate. He opened it remotely and went outside to meet the delivery guy. Right away, he was back with two enormous bags of fragrant food. Willa's tummy began to growl.

Over dinner, they continued to laugh and bond. They discovered they both had a decent tennis game, but didn't feel the urge to play very often even though they enjoyed it. They thought golf was too boring to use up the better part of a day to play. Neither was particularly compelled to surf—though they'd both learned how when they teenagers. But they did enjoy watching the surfers and loved the beach.

And they talked about running. Willa sometimes ran in the evening to relax after a long day of writing, but Jackson was an early riser who ran on the beach at dawn. Jackson said he'd love to try hang gliding at the nearby gliderport up the coast a way, but Willa wasn't so sure. "I'm not so crazy about that idea," she explained, "mostly because I hear the equipment weighs a lot when you have to drag it around." She gave him a friendly look and continued, "I'll be glad to watch you do it, though."

Shocking her speechless, Jackson suddenly asked, "So, what should we do on our second date?" His blue eyes twinkled as he bore into her gaze.

"Second?" was all she could manage.

"I'm counting tonight as the first. I invited you for a drink and then fed you dinner. I'm enjoying your company immensely, so this is a date."

"Wow. I didn't even realize." She laughed, "I guess I should have dressed a little better and not wiped my runny nose so much."

"Nonsense. You look gorgeous. And I don't mind saying that I'm already developing quite a crush on you."

Willa blinked at him in surprise. "Uh... thanks?" She was also wildly attracted to this tall, handsome neighbor of hers with his dark scruff and wavy black hair that she wanted to run her fingers through, but she was too nervous to say so.

With a tiny smirk, Jackson stood to clear the dishes away and packed the leftovers into his refrigerator. Looking over his shoulder, he asked, "So?"

"Uh... so? So what?"

"Alright, I'll take the pressure off. I've been invited to a party in a few weeks. Will you come with me as my date? I'd like to take you out sooner than that too, though." Jackson got a thoughtful look on his face and went on, "Maybe that could be our third date, or... fifth or sixth..." his voice trailed off in a hopeful sounding way.

Willa shook herself a bit and then laughed. "Are you always so sure of yourself?"

"Never once. This is a complete first for me. You are bringing me to my knees, Willa."

"Huh." She gave him a serious look and then a beaming smile. "I'd love to go to the party with you. In the meantime, I don't know what to suggest, though. What do you like? Galleries? Theater? Sporting events? There might be a Gulls game this week."

"Oh! You're a hockey fan?"

"Mm... not really a *fan,* per se. At least I'm no puck bunny. I don't actually know much about ice hockey, but I played a mean game of field hockey when I was a teenager," she said with a grin. "I'm just thinking about possible new experiences. Do you like hockey?"

"Actually, I love it. Let's do it. I'll get us some tickets right now. Meet me in the living room in a minute." Jackson headed to another part of the house where he quickly brushed his teeth and then grabbed his laptop. When he made it back to the couch, he thought to himself how right Willa looked with her feet tucked under herself on his big sofa. He quickly moved to her side and sat down close enough to touch her. "I'll pull up the seating chart so we can choose our seats." It was a good excuse to scoot closer. She had to see the screen, obviously.

While he was perusing the ticketing site, Willa asked, "So... Jackson? I thought that maybe you had a girlfriend."

Shaking his head, he turned to look at her. "What gave you that idea? I don't, by the way. Not yet, anyway." He winked.

"You said something about your friend who decorated for you, and I thought maybe..." her voice trailed off as he laughed.

His mouth curled into a crooked grin and he said, "Casey."

"Um, yeah?"

"First of all, Casey is my best friend, and we grew up together. He's a guy. He lives out in Rancho Santa Fe now where he has this amazing import and design business and an incredible house. It's gorgeous out there, but I wanted to be closer to the beach. Anyway, I guess you could say that we're close, but he's certainly not my girlfriend." Jackson laughed at his own joke.

Letting out a breath, Willa smiled sheepishly. "Oh, I see. Sorry for jumping to conclusions."

"It's alright. My turn to ask you something."

"Oh. Go ahead."

"How about these two seats? Look good?" He pointed to the arena seating map.

"Sure. They look great. That was your question?" Willa's brow furrowed.

Jackson punched a few buttons on the site and sat back contentedly. "There! Now we have tickets to the game this Wednesday night." He put the laptop aside and took Willa's hand in his large one as he looked straight into her eyes. "No. That wasn't my question. Willa, I'm attracted to you, and I like your personality and brains. A lot. You already know I want to take you out. I want to see where this might go. Are you with me at all on this?"

Enjoying the feel of his warm hand, she regarded him back and said softly, "Yes."

"Wonderful." Jackson looked happy and pensive when he added, "I wasn't going to be so forward, and this may be bad—or rude—timing, but I'm dying to know... when you write about sex, how much of it is from personal experience and how much is just imagination? I'm sorry if that's too nosy."

"Oh, well. Um," she stammered. "Obviously, I've had sex. Some of it has been great and other experiences not as exciting. I've done a lot of reading and research, so I know what sounds good to readers. They don't always want the most factual or realistic scenes, but as a writer I have to make things plausible and steamy enough to keep them interested. As for my own experience, it depends on the book. I've certainly never experienced any kind of a ménage, though they are loads of fun to write about." Jackson smiled at that, and she continued, "I'm not so much into writing about BDSM—and that craze seems somewhat passé now anyway—but I've written about a little light bondage in the spirit of keeping things fresh and unique from book to book. Each partnership needs to have their own sexual chemistry and bedroom personality, or it comes across as cut and paste. Does that make sense?"

"It does. I'm still not all that sure about your experience, though."

"Hmm, well, like I said, I've had sex." She started to laugh and added, "Not for quite a while now unfortunately. But seriously, I haven't made any conscious effort to recreate any of my personal experiences in my books because I see the characters as separate individuals from me. They all sort of live in my head all fully formed, you know?"

Jackson laughed and answered, "Nope. I can't say I do know. It sounds a tiny bit crazy to have all of these people talking to you in your head."

"It's not like they talk to *me*, although some authors do feel that way. Mine act things out more like a movie scene in my brain. I guess it's more visual imagination rather than auditory." She looked down for a second. "Maybe I need to have my head examined." Then she burst out laughing and Jackson joined her. As she quieted, she looked at him with narrowed eyes. "When you're dreaming up an app to invent, don't you see the possibilities and how to make it happen in your head?"

"Of course."

"Well, it's basically the same thing then. A creative mind. Only you build and program things and I write them. You didn't have to experience what your app accomplishes before you invented it, right?"

"You're right." He leaned back against the couch and studied her. "You know you are a fascinating woman, right?"

"I'm glad you think so," Willa said with a small blush. "You're pretty interesting yourself."

"It's killing me not to kiss you now," he said in a gravelly voice.

With a shy smile, Willa whispered, "What's keeping you?"

"Come here." He brought her closer and scooped her onto his lap as she gave a startled gasp. Sweeping her hair back on one side, he began to gently kiss her neck.

A buzz went through Willa as she felt his warm lips nibbling her neck and along her jaw. Turning her face, she met his lips with hers.

After a few minutes of some fancy—and most enjoyable—lip-locking action, Jackson pulled back and leaned his forehead against her. "Kissing you feels as good as coming home after a long, tiring business trip. God, that sounds so stupid, but do you know what I mean?" Willa nodded, so he continued. "It feels so right. Now I'm really sorry I didn't come looking to borrow that cup of sugar sooner."

Willa chuckled softly. "I probably don't even have a cup of sugar in my pathetic pantry, but it would have been fun to meet you sooner anyway—maybe before I left on the book tour. I'm sorry if I came across like a hermit of a neighbor. Still, you've certainly helped turn what started out to be a horrible evening into a spectacular one."

"Spectacular, huh?" He gave her a smug, cocky grin.

"I'd be a fool if I didn't think your kissing skills were superlative, but don't get full of yourself now," she laughed softly.

"I'd like to get you full of *me*, actually, but not quite yet, I think. Are you a 'third date' kind of girl?" He chuckled and gave her a squeeze.

She narrowed her eyes at him in a mock frown as she tried not to laugh and answered, "We'll see." Looking around, she asked, "Do you know what time it is? I need to get up early tomorrow for a phone call to the east coast. They think they're doing me a favor by scheduling the meeting for nine am, but that's still only six here. And since we'll be using this trendy app called Face-to-Face," she winked at him, "I'll need to be dressed and awake enough to appear presentable."

"Bummer. I'm definitely not ready to say good night, but it is after midnight and I understand. I'll walk you home." Jackson gently lifted her to her feet and stood.

"It's okay. I'm just next door," she protested.

"Doesn't matter. It's what I was raised to do." He took her by the hand and asked, "Where are your shoes anyway?"

"Oh, um, I kicked them off before running outside. They're at home by the back door."

Taking her hand, Jackson ordered, "Let's go then." But when they reached her door, and he watched her open it without using a key, he was shocked. "Willa! Don't you lock your doors? It's nighttime, and you never know who could be hanging around the beach." He scowled at her, holding more tightly to her hand.

Looking away, she said in a small voice, "I guess I was too angry to think straight. And I only meant to be outside for a few minutes. Still, the property is gated, so it should be pretty safe."

"And you ran through the beachside gate, leaving it open, too. Willa, you need to be more careful. Let me come in with you and make sure everything is safe, okay?"

Leading him inside, Willa looked around. Nothing seemed to be out of place. Her laptop was on the table where she left it, and the TV was still on. "I think it's all fine, Jackson. You can go home now. Nothing's been disturbed."

"Humor me. I'm going to take a fast look around. Someone could be in here waiting for you, for all you know."

Willa made a sharp intake of breath. "Okay, now you're just scaring me."

"You can never be too careful." Jackson wandered through her house, opening closet doors and looking under and behind things. "I ought to volunteer to stay with you tonight to keep you safe," he said with a wink when he returned to her side. "But everything seems to be fine." He wrapped his arms around her and pulled her in for a kiss. "Goodnight, Willa. I'm looking forward to Wednesday. Would you like to have dinner somewhere before the game?"

"Um, sure. That sounds great. Thank you for everything tonight. You put up with my sob story like a boss." He chuckled at her. "Despite all of that, I had a wonderful time with you. I'll see you Wednesday, if not sooner." She smiled and stood on her tiptoes to give him another quick kiss, thinking, *this guy is addictive.*

♡♡♡

Despite the afterglow of kissing Jackson, Willa was somewhat put out with herself over the next couple of days. She found herself staring out the window far too often when she ought to have been writing.

The jumbled thinking started in the middle of her conference call the next morning. She was distracted by the sight of Jackson running on the beach and bounding up the steps and into his house. He wore earbuds that seemed to be making him smile at something, and he was a sweaty mess with his shirt sticking to his beautifully toned body and his hair plastered to his forehead. Sighing like a lovesick nutcase, she had this sudden urge to brush that lock of hair back when she heard someone on the conference call try to get her attention.

"Earth to Willa! Where did you go? What do you think?" someone asked.

"Oh, sorry. Um... yes, of course," she spluttered, hoping it was an appropriate response.

It wasn't. The call ended up taking longer than she expected, given her lack of focus.

Often, she caught herself daydreaming about Jackson rather than concentrating on her book characters and what she planned to do with them. What was a girl to do with a neighbor like that? Handsome, smart, chivalrous, and a great kisser. She had a terrible time reining in her imagination about what could happen next...

Chapter Five

Wednesday seemed to take three weeks to arrive. Jackson had more productive dreams about what he wanted to do with Willa than he did dreaming up his next great invention, but he didn't want to crowd Willa by imposing himself on her while she was working. He itched to make the short walk over to her place and kiss the daylights out of her... as a starter.

They had to make do with some flirty text messages back and forth and a couple of phone calls.

Wednesday finally arrived. It was a sunny winter day that was freakishly warm for February due to the Santa Ana wind that blew sometimes coastward off the inland desert.

They both felt silly grabbing gloves and jackets to wear inside the arena, considering how hot it was outside. But they knew the rink would be chilly.

Over burgers and beers at a local hot spot, they got to know more about each other. Finally, Willa asked, "So who's throwing the party you mentioned, and what's the occasion?"

Jackson swallowed his beer and answered with a smile, "It's Casey. I'm anxious for you to meet each other actually." When Willa gave him a questioning look, he elaborated, "I think the two of you will hit it off." Then he explained, "The party is to celebrate the success of his business. He's had it now for five years, and he's pretty proud of where he's taken it. I guess it's sort of an anniversary party for himself."

"Cool. I'm looking forward to meeting him too then. Do you think, if I ask nicely, he'll tell me any dirt about when you were a rebellious youth? Stories about old girlfriends, that kind of stuff?" Her eyes twinkled with mischief as she explained, "As an author, I like to probe and hear the good stuff, you understand."

Jackson just threw his head back and laughed. "My life is an open book to you, Willa. No need to ask Casey. You can ask me anything."

"Hmm, okay." She pondered her question before asking, "What was your longest relationship and why did it end?"

Jackson laughed again, "Going straight for the good stuff, aren't you?" She gave him an unapologetic grin, so he went on. "Okay. My longest relationship with a woman was just under two years. We broke up because I wanted to move out of Silicon Valley and she didn't."

"Huh." Willa looked less than impressed. "That's it? Surely there is more to it than that. Did you ask her to move with you?"

"No."

"I see. Did you move to get away from her?"

Looking away for a second, Jackson thought and then answered, "That's possible, though I never consciously thought about it like that."

"So, what was wrong? You spent a long time together. Did you live together?"

"No, we didn't. I don't think anything really went wrong. It was just that nothing was particularly right about us either. I think we just lost interest in each other. I said I was moving, and she said have a nice life." He paused. "I guess the relationship just ran its course and it was time to move on. Maybe I spent too much time running my company, and she got bored. And maybe she didn't want to be with someone who was suddenly unemployed when I sold the business. Honestly, I didn't get into it with her enough to ask. I just moved on."

"Pardon my saying so, but it doesn't sound like much of a relationship. Do you ever expect or want to have a more serious one with anyone?" Willa asked a little nervously.

"Yes, I do." He looked at her pointedly, causing her to blush. "We'll see how this goes." Reaching for her hand, he gave her a squeeze. "I don't want to perpetuate a stereotype about Silicon Valley, but there are a lot of people living there with less-than-stellar social skills, and, as a programmer, she fit right into that mold. She was attractive and convenient, and admitting that probably makes me sound horrible. But I think living here at the beach will broaden my horizons in many ways."

Taking his credit card out of the restaurant folder he asked, "Ready to go?"

The hockey game was loud and entertaining—in many ways.

"Did you know," Jackson asked, leaning close and talking in her ear, "anytime someone scores a goal, it's a tradition to kiss your date?"

"I didn't know that," Willa answered with a laugh.

"Oh, yes. And the same thing goes for when someone is sent to the penalty box."

"You're making this all up, aren't you?"

"Nope. Time-honored traditions where I come from," he laughed. She looked down and saw he had his fingers crossed where she could easily see them.

"So, there's a lot of ice hockey in Castroville?" she asked skeptically.

"Mm-hmm, more than you'd expect, actually." Jackson flashed her a grin that made her insides feel hot and mushy.

Seven goals and five penalty box visits later, Willa's lips were swollen and her head was swimming with arousal. When they appeared on the kiss-cam via the jumbotron, the crowd cheered wildly for them.

Jackson looked smug after that.

On the way home, Willa observed, "I don't think I could ever get used to driving a car that's this silent, or one that can drive itself. Doesn't it freak you out?" Jackson had a gorgeous new 2019 Tesla Model S Performance in a zippy bright blue.

Jackson laughed. "It took some getting used to when I first got it, but it's so much more relaxing when you drive long distances when you know the car is looking out for you. Sometime I'll have to show you the Ludicrous mode."

"Um, maybe not. That's okay."

Jackson remembered suddenly that she'd lost her parents to a car accident and felt like a heel for bringing up doing something reckless. The ride was quiet for a while after that until he asked, "Are you busy this weekend?"

Willa brightened and answered, "Nope. Just the usual stuff. Writing, sleeping, neglecting housework, going for a run."

Looking at her with a sincere expression, Jackson announced, "I'd like to take you out again. I've been having a great time tonight."

Laughing, Willa answered, "This date isn't even over yet, and you're already planning ahead?"

"Yes. I wanted to make sure you understand how much I enjoy spending time with you." At that, he pulled the car into his garage, shut it down and leaned in to give Willa a kiss.

When the kiss ended, Willa smiled. "Would you like to come over to my place and have a drink? I know it's late, but I'm still feeling kind of wired from that game."

"Great idea," Jackson agreed happily. He hopped out, opened Willa's door like a gentleman, and then plugged in his car for the night. Just then his phone buzzed in his pocket. Pulling it out, he grinned at the screen. A text message said:

Casey: Watched the Gulls on TV tonight. Saw you on the jumbotron, you dog. Who's the knockout?

Jackson: You'll meet her at your party.

Casey: Nice. She's... wow!

Jackson: Very. See ya. Busy now. ;)

Casey's response was a series of kissing emojis that Jackson ignored with a laugh as he pocketed his phone.

Chapter Six

He followed Willa into her house. They both dropped their jackets and cold weather paraphernalia onto a chair, and he wandered into the kitchen close on her heels.

"Let's see... I have white wine..." she trailed off as he wrapped his arms around her from behind and nuzzled her neck. She purred and then asked, "Would you like some?"

"Some what?" he asked, dragging his lips down her neck and back up again, nuzzling behind her ear.

"Some wine?"

"Some Willa sounds better." He gently spun her around in his arms and leaned in for a kiss. Chuckling at the hungry little moans Willa made, he grazed her lips and then squeezed her to him as his kisses intensified. His tongue probed her with greater and greater force, and Willa could feel his hardness as they pressed their bodies together. "Let's just go sit down for a while, Willa. I don't need anything but you, and as much as I'd like to hoist you over my shoulder right now and haul you off to the bedroom, I'll wait until you tell me you're completely ready for that."

Willa pulled back and her blue eyes bore into his like lasers. He saw in them every bit of his desire reflected right back at him.

"Would you think any less of me if I told you I'm ready right now?"

Jackson laughed. "*Less* of you? I'd say you're the woman of my dreams." Quickly he bent down and hoisted her up over his shoulder just as he'd threatened to do.

This brought on a barrage of giggles from Willa. "Stop! Put me down. You'll hurt yourself, and then what good will you be?" He ignored her words and her laughter and made his way down the long hall to the big, softly lit bedroom at the end. He tossed her gently onto the enormous bed, toed off his shoes and lay down beside her.

"Oh, Willa." He looked at her reverently. "I don't even know where to begin. You're so perfect."

Willa scoffed. "Sweet talker. I'm already a sure thing." She flung her arms around him and kissed him.

As their tongues dueled and tasted, their hands wandered. Jackson's large, warm hand slid under Willa's shirt and caressed her bare skin. "You're so warm and silky—your skin feels like velvet," he told her between kisses.

Willa also snaked her hands inside Jackson's shirt, and she purred with delight at discovering his firm abs and muscular, smooth back. "You must do more than just running to keep this physique of yours," she observed.

Jackson sat up and yanked off his shirt with a soft laugh. "Push-ups and sit-ups every day." He winked at her.

Willa moaned happily at the sight, and her eyes dilated with desire. Jackson was seriously ripped—pretty amazing for a self-proclaimed nerd.

Jackson's eyes turned serious for a moment. "Let's do the responsible thing for a second and have a little chat, alright?'"

"Umm... a chat about...?"

Nodding, he explained, "Birth control, condoms... you know."

Willa also sat up then and looked serious. "Oh, that stuff. Yes. Well, I have a five-year IUD in place that I've had for two years, so I'd say we're good. I haven't had a boyfriend for about a year now and got tested back when we broke up even though we also used condoms. What about you?"

"I've always been a condom kind of guy—religiously, but I didn't bring any with me tonight, so I guess I ought to run home for a minute to grab some."

"It's okay. I have a new box of them in the nightstand." She smiled. "I had to make a drugstore run today anyway and thought, 'Why not?' Better to be safe than sorry, and it's good to be prepared..." She looked away for a second. "You must think I'm pretty eager."

Jackson gently took her chin in his hand and turned her face to look at him. "I'm beyond flattered, Willa, and believe me, I'm just as eager." He gave her a soft kiss this time. "Now where is that box of condoms?"

Willa indicated the bedside table and answered with all sincerity, "In that drawer behind the dildoes, handcuffs, cock rings and butt plugs."

Jackson's jaw dropped momentarily before he leapt from the bed to wrench open the drawer with so much force, Willa was afraid the entire contents would land on the floor. She fought to stifle her laughter, pressing her lips together.

He burst out laughing when he found the box sitting next to a sedate little black vibrator, and that was all. When he could stop cracking up, he asked, "So were you embarrassed by the sex toy and wanted to make it seem like nothing in comparison?"

"Well..." she shrugged her shoulders and let her laughter loose finally. "Not really, but I guess your reaction says something about you."

"I do like an adventure," he said pointedly, looking into her eyes. "But I also need to finish letting you know that I was tested before leaving Silicon Valley. When I thought about my girlfriend's nonchalance regarding me leaving, I wondered if she'd been cheating. My tests came back just fine."

"Thanks for your honesty. Now come back and kiss me some more before I positively melt into a puddle of want."

Flopping onto the bed, he laughed. "You're such an author. A 'puddle of want?'"

"That's exactly what it feels like." She grinned at him and whipped her shirt off over her head, tossing it away. Her breasts were barely contained in a sheer, lacy bra. Opening her arms to him, she commanded in a silly brogue, "Take me, milord!" Then she snorted. "Did that sound romance-y to you? All the Scottish women probably yell that to their Highlanders, I think. But I don't write that kind of stuff."

"You're in quite a mood, Miss Erotic Romance Writer." He leered at her and then buried his face between her breasts. He kissed and nuzzled them as he reached around to undo the clasp of her bra. As soon as her boobs were free, he grabbed a nipple with his lips.

Willa let out a barrage of moans and encouraging noises that turned Jackson on no end. He switched to the other breast and gave it a playful bite, as Willa burst out with a loud, "Yes! Don't be afraid to get a little rough. I'm not fragile." He held her nipple with his teeth and tongued it quickly. "Oh, yes, more of that please," she ordered. She jammed her fingers into his hair and held him even closer. She toed her shoes off, and Jackson heard them thud onto the floor as she kicked them out of the way.

When it seemed that neither of them could take it any longer, Jackson reached for the zipper on Willa's jeans. Looking straight into her eyes as he slowly lowered it, he asked, "You're sure?"

"Absolutely." She raised her hips to help him drag the jeans down over her hips. They hit the floor along with the rest of her clothes. All she had on now was a lacy pair of bikini underwear that had a tiny bow right over her pussy.

"This looks like a pretty little present," he observed with a crooked smile. "Lucky me."

"Better unwrap it then. But take your pants off too first, please."

Jackson stood and quickly got rid of his jeans and boxers all in one swoop. His erection stood out, proud and glistening. He squelched a tiny snort as Willa's jaw dropped. His arousal grew as her eyes lit up with eagerness. He quickly yanked off his socks and then bent over to drag Willa's panties down her long, smooth legs. He spread her legs apart and lay down between them.

"Gorgeous," he muttered as he reached for her pussy. "You're so wet, Willa. I'll take that as a compliment." Then he dragged his lips along her inner thigh, licking and nibbling as he went.

"You should," she groaned contentedly as she felt his fingers exploring her sensitive places.

He dipped a finger into her a little and then spread her moisture around in the most delicious way. He stroked her clit softly and listened to her sigh and moan happily. "That feels *so* good," she said with her eyes closed and a look of pure contentment on her beautiful face. After a minute, she ordered, "Harder, please."

Jackson chuckled and bent down to bury his face in her. His tongue took over where his finger had been, and his finger slid deep inside her, eliciting a loud gasp from Willa. He added a second finger and began to fuck her with them as he sucked her clit between his teeth.

Willa let out a surprised cry that would have worried him, had she not followed it up immediately with, "Ohmygod, *yes!* More, please."

He lapped at her clit over and over with a firm tongue and thought she might be getting ready to come when she surprised him by saying loudly, "Wait. Stop!"

Dumbfounded, Jackson pulled away from her, expecting to see her upset expression. Instead, he saw one of pure greed and lust. She reassured him by saying, "Spin your body around. I want to play too." He blinked at her for a second, letting that sink in when she clarified, "You know, some sixty-nine fun?"

Not one to turn down fellatio, Jackson immediately scooted around so that Willa could access his junk. He watched as she reached for him, stroking and getting a feel for him with both of her hands. When she took him into her mouth, she let out a long, contented "mmm" that made his balls tighten. *This woman certainly enjoys the heck out of sex. How did I get to be so lucky?*

Jackson went back to his sucking and finger fucking, admittedly feeling somewhat distracted this time by the delicious sensations Willa was creating. The woman was positively voracious.

If Jackson thought he'd been stiff before, he was now as hard as a diamond. He relentlessly sucked her clit, and in less than a minute he had her shaking and bucking uncontrollably. His fingers could feel her baring down on him as her orgasm barreled through her.

Not able to stop himself, Jackson let go too. With a groan, he filled her mouth with hot spurts of cum. He could hear her alternately chuckling and moaning in appreciation. He was amazed as she swallowed everything he gave her and kept sucking long after he was drained. Finally, he was too sensitive to let that continue, so he pulled away and flopped onto his back.

Willa also lay back panting. "Holy cow. Are you always this good, or are you just showing off?"

Jackson laughed softly. "That was off the charts, and we haven't even screwed yet. You're amazing, Willa. Is it too early to pledge my undying love to you?"

"Uh, yeah. A little," Willa chuckled. "But I understand the sentiment." She closed her eyes for a second and shook herself briefly. "I kind of feel the same way." Leaning toward him, she fell into his kiss. Pulling back finally, she explained, "In Romanceland, we call this instalove."

"Well, whatever it is, I'm glad you're on the same page." He excused himself for a minute and walked toward the bathroom, giving Willa a delightful view of his delicious backside as he sauntered away and his equally delectable front side as he returned to her. He had a glass of water in his hand that she gratefully accepted.

Jackson could feel himself stiffening as he watched her drink. She was looking up at him through heavy lashes, her face flushed from sucking his cock. She set the glass aside and licked her lips. He took that as an invitation to kiss her again, and he felt his arousal growing and growing.

Humming her approval, Willa took him in hand and began stroking his length. "I think we're ready for the big event now," she encouraged with a grin. She reached for the box of condoms, and Jackson watched with rapt attention as she quickly sheathed him and spread her legs. She opened her arms invitingly, and he lay atop her without hesitation. He rubbed his erection against her until she was writhing and begging for him to enter her. Finally, he slid into her slick heat. Both of them let out long, happy groans as he slowly retreated and slid in again.

"You're amazing," Jackson whispered. "I feel like I'm where I was always meant to be." He kept up a slow, tantalizing speed as Willa arched her back and ground against him.

"Yes," she panted. Jackson couldn't be sure if she was agreeing with him or commenting on how things felt. Either way, it made him happy.

Wanting to make things last this time, Jackson didn't speed up until he felt Willa squeezing him like a vise. With that, he pulled out and flipped her over on her belly. "Raise up your sexy ass, gorgeous," he ordered as he encouraged her to get up onto her knees. Once she was situated, he rammed his dick into her with a force that made her holler with surprise and want.

"Yes! Like that. Fuck me *hard*, Jackson. I love it," she cried.

Eyeing her beautiful, toned butt, he decided it was time to go to the next level. Gripping her hip firmly with one hand as he pounded into her from behind, he put a finger into his mouth and then circled her anus with it. This elicited another happy moan from her so he asked, "Have you ever been fucked here?"

Willa looked over her shoulder with a coquettish look. "Not yet," she purred.

With a lustful smile and thoughts of many possibilities swirling through his brain, Jackson carefully slid his finger into her puckered hole. The sound she produced was somewhere between a word, a gasp, and an unearthly utterance, and it immediately made him feel like the king of the universe. He created a rhythm of fucking her pussy and probing her bottom, all the while listening to the noises of approval that continued to flow from Willa. Harder and faster he fucked her, and she ground her fingers against her clit. Watching her enhance her own pleasure turned him on like he'd never been before.

When Willa broke out into a full-body sweat and her legs shook uncontrollably, Jackson stepped up his pace and force to a seemingly impossible degree. Unable to stop the orgasm that was crashing through him, he cried out, "I'm coming!"

Willa moaned deeply as her own orgasm took over, and together they shook and cried out in release.

Total euphoria.

Reluctantly, Jackson retreated once again to the bathroom to dispose of the condom and wash up. When he returned, he found Willa curled on her side with her eyes closed, looking completely blissed out. He scooted against her and spooned her, wrapping her in his strong embrace. He kissed her damp shoulder and neck as she muttered on a sigh, "Yep. Instalove. I think I need to rest for just a moment, and then we ought to go take a shower, okay?"

"Sounds perfect."

Twenty minutes later, they were warm and refreshed from the shower. Willa looked into Jackson's eyes and asked, "Want to spend the night?"

"Absolutely."

And so, he did. Neither of them stirred all night long, co-cooned in her comfy bed and wrapped tightly in each other's embrace. They were exhausted, but also more content than either had ever imagined.

Chapter Seven

Early the next morning, Jackson woke Willa with a kiss. "Ready to go for a run on the beach?"

"You have to be kidding," she grumbled as she squinted at the bedside clock. Six am wasn't her idea of fun. "It feels like we just went to sleep. Can't we run this evening instead?" She turned to him then and grinned. "There are other ways to get your heart pumping at dawn if that's what you want."

Jackson considered this for a moment and then capitulated as he reached for the box of condoms. After their "heart-healthy exercise," they went back to sleep for two more hours.

Eventually hunger drove them from the bed, and Willa wandered to the kitchen to make coffee. As she ground the beans, Jackson examined the contents of her refrigerator. He ended up making them scrambled eggs and toast.

"Sorry I don't have a lot of offer. I usually just have cold cereal," Willa explained. Or sometimes I buy a bunch of muffins or bagels and freeze them."

"This is fine," Jackson assured her with a kiss as he placed the plates on the table. "Do you have any fruit, though?"

They ended up splitting an orange, and Willa voiced the obvious, "I really do need to buy groceries if you're going to keep making mc breakfast."

"You'd better get some groceries then," Jackson replied with a flirtatious smile.

Over the next couple of weeks, they spent as much time together as possible, flowing back and forth between the two houses as naturally as the tides of the Pacific right behind them. It amazed them both how comfortable they were together after such a short time.

Willa needed to spend several hours a day working on her current book and discussing issues with her publisher and agent, and Jackson was worried at first that having him around would be too distracting for her. She assured him, "I love having you here, and you're very quiet while you're working too, so it's fine, I promise." Jackson was working on a new brainstorm and spent long hours at his computer. He found working beside her comforting and inspiring.

At the end of each day, they would both close their respective laptops and laugh about how driven they were for a billionaire and a multimillionaire.

"I'm way too young to retire," Jackson said as they fell into bed one night. Tapping his temple, he added, "Gotta keep the brain working."

"I know just what you mean," she answered as she snuggled closer.

Sometimes they went out or had take-out delivered, and sometimes Jackson showed off his newly acquired, YouTube-inspired, cooking skills. They decided he was best at grilling, since that was basically a guy thing anyway. His other results were so-so, but they didn't starve. At one point he suggested, "You know, I could hire us a chef." They both thought that idea had merit and decided to start looking for one. "After all, what's the use of all of this money if we don't live it up a little?" Jackson also thought to himself that it would be fun to remodel their two houses into one extremely large one, but he kept that idea to himself for the time being.

His newly found wealth hadn't changed him much, so he was trying to be creative about using it. He'd already invested a few million into his parents' artichoke farming business, thus making life a lot easier for them, and he quietly gave a few more million away to charities he valued. Neither of these things made much of a dent in his fortune, but so far, he wasn't used to his billionaire status. In a way, he hoped he never got used to it. Being wise about money was a virtue, in his opinion. Although now that he was with Willa, he thought it might be fun to splurge on things they might both enjoy.

One afternoon, Willa and Jackson sat side by side at his table. She was typing away happily while he stared at a blank screen. His thoughts wandered to his money, and how he might use it to increase their enjoyment. *Maybe I could buy an NHL hockey team... or better yet, a football team! San Diego needs one of those since the Chargers left town. But maybe that's not really something I want. I like football, but I don't necessarily want to immerse myself in it on a daily basis. Nah... no football team.*

Willa muttered something to herself as she wrote. Jackson glanced up at her, smiling at the image she presented in the afternoon sunshine, her hair curling around her neck and her eyes focused. She was biting her lip in concentration. He couldn't think of anyone else he'd rather have by his side. She really was his perfect match.

...And then a truly awesome idea struck. *Maybe I could be the financial backing for one of Willa's books to be made into a movie. I love the way that sounds; I know it's been a dream of hers.*

And so, his new computer app took a backseat to his research on how to be the producer and backer for a movie. He wanted to get a few ducks in a row before discussing it with her. He had a purpose now—and lots of calls to make.

♡♥♡♥♡

As happy as she was with Jackson, Willa had some demons to deal with. Once Jackson awoke in the middle of the night to find Willa gone from the bed. When she didn't come back right away, he got up and found her in the living room staring out at the moonlit ocean. So as not to startle her, he whispered her name before wrapping his arms around her. He had a pretty good idea of what bothered her, and this became crystal clear when she turned and buried her face into his warm chest and sobbed. "Sometimes I just miss them so much. They were so young; it just sucks. They were the best parents I could have asked for."

Jackson stroked her back and kissed the top of her head, telling her how sorry he was for all that she'd lost. "You're so brave, Willa, but I'm here now. I'll keep you safe."

Daytimes could also be difficult for her. Generally, she was able to get her ideas sorted out in her manuscript with no trouble, but now and then visions of Deb Abbey's violation crept in and derailed her thoughts. Willa had never felt hatred for another soul in her entire life, but she detested everything about Deb and what the woman represented. She hated Deb for making her doubt herself before she ever published a book, and she hated Deb even more for taking advantage of her when she was so young and naïve. The whole mess depressed Willa.

When those thoughts crippled her creative thinking, Willa generally sought out Jackson's company. His solid warmth and comforting nature were like a balm to her tortured brain. She would crawl into his lap and let him hold her or tell her about his family and the many wonders of artichokes. Eventually she'd laugh and call him Bubba when he recited too many recipes for them. He never failed to bring her out of her funk.

Chapter Eight

Besides working on his new plans, Jackson spent a lot of time simply thinking about Willa. A few times here and there, he couldn't resist snapping a selfie with her that he would ogle while she was busy writing. He sent a couple of them to Casey which set up the perfect opportunity for texting between the two men. Casey was apparently just as awestruck by Willa's beauty as Jackson.

Casey: You are one lucky SOB. She is incredible. I can't stop looking at her photo.

Jackson: She's beautiful inside and out. Just wait 'til you meet her.

Casey: Lusting from afar...

Jackson: LOL

Jackson also wondered about Deborah Abrams or Deb Abbey—whatever her name was. He knew the subject preyed on Willa's mind, so he didn't want to bring it up to her without having anything to offer to the conversation other than his opinions. He planned to delve into the topic a lot more and see if he could offer some concrete help.

Another nice thing Jackson discovered about Willa was that she had a lovely, generous nature. He came home from an appointment late one afternoon and found her conversing with several eager teenagers via Face-to-Face.

She turned to greet him and smiled happily. "Oh good, you're back. Come and meet my kids," she laughed.

When he sat down next to her, he saw a screen filled with smiling faces and a few raised eyebrows.

"Everyone, this is my boyfriend Jackson," she announced. This elicited a chorus of oohs and a few whistles and cat-calls. Apparently, the kids approved. "Jackson, these talented young people are a group of aspiring writers. We get together and critique each other—*kindly*—and discuss various writing techniques."

After a few more words with them, Willa told them all, "Terrific work today, everyone; I'm really proud of you. Have a great week and remember to 'show not tell' in your next assignment." She disconnected and turned to Jackson to explain, "They're a group of bright fifteen to eighteen-year-olds nominated by their schools to participate in this mentoring program. I've been doing it now for about two years."

"Side job?" he asked.

"Pfft. No. It's volunteer work for me, but I enjoy it so much, I'd pay them to let me work with these kids."

When it was time to set the computers aside, they dove into bed together, eager to revisit the sheer bliss they found in each other's bodies. Their adventures were so enjoyable that they found their work days ending earlier and earlier.

One afternoon, after they'd spent hours in bed together, they made a pact that they had to wait until after dinner to partake in any more sexy romps. It had become far too tempting to blow off work and play in bed. As a result, bedtime began to creep earlier into the evenings. They both positively craved each other, and the sex was incredible.

One night, as they lay curled around each other in a sweaty, post-coital embrace, Jackson asked, "Are there any fantasies you have? Anything from your books you'd like to try?"

Willa chuckled. "Theoretically yes, but in a practical sense, probably not. Most fantasies are best left in your head and not attempted, I'm afraid."

"Why's that?"

"Because the possibility for hurting someone's feelings or doing something that sounds better on paper than in real life is a real concern."

"Do you think you'd hurt my feelings if you said you wanted a man with a bigger dick or something?" Jackson asked with a laugh as he squeezed her.

Scoffing at him, she answered, "No. You have that one covered just fine. I was thinking more in terms of what if I told you my fantasy was to have sex with another man *and* you? You know, like in the book of mine that you read."

"I'd say that one has some seriously great possibilities." *Yes! Now we're getting somewhere,* he thought to himself.

Willa sat up and stared at him for a few seconds. "I don't mean two men 'servicing my needs,' Jackson. I mean two men in a ménage with me, all three as equal partners. That idea turns me on like..." She closed her eyes for a second. "You have *no* idea."

Jackson seemed to ponder that, and Willa decided he was probably going to drop it when he finally answered quietly, "I might be able to arrange that for you—if you're serious."

Willa's eyes popped. She blinked up at Jackson, sure that he was misunderstanding her. "I seriously would not want two straight guys trading me back and forth, you get that, right? And I also don't want to get into the middle of some macho demonstration for my supposed benefit. I would only be into it if you were... really into it."

Jackson smiled enigmatically and reached for her, pulling her back into his embrace. He kissed her and took a deep breath. "Okay, well... I have to tell you something. Something maybe I ought to have mentioned before."

"What is it?" Willa could feel the tension in Jackson's body and it worried her. "Is this going to piss me off?"

"Not in light of what you just admitted to me, no. Or at least it shouldn't." Again, Jackson took in a deep breath and seemed to be settling his nerves. "I wouldn't actually go so far as to say I'm bisexual, but I'm not completely straight either. Maybe just a little... bent. I've had some experience with... um... another guy."

"Oh!" Willa blinked in surprise. A slow smile spread across her face.

"You're not horrified?" Jackson asked, still tense against her.

"Not at all. On the contrary, I think it's pretty hot that you're so open to exploration and willing to admit it. Tell me about it—will you, please?" She felt the stiffness exit his body, and he went back to feeling like the big, warm, protective man she was falling for. Then a thought crashed into her brain, and she blurted out, "Would this possibly have anything to do with your friend Casey by any chance? I remember you saying you were very close."

"It does. Very perceptive of you. We both love women, but back when we were around thirteen or so, we started messing around a little. Experimenting, I guess you would call it. It was just kid stuff."

"What do you mean, 'kid stuff?'" she asked.

"Well, once I... uh... 'borrowed' one of my brother's *Playboy* magazines and we jerked off together looking at the pictures. Like I said, we love women. But, after that experience, we'd get together and look at the magazine and talk about what we thought sex might be like. We were both skinny, pimply kids who weren't likely to experience it first-hand anytime soon, and we had limited knowledge and a lot of curiosity. We'd both get turned on and start jacking off. It got to be kind of a regular thing. I remember eventually thinking it excited me like crazy to see him blow his wad. And I kind of liked showing off for him too."

Willa swallowed hard and reached both for Jackson's face. She pulled him towards her, laying a scorching kiss on his lips. As if she couldn't believe her own actions, she stopped suddenly and gasped, but Jackson took full benefit of her open mouth and plunged his tongue inside as he ground his lips onto hers. He wrapped his arms around her and kissed her like he'd invented kissing.

When they finally came up for air, Jackson asked, "So, this turns you on?"

Willa clamped her thigh muscles together and answered with a little moan, "I guess it does. What else did you guys do?"

Taking a deep breath, Jackson thought for a second and then answered, "I've never told a single person this before, but we wondered what it would feel like to have a blowjob—so we tried it out on each other. After a while I realized I didn't have to imagine he was a girl doing it, and finally just embraced whatever this was between us. We never actually said we were bi or gay, just that we liked doing it together."

Willa studied Jackson's face and said, "Interesting. Did you guys ever fuck each other?"

"Not back then, no."

"Oh! So, this relationship or whatever you have together is still going on?" Willa suddenly felt a bit less comfortable with this idea.

"No, not exactly." He looked a little uncomfortable suddenly as well. "But later on, when we were older, we just got to be more and more curious. When we weren't actively dating some girl, once in a while we'd... um... experiment some more.

It hasn't happened for a long time now, though, and I promise I've never done anything with any other guy. I couldn't swear to it, but I doubt Casey has either."

Willa took Jackson's hand and looked into his eyes. "It's nothing to be ashamed of, and I'm proud of you for being able to act on your feelings. A lot of guys aren't brave enough to do something like that." She paused, pressing her lips together nervously before asking, "Do you have feelings for Casey?" She steeled herself for his answer.

"Oh, well. I suppose. To be honest, I've always kind of had a little crush on him." Jackson looked away and then hastened to add, "He doesn't know it, though. I'd never tell him. We both want straight lives with women, and... um, you can probably tell how much I truly enjoy sex with you. And, well, everything with you."

"Hmm, this is a lot to take in, and I hope I'm not getting into the middle of a relationship you ought to work on with Casey. I have to admit, though, that even though I've never met him, the idea of *you* fucking another man is extremely arousing. Who knew, huh?"

"It's pretty sexy to me to hear you say that."

Willa got a thoughtful look on her face and asked, "Well... if men weren't supposed to be with other men, then why were they created with their G-spot up in their butts?"

Jackson's jaw dropped momentarily and then they both laughed at the hilarity and appropriateness of her question. Finally, they calmed down and kissed each other.

"Willa? Remember when I told you I was feeling what you called 'instalove' for you?"

She laughed, "Yes, of course."

"It's the real thing now. You have to be the most perfect woman ever. I'm so head over heels gone for you; you have no idea."

"Aw! Jackson! All it took was for me to horn-dog about your man-on-man fantasies?"

"No, though it doesn't hurt. It's everything about you. I've never felt like this in my whole life. I love you, Willa Camden."

She buried her face into his chest and answered, "Good."

He kissed the top of her head and asked, "Not to break the mood again, but do you think you'd like me to talk to Casey about a threesome sometime to satisfy your curiosity? He'd probably be up for it."

"Let's wait until after he and I meet each other, okay? I mean, there ought to be at least some chemistry between us, don't you think? And there's no sense in rushing into something while you and I are building our beautiful relationship."

"You think it's beautiful?"

"I do. And my feelings for you grow every day."

"Do you feel like *pretending* we have another guy with us?" he asked with a leer.

"How's that?"

"I, um, bought us some equipment so we could simulate DP."

Willa gasped. "Was that what was in the box the FedEx guy brought this morning?"

"Yep."

"You dirty dog, you! Show me!"

Since they were at Jackson's house this particular night, he strode out of the room in all his naked glory and came back a couple of minutes later with a bottle of lube and a dildo shaped like a large penis. "Here we are. We can practice and see if you like it."

Eyeing the dildo, Willa furrowed her brow a bit. "You're such a guy," she laughed. "I don't think most women would pick out a dildo that looks like that one. But, if you think we're ready for it, I'm game. Does it vibrate or do any tricks? Whistle? Squirt?"

"Uh..."

She cracked up. "I'm just kidding. Why don't you show me what you have in mind?"

Her question had an instant impact on Jackson, and he was already at full staff and ready to play. He set the toy and the lube on the bed next to Willa and pulled her into his arms again. "I've played with your ass enough now that I think you're ready to take me. Are you prepared for this?" he asked as he nuzzled her neck. He could see goosebumps break out on her arms and thought that was a good indication of her acceptance.

"Yes," she replied in a breathless voice. That one little word held a lot of desire.

"Get on your hands and knees," he ordered.

Jackson grabbed a condom and popped the lid on the lube. Willa watched over her shoulder as he sheathed himself and then poured lube into her butt crack. He used his fingers to gently massage her, slowly probing the tip of his finger inside. He added more lube as he pushed up more deeply, always retreating to lube up his finger.

Willa sighed with pleasure as this massaging and probing went on. Then with a little start, she felt a second finger enter her. It caused a tiny, momentary sting that immediately went away as Jackson spread more lube around. All the while, he stroked her with his other hand, touching her neck, her breasts, and finally her clit. All the while, he continued to stretch her rear entrance.

"Remember to stay relaxed. I won't ever push you too hard. If it hurts, say so, and I'll stop, okay?"

Willa groaned, "It's fine. I promise. Don't stop. I like this."

Chuckling, Jackson pulled out his fingers, and this time he slowly, ever so slowly, inserted three of them.

"Oh!" Willa gasped.

"Too much?" he asked in a worried tone.

"Um, just more than I expected. Don't stop."

So, Jackson moved his three fingers in and out of her slowly and carefully. Her tight ring of muscles squeezed him and then finally relaxed. "I think you're ready," he declared. "Is it alright to go ahead?"

"Yes, please," she moaned.

So, Jackson removed his fingers and brought his throbbing dick to her. He never stopped manipulating her clit with one hand as he carefully positioned himself. "Now take a deep breath in and tense up your muscles as hard as you can. Good, like that. And now quickly let it go and breathe out," he told her. As she softened, he slowly guided himself into her body.

Willa's eyes practically rolled back in her head at the sensation of Jackson entering her this way. She could feel the warmth of his body against her as he finally pushed all the way inside. He didn't move yet, letting her relax enough to accommodate him.

"Are you alright?" Jackson asked, his voice sounding strained.

Breathing heavily, Willa shook a little as she answered, "I had no idea it would feel like this. I'm fine, but don't make any sudden moves, okay?"

Jackson bent down and kissed her shoulder. "You set the pace, sweet cheeks."

Willa chuckled at his endearment.

Finally, Willa indicated that she was ready, and Jackson began slowly, lovingly moving in and out. "Wow," she breathed.

"Are you ready for the other guy now?" he asked. He was using all of his concentration to make sure he didn't come too soon and ruin her experience. "The dildo's been washed. Do you need some lube on it?"

Snorting, Willa replied with a smile in her voice, "Hardly. I'm positively dripping down my legs. You have no idea how turned on I am right now. Hand it over."

Jackson chuckled and passed the dildo to her, saying, "You are absolutely the woman of my dreams, Willa. God, I'm so in love with you." He kissed her back again.

Willa maneuvered the phallus into herself and they both gasped simultaneously as they felt it meet up with Jackson, bumping him deep within her.

"Use the switch on the base, and it'll vibrate," he told her, his voice raspy with arousal.

"Ohh, God," she moaned. "I think I'm in heaven right now. I've never felt so completely... so totally... aahhhhhgg!!"

"That's amazing. I feel it vibrating me through you," he moaned. "I'm going to pick up the pace a little now, is that okay?"

"Do it." Willa was sliding the dildo in and out more and more rapidly as Jackson's manipulations on her clit sped up and his body moved faster and faster behind her. Within minutes, Willa felt her orgasm beginning and she moaned, "I'm going to come now. Come with me."

Willa's body shook from head to toe with her release, and Jackson had to hold her with both hands firmly grasping her hips. He shoved into her two more times and suddenly let out a war cry as his own release exploded from him. He smashed his eyes closed and threw back his head, hollering.

Exhausted and satisfied, they both landed in a heap onto the bed. Jackson kissed her and then excused himself to get rid of the condom and clean up. When he returned, he snuggled against her, wrapping her into a tight embrace.

"That was pretty amazing," Willa murmured into Jackson's neck.

"You make me so happy." He kissed he and held her close to his warm chest. Their hearts seemed to synchronize their beats.

"Jackson?" she asked sleepily.

"Hmm?"

"I love you."
"Good."

Chapter Nine

The day before Casey's party, Willa was in the middle of writing when she thought of a question she wanted to ask Jackson about computers. She remembered he'd said he needed to go home that morning, but she was deeply involved in her writing and couldn't remember anything about why he couldn't stick around at her house. She decided to pop over and ask him in person rather than calling him. Any excuse to see the man was a good one, she reasoned, and she wanted to write about the subject correctly. It was certainly his area of expertise.

As she reached the front door, a strange man opened it and locked it behind him. He turned to face her, as surprised to see her as she was to see him.

At roughly the same height as Jackson, this man was just as handsome in a completely different way. He had that California surfer boy appearance about him with extremely broad shoulders, bulging biceps, narrow hips and thick blond hair. Green-eyed with a sexy scruff, he looked like he could take care of himself by breaking you in half—or wooing you to his bed just as easily.

Willa scolded herself for ogling him. It was terribly uncomfortable to be attracted to someone else while standing on her boyfriend's doorstep. Or anyway, she was attracted to him, until he started speaking.

Scowling at her suspiciously, the man said, "So, you must be the famous Willa who has stolen Jackson's heart and apparently his sense of reason as well. I recognize you from your picture."

Willa stepped back and blinked. "Excuse me?" She assumed he must have seen her photo on one of her books and wasn't sure she liked the sudden gleam of interest in his eyes. *Maybe this asshole isn't all that attractive after all.* "Who are you?" she demanded. "I was just coming to ask Jackson a question."

"Casey Melrose. Jackson's *best* friend."

Great. This jerk is the one Jackson is proposing as a possible third? Forget it. "Pardon me. It's... nice (*no it isn't*) to meet you finally, but I need to talk to Jackson. Can you let me by, please?"

"He's not here."

Willa raised her eyebrows at that news. "Then what are you doing here?"

"I was dropping off a painting he's been waiting for that he wanted to hang in his dining room. Jackson was here, but he had to rush off as soon as I arrived. Dentist appointment. I hung the picture, and now I'm leaving too. But I'm glad I ran into you because this will give us a chance to have a little chat. I was thinking about coming over to your place and introducing myself actually." Casey gave her a penetrating look. "I'm sure you realize he's enormously wealthy, and I know he's completely hung up on you. Since he's my best friend, I want to make sure you're in this with honest intentions, and you're not a gold digger."

Willa glared at Casey. "How dare you? You know nothing about me, and you assume I want Jackson for his *money*? Don't you realize there's so much more to the man than that? He's brilliant and kind and the sexiest man alive." She hadn't meant to admit that last part, and she suddenly blushed a deep pink. "You think so little of your best friend that you assume I see only dollar signs? I don't want—or *need*—his money, and I'm definitely in it for the long haul with Jackson. I'm in love with him, and if you can't handle that, then fuck you!"

Willa spun around and stomped away but only got a few steps when Casey burst out laughing and called after her in a light voice: "Atta girl, Willa. You pass inspection!"

Still supremely irritated, she faced him again and huffed, "I don't need your approval."

"Well, you have it anyway. Good for you." He beamed at her. "I'm delighted to hear you stand up for him. He's a very special guy and I never want to see him get hurt."

Baffled at Casey's mood swings, Willa stared at him and didn't know what to think. She didn't like being manipulated, or forced into anger. And she wasn't sure she could completely trust that Casey was just "testing" her, anyway. Angrily she stepped forward and blurted out, "One more thing, buster. If you are so concerned about this man—who loves you—then you better not be trying to undermine a relationship that's important to him. He loves me too!"

"Loves me?" Casey looked quizzical and taken aback.

"A figure of speech," she muttered, not looking at him. *Maybe.*

Casey narrowed his eyes again, cocking his head thoughtfully. "I think we're off to a bad start. I'm sorry. I'm not... the best with people sometimes. And Jackson is really important to me."

"Why do you think you need to look out for him? He's a grown man."

Casey sighed. "When we were kids, he tended to get bullied because he was so smart and often had his head in the clouds. I just got used to watching his back, I guess. Old habits die hard."

"Jackson did mention that the two of you had a pretty special relationship. He explained how... close you've become over the years."

At that, Casey's head jerked almost imperceptibly, and he narrowed his eyes at her. "Just what exactly did he tell you?"

"He told me that you were very good friends, and I'm not going to say anything else without him here with us. I don't want to speak out of turn. We've said enough about him without his being here."

"Fair enough," Casey said quietly. He looked suitably chastened by Willa's words. "I apologize again for coming off like a jerk. I can see now that you aren't the gold digger I worried about. He's just such a special guy, and he's completely head over heels about you. I just worry sometimes, you know?" He extended his hand like an olive branch. "Friends, yeah?"

Willa narrowed her eyes but took his proffered hand anyway and instantly felt the strength of his warm grasp. It was a lovely hand, she thought to herself. And that attraction she'd felt when she first saw him returned with a vengeance. They stood there, hands clasped, for way too long until both of them began to look a little sheepish about it.

Finally, Casey took his hand back and said, "I look forward to seeing you at the party tomorrow night, Willa. It was good to meet you, even if I made things uncomfortable. I think Jackson is a lucky man after all. And I don't mind saying that I'm just a tiny bit jealous of that."

Willa nodded. "Uh-huh." She wished she could have come up with a better response, but the man scrambled her circuits. She knew for a fact that she wanted more of that touch and more of his hands... all over her.

Chapter Ten

The night of Casey's party finally arrived. Jackson told Willa that it would be at Casey's house, "or estate if that's what you wanted to call it," so all of his friends and clients could enjoy its beauty.

"Casey is quite the world traveler," Jackson explained. "He goes on buying trips all over, looking for special things to import. Sometimes he comes home all excited about a new discovery he's made. It's fun to be around him when he's all fired up about a new artist or craftsman. Actually—it's always fun to be around him. You'll see."

"He sure did an amazing job with your house. I'm anxious to see him again." She winked at Jackson, and he took that to mean that she was interested in more than Casey's house. She'd told Jackson that she'd met Casey briefly the day before, but hadn't said anything else about their conversation. He assumed they'd just shared a friendly, quick greeting.

"You look stunning tonight, Willa." She was dressed in a short, slinky red cocktail dress that was curve-hugging, and she wore heels that made her legs look even more amazing than usual. Her long hair was down and curled in waves he wanted to bury his face into. Not wanting to mess her up, however, he just stood close and breathed her in. "You smell delectable," he murmured and kissed her neck. "Let's hit the road. Do you have a coat?"

Jackson looked pretty magnificent himself, dressed all in tailored black. He wore a soft cashmere sport coat over a silk shirt that begged Willa's fingers to reach out and stroke. His wavy hair was tousled just right, and he smelled divine.

Forty minutes later, Jackson pulled his Tesla into a gated estate with ample parking in front of a magnificent Hacienda-style mansion. Willa smiled as she took in the traditional adobe brick and red-tiled roof of the house that sprawled seemingly forever on one level. The artfully illuminated landscaping around the house was a breathtaking combination of lawn, colorful groundcovers, fragrant eucalyptus trees, and beds and pots of desert plants in an amazing array of colors.

Guests arrived in droves, and Willa observed how stylish and lovely everyone looked. It was obviously a well-to-do guestlist.

"Ready?" Jackson asked.

Willa nodded, and Jackson grinned at her. He leaned across the car and kissed her tenderly on the cheek. "I can't wait to show you off," he murmured in her ear. Then he hopped out of the car and raced around to her side, opening her door for her. Willa grinned as he offered her his arm, a wave of affection buzzing through her. This guy was serious Forever material.

They didn't find Casey right away, so she and Jackson mingled with the crowd, making polite conversation with people. Jackson seemed to know a few of them, though not particularly well. Willa was happy to laugh and chat with the wide variety of guests. For someone who didn't do well with people, Casey sure seemed to know a lot of them.

Willa decided to keep that thought to herself.

♡♡♡

They hadn't caught sight of Casey yet, but Casey knew as soon as they walked in the door. Jackson was his best friend in the whole world, and as pleased as he was to see Jackson looking so happy with his arm around the waist of such a stunningly gorgeous woman, he couldn't help but feel a little envious. From across the enormous living room, Casey observed the couple. He could see how Willa smiled and was polite to everyone and how she ignored the stares of men who ogled her cleavage or her legs.

Good lord, those legs! Wouldn't it be something to have those wrapped around your waist? Stop it! Casey told himself. *She's Jackson's girlfriend. Speaking of Jackson, he looks good enough to eat. Oh, stop.*

From this distance, Willa came across as regally beautiful. Polite to a fault, and relatively reserved unless she was speaking to Jackson. When she did that, Casey imagined he could see the love pouring from her heart. He just hoped it was genuine and not a carefully crafted act.

Casey mingled, making polite small talk and accepting everyone's compliments on his home, all the while keeping his eye on Jackson and Willa. He moved closer and closer to them in the enormous, crowded room.

Eventually they made their way to each other, and Jackson let go of Willa long enough to give Casey a tight hug. "Case! Great to see you finally." He kept his arm around Casey's shoulder as he said, "I understand you've already met Willa Camden, the woman of my dreams. Willa, as you know, Casey Melrose is my closest and oldest friend."

A few heads turned to stare at Willa when Jackson made his announcement. Willa ignored the looks. Casey assumed women were jealous that Jackson had basically called Willa the love of his life. He was unaware that the people staring were more likely readers of her work and were amazed to be in her company. Jackson had not filled him in.

Casey was pleased to see the ice melt from Willa's gorgeous blue eyes as she stared up at Jackson. "Good to see you again, Casey," she said with a smile. She regarded him with genuine interest and delight, which set Casey's heart pounding. When she leaned forward to hug him and give him a peck on the cheek, he couldn't stop himself from breathing in her feminine scent. "Jackson has nothing but the best things to say about you, and I've been dying to get to know you better."

Her smile and the look in her eyes penetrated him so profoundly, Casey was momentarily at a loss for words. He mentally shook himself and gave her a blinding smile.

Willa smiled back. She was drawn to the way his face crinkled around his eyes when he smiled. It was as if his smile was so big, everything else had to move out of the way. She couldn't deny her attraction to him. *So far, so good.*

People moved in and out of their circle for the next hour, and servers drifted by with trays of food and drinks that the three of them ignored—too engrossed in conversation to notice the lobster toasts with avocado or paté de foie gras with truffles. Instead they stayed put, pulled from one topic to another, fascinated with each other.

Eventually, Casey announced, "Jax, I know you've been looking for some investment opportunities, so I want to introduce you to a guy before he leaves, yeah?" Turning to Willa, he asked, "Will you excuse us for just a moment?"

Willa decided to take that opportunity to find a bathroom, so she wandered off down a hall, admiring the house in all of its stunning glory. When she exited the powder room, she was surprised to find Casey standing in the hall, apparently waiting for her. "I told Jax to come find us in my study when he's done with the guy who wants a chunk of his money," he laughed. "Would you like to sit down awhile and talk?"

"Sure, that would be nice, but don't you have other guests you need to visit with? I feel like Jackson and I have been monopolizing you all evening."

Casey gave her a warm look and took her by the arm. "It's fine. These people aren't nearly as important as the two of you. And they're getting what they wanted out of my party. They came to see the house and to be seen here by each other. I know the game they're playing, and it bores me."

Opening a heavily carved wooden door, Casey urged Willa inside. It was a stunning library with an enormous tiled fireplace at one end. It was all done in Southwest design like the rest of the house. Casey gestured to a plush sofa in front of the fireplace. "Please, have a seat. I'll get us some champagne and something to eat." He went to an intercom near the door and quickly made his wishes known. He sat down, and within less than two minutes, a server brought them a cart laden with food and drinks. The man quietly rolled it to a convenient distance and left the room.

Casey handed her a glass of champagne and said, "Please, help yourself to anything that looks good." He then picked up his own drink.

Willa looked questioningly at Casey and asked, "Did Jackson say something to you?" She was a little miffed if this was the case, but why else would the host of a large party want to have a private conversation with her and leave his other guests behind?

Casey's brow furrowed slightly, and he said, "I'm not really sure what you mean. Said something about what?" He saw Willa's posture relax and the happiness return to her eyes.

"Nothing. Never mind."

Peering at her closely with his sea-green eyes, Casey asked, "You're not still angry with me about yesterday, are you? I'd hate for any animosity between us to rub off on Jackson and make him uncomfortable."

"No, it's fine, Casey. I understand, and I think it's great he has someone looking out for him like that, actually. He's a tender-hearted guy, and maybe he needs a ball-buster like you to scare off girls with nefarious intentions."

Casey grinned. "Nefarious intentions, huh?"

Willa shrugged. "I'm a writer."

"Are you?" Casey asked. "Jackson hadn't mentioned that." He handed her a plate and indicated the food spread out before them. "Please, help yourself. I noticed you weren't eating anything when we were in the main part of the house with the other guests."

After selecting a few things, she took a bite of a canapé and chewed. The delicious flavor burst in her mouth, and she let out a whimper of pleasure.

Casey smirked at her and was about to say something inappropriate about her moaning when the door to the study opened and Jackson sauntered in saying, "You asshole, Case. That guy is full of shit. His investment strategy is for the birds, and I couldn't get away from him. Did you have any idea he was such a blowhard before you sicced him on me?"

"Sorry man," Casey said without a trace of remorse. "I wanted a private word with your lady friend here. I'm pretty jealous that you had the chance to meet her before I did."

Willa huffed quietly, and Casey chuckled at her, saying, "She's quite the tigress."

Jackson sat on the couch between them and answered, "You have no idea. Oh wow, you have my favorite shrimp kabobs." Grinning, he grabbed a plate and snagged a couple of them off the food cart. "People are starting to wonder where you disappeared to, Case. Some of them are leaving because the fog is rolling in and the driving is going to be tough if it gets any worse out there."

"Yeah, well it wouldn't be Rancho Santa Fe without the occasional nighttime pea soup. I guess I ought to go say goodnight and send them on their way." He looked at Willa then and noticed she was visibly distressed. "Are you okay?" he asked.

Ignoring Casey's question, Willa turned to Jackson with a pleading look. "Can we also leave *right now*? I'm rather terrified about the fog... you know..." She trailed off.

Jackson looked at her with understanding in his eyes. "I get it, Willa. I'm sure Casey won't mind if we stayed here to-night and drove home in the morning." Turning to Casey, he asked, "That okay with you? Willa's not too crazy about driving through fog at night."

"Absolutely," Casey replied. "We'll have more time to catch up this way. And the house has plenty of room in it, that's for sure. Relax. Have some more shrimp or... whatever, and I'll be back in a few."

Chapter Eleven

"So, care to tell me what that was all about?" asked Jackson. "Why did he set me up with that jerk so he could spirit you away?"

In a flat tone, Willa answered, "He's looking out for you. Yesterday he took me for a predatory woman who was only out for your money."

Jackson raised an eyebrow. "Did he? And what did you say to that? I assume you mentioned that you didn't need my money."

Willa scoffed. "I may have pointed that out, though I'm not in the habit of discussing my finances with strangers who accost me at my boyfriend's front door. But apparently, I passed his test anyway. I think he wanted a minute with me to make sure we're cool." She paused a moment and let that sink in. "He's an attractive and... interesting guy, but he's a little volatile, and he's certainly protective of you. He reminds me of a mother grizzly bear."

"He means well. But I hope he didn't hurt your feelings."

"I can see that you mean a great deal to him, and because of that, he didn't hurt my feelings. Well, much anyway. I'd scratch anyone's eyes out who tried to hurt you too." She peered into her glass of bubbling champagne as if it held all the answers, and continued, "He was very worried that I didn't really care about you. That I was just pretending, while you were falling in love."

Jackson drew in a startled breath and asked, "You don't think I'm worried about that, do you? You know I trust you, right?"

"I do know that," Willa said with a small smile. "It's fine, really. He just floored me a little. The man obviously has just as strong feelings about you as you have for him. I hope you realize that. I'm... I'm a little worried that I'm going to forge a wedge between you somehow."

"Oh, Willa." Jackson pulled her against him and kissed the top of her head. "The heart has an infinite capacity for love, and there are different kinds of love we feel, you know."

"Yeah, well, I believe that the kind of love you guys feel for each other is the same kind you and I have. You need to think about that."

Jackson did think about that for a moment and then said, "Well, if that's the case, then it will make our proposal all the more interesting, wouldn't it?"

She pondered his question for a bit and answered, "I just don't want anyone to get hurt. But I can't pretend that I'm not interested. He's very attractive, and I honestly think his protectiveness of you is sexy."

Jackson looked lovingly into her eyes and set their drinks aside. He took her into his arms and began kissing her. She was so warm and pliable he just couldn't get enough of her. One of his hands went to her thigh and gradually slid up between her legs. He chuckled victoriously when he realized she was sans undies and pulled back for a second.

"Naughty girl! Did you plan on flashing anyone tonight?"

Purring her delight as Jackson caressed her, she whispered, "No. I just hate the feel of wearing a thong, and this dress is so tight, I didn't want panty lines. But keep doing what you're doing, and I may be inspired to wear it every day." She gasped then as his long finger slid inside and stroked her. "Jackson!"

They kept up the kissing and the playing for a while as Jackson manipulated her clit with his thumb and pushed in and out of her. She squirmed and writhed in her seat to get more friction. It was nearly enough, and she was almost there when they both heard a throat clearing behind them. Casey had made his way back into the study, and they hadn't heard him.

Willa's eyes popped open. Jackson hesitated for a moment, but when she didn't move away from him, he moved inside her again, tentatively. She moved against his hand. It was as if they had communicated something between them—as if they had decided to see this through.

When she made no move to stop kissing Jackson or to tell Casey to go away, he continued to walk toward them. Her eyes remained locked on his as he approached. Hers held a mischievous expression.

Casey's attention finally shifted to where Jackson's hand played between Willa's thighs. It glistened with Willa's arousal. Reverently he whispered, "Beautiful."

Being caught in the act by Casey was the catalyst that tipped Willa over the brink. She let out a colossal moan as her orgasm overtook her, crying out, "Casey! Ohh, Jackson." She squeezed her eyes shut as she bucked against Jackson's hand for at least a full minute before she could relax and catch her breath. When she opened her eyes again, it was to see Jackson grinning like the Cheshire cat at Casey, who was staring at them with lust in his eyes. He'd removed his tie and his jacket, and his arousal was quite evident in the front of his dress pants.

Casey blinked at Willa when he realized that maybe she ought to be mad at him for watching, but she was still smiling at him as broadly as Jackson. *What the...?*

Willa broke the silence with, "Casey, I know we sort of got off on the wrong foot yesterday, but Jackson and I were just curious...um..."

Jackson laughed and added, "Kind of like when you and I were *curious* when we were teenagers, if you get my drift."

Casey's eyes went dark with lust, and he sat down with a plunk next to Jackson as if his legs couldn't hold him for one second longer. Then in a strangled voice he croaked, "I think you two need to explain exactly what you mean."

"It's one of Willa's fantasies to have a ménage experience."

You could have heard the fog rolling around outside, it was so quiet in that study until Willa added, "Not just any ménage. I'm interested in a male/male/female triad. Equal partners. And I understand from Jackson that you two have... experience together."

A shocked expression crossed Casey's face as he blurted out to Jackson, "We promised each other no one would ever know about that!"

Jackson reached for Casey's hand and took it gently, saying, "Willa isn't just anyone, Case. We love each other, and she'd never betray our confidence to anyone. What you don't know about Willa is that she's an extremely well-known author."

"She said she was a writer," Casey said vaguely, staring down at Jackson's hand. It felt so right to touch him. So natural.

"Well, I'm guessing she under-sold herself," Jackson replied. "She writes erotic romance books, and she realized her interest in ménage after researching it for a book. I'd love to facilitate that for her, but it could only be with you."

The light went on in Casey's eyes and he asked, "Is that why people were staring at you when Jackson said your full name out loud earlier? You're famous?" He snorted, "Where have I been?"

"It's okay. It's probably not your genre," Willa soothed as she waved off the worry with her hand.

"But you ought to read some of it anyway. It's good stuff," Jackson chuckled and wiggled his eyebrows.

Casey sat quietly and stared at them. He was deeply aroused, and the idea of being with both of them filled him with lust, but he didn't know what to do.

Jackson finally made the first move by standing up and switching places with Willa on the couch. She immediately picked up on his silent message and leaned forward to kiss Casey.

Casey couldn't deny his interest, and when Willa's tongue met his, it was all over. Whatever guilt he'd been feeling for lusting after Jackson's girlfriend evaporated as his arms went around her. He could feel Jackson pressing up behind her, and that turned him on even more. Jackson reached around Willa and began to stroke Casey's hair and neck at the same time he caressed Willa's exposed thigh.

Jackson let out an approving sigh as he watched Casey kiss his woman. He was so hard, he desperately needed some relief, so he let go of them and unzipped his pants. He pulled out his throbbing dick and began stroking himself.

Willa pulled back and turned to see what Jackson was up to. When she saw his exposed member, she scooted off the couch and got to her knees. Leaning in, she took Jackson into her mouth for a moment as both men moaned at the sight. Then she pulled away and reached to unzip Casey's slacks as well. Reaching into his boxers, she released him from his confines. Looking up into Casey's eyes, she saw disbelief and lust, so she pulled him into her mouth as she had done to Jackson. She had Jackson in one hand and Casey in her mouth. It was almost too much to take in.

Not wanting Jackson to feel left out, she switched back to fellating his dick, and with a nearly imperceptible jerk of her head, gave Jackson a suggestion. All the time she kept stroking Casey with one hand.

Grinning, Jackson leaned over and pulled Casey's erection into his mouth. Willa's hand slipped down to play with Casey's balls, massaging the sensitive area just behind them.

It didn't take long before both men were erupting like volcanoes.

"Ohmygawd!" cried Casey. "You two are unbelievable."

"Is that a good thing or a bad thing?" asked Willa. She couldn't tell by Casey's incredulous expression.

"It's... ah... let's all go to my bedroom, yeah? The last thing we need is for the servers to come looking for dishes and stuff to clean up. Come on." He stood and did up his pants and led them further down the hallway past several bedrooms until he finally reached the enormous master suite. After he made sure the door was locked, he turned to Jackson and asked, "Are you really cool with this, Jax? You won't be mad if I see your girl-friend naked?"

Casey wanted to be certain that Jackson wouldn't have any regrets later, so he let him think about it a moment. Jackson looked down for a few seconds and then turned to Willa. Seeing the unmistakable lust in her eyes, he grinned and turned back to Casey. "It's fine. She wants this, and I want to do this for her. I'm not going to hate you for it—don't worry. And understand that I'd *never* consider doing this with any-one else."

Casey nodded solemnly and then looked at Willa, "And you won't be mad if I do something to your boyfriend, yeah?"

"That's kind of the point, Casey. We're all free to do what comes naturally to us. If you want to fuck me or fuck Jackson, it's all good."

"Unfuckingbelievable,'" he breathed out on a sigh. Look-ing at them he commanded, "Well, don't just stand there—get your clothes off! We have new experiences to explore!"

With just her shoes, dress, and bra to contend with, Willa was the first one undressed, so she crawled to the middle of the bed and tried to look seductive instead of nervous.

Casey was next, and he crawled to the middle of the bed in a lower position that put him between Willa's spread legs. He murmured at the glorious sight of her smooth, wet pussy and kissed his way up her thigh to her clit. Willa let out a long sigh and said, "Yes! Right there," as he latched onto her. Soon he had her thrashing against his talented mouth, so he shoved a finger inside of her as well.

Jackson, also now naked, scooted next to Casey, put his arm around his friend, and whispered, barely discernable over Willa's cries of ecstasy, "She loves ass play, so don't neglect her there."

Casey groaned and nodded, which added pressure to Willa's clit, and she hollered, "Yes! Don't stop!"

Jackson had a condom in his hand that he'd taken from his wallet and placed it on the bed. He opened the bedside cabinet, rooted around, and made a harrumphing sound when he came away empty-handed. He slipped off the bed and headed to the ensuite bathroom, returning immediately with a bottle of lotion. He sheathed himself with the condom, staring at Casey's ass. He then squirted a healthy dollop of lotion into his hand.

Willa was beside herself with tingling lust, but when she realized what Jackson had in mind, she let out a low moan. She watched as he scooted behind Casey, whose butt was raised invitingly. And she heard Casey make a strangled moan as Jackson's hand disappeared from Willa's view behind Casey.

Casey's mouth and fingers continued their unceasing assault on Willa. She had never been so turned on in her life. But when she saw Jackson thrust into Casey's body from behind, and she recognized the strained ecstasy on both their faces, she exploded. Spasm after spasm of euphoric bliss burst through her body as she bucked and strained against Casey's mouth and hands.

Panting, she watched as Casey finally pulled away from her body and squeezed his eyes shut as Jackson pounded in and out of him. He was breathing hard in short blasts. Casey was still on his hands and knees, so she scooted around beneath his body to get her mouth on his erection. She intended to help him to his climax, and she loved the power she felt when sucking cock.

Casey's mind was in a tumultuous state of passion overload. He'd had Jackson inside him before, but this time Jackson pounded into his prostate and drilled him from behind at the same time as this gorgeous woman had his dick in her mouth, sucking him for all she was worth. It was the most incredible sensation in the world, he was sure.

Jackson howled his release just as Casey hissed out a long stream of swear words that somehow sounded like a prayer of thanksgiving.

Finally, they all collapsed in a heap.

"Incredible," whispered Willa. "Thank you, both."

"Amazing," agreed Jackson.

"Can we do it again?" asked Casey with a laugh.

♡♡♡

After a quick shower, they all snuggled into bed with Willa sandwiched between two hot, hard bodies. She kissed Jackson and then Casey. Groggily she muttered, "I could seriously get used to this, you guys."

Casey and Jackson stared at each other. Finally, Jackson winked at Casey, and they all fell asleep.

Chapter Twelve

The next morning could have been awkward, but the two men awoke as they felt a gentle hand caressing their morning wood. Clearly, Willa was not done with their shenanigans. What developed fulfilled more of her fantasy. After kissing her deeply, Jackson made love to her sweetly and almost sleepily while Casey carefully prepared Jackson's ass. She watched with rapt attention as Casey kissed Jackson's back and shoulders and gently probed him with well-lubed fingers.

Jackson repeatedly made hungry little noises in his throat, and Willa could tell he was in a state of bliss. His arousal turned her on like nothing ever had before, and she could feel how wet she was as he slid in and out.

"God, you're tight, Jax," Casey murmured. "Relax. I know it's been a long time, and I know how much you love this. Willa's going to enjoy it too." He kissed Jackson on the neck and gave him a little bite.

Jackson gasped then, and Willa could tell from the way he tossed his head back that Casey had just entered him. Suddenly, nothing was sweet and gentle at all. Propelled from behind, Jackson pounded into Willa as Casey drilled into him, hitting Jackson's prostate with each thrust. All three of them cried out over and over as their combined passion grew.

Willa felt closer and closer to heaven with each mighty thrust, and she could tell her release was imminent as Jackson ground against her. Jackson cried out, "Coming," at the same time as her spasms began.

"Yesss," she sighed on a long breath as Casey began what she would come to find out was his normal orgasm chant. He closed his eyes and muttered a string of curses that were nonsensical, profane, and completely heartfelt.

It blew everyone's mind once again.

Utterly exhausted, they all went back to sleep and didn't budge again until nearly noon.

♡♡♡

The fog from the night before had burned off, and they were having a beautiful seventy-four-degree day. Typical San Diego county weather, even for winter.

Being the consummate host, after showers, Casey offered them clean clothes to wear that they'd be comfortable relaxing in. He presented Willa with some drawstring shorts and the smallest T-shirt he could find. It didn't fit too horribly. He loved the way she filled it out, in fact.

"You can pick out whatever you want to wear," he told Jackson and pointed him toward the closet for shirts and pants. While Jackson looked for pants that would fit, Casey and Willa wandered toward the kitchen in search of coffee.

Jackson joined them in the kitchen, barefoot in jeans and a rock band T-shirt with a quizzical look on his face. Addressing Casey, he asked, "Have you had this Back-Trick shirt of mine all along? I thought I lost it. I got it when we went to that concert in Monterey, and then I wore it a while and it disappeared." He turned to Willa and explained, "That was the summer after we graduated from high school." Looking back at Casey, he said with a laugh, "I looked everywhere for this thing. It was a great concert, and I remember the trip being a lot of fun. Did I leave it at your place somehow?"

Casey stared into his mug of coffee. His cheeks had turned pink, and the tips of his ears were bright red.

"Case? It's no big deal, I'm just curious, that's all," Jackson assured him.

Heaving a sigh, Casey admitted. "Okay, I swiped it from your laundry basket one day when I was over at your house. I knew we were going off to different colleges, and that made me sad. I saw the shirt, and it made me think of the good times we'd had, so I took it as sort of a souvenir. I'm sorry if you missed it." He laughed then and went on, "You can have it back now. It's been washed."

"I can see that. Clearly it's been worn and washed hundreds of times." He sat down on the breakfast nook bench next to Casey and scooted up next to him. "I missed you too. At least now we're back together now, living in the same place. That is, when you're not off traveling the world like you have been for the past several weeks."

Willa's laughed softly and said to Casey as she bumped his knee with hers, "If you were a woman in a romance book, you'd have kept the shirt and sniffed it all the time instead of laundering it." She noticed how her statement made Casey's blush return. She gave him a knowing look but did not comment on it. Ready to change the subject, she asked, "You guys did see each other during those years though, right?"

Jackson explained, "Absolutely. We saw plenty of each other during school breaks and over the summer. But now that we live closer to each other, this is much better." He put his arm around Casey's shoulders and squeezed him.

Looking relieved, Casey did something they'd never done in all the years they'd known each other. He kissed Jackson. On the lips.

At first, Willa could see the shock in Jackson's eyes, and then the acceptance. It was one thing to mess around with each other, but kissing represented a whole new level of intimacy. The kiss deepened and the two of them slid their arms around each other. Willa could feel herself becoming aroused at the sight and squeezed her legs together. She knew she was right; they obviously harbored strong feelings for each other.

Well... now what?

Casey eventually pulled away. He and Jackson leaned their foreheads together for an instant and then grinned at each other.

"Anyone else as hungry as I am?" Seeing both of his guests nodding and smiling, Casey said, "The chef has Sundays off, but he always leaves Belgian waffles to heat up and a bunch of fresh fruit. Or, I also have a fantastic artichoke frittata he makes that heats up really well." He winked at Jackson as he began hauling things out of the refrigerator, and they all set to arranging brunch for themselves.

During their meal, they kept things light and talked mostly about the people they'd had conversations with at the party the night before, but when they were all done and the dishes were put in the dishwasher, Casey suggested, "Let's take our coffees outside. It's nice enough to sit by the pool, even though the water's too cold right now for a swim." They sat around a table and let the sun warm them.

Willa was the first to break the ice. "Guys, I have to say this, and you can respond however you feel, as long as you're honest about what you answer." Jackson looked serious and Casey looked a little worried, so she didn't take any time getting to the point. "This experience with the two of you has been mind-blowing and beyond my wildest expectations." She looked at Casey and added, "And you and I haven't even fucked yet." She winked at him. "I'm a tiny bit worried, however, that I've stepped into something that's been brewing between the two of you for years, and maybe I ought to back off and let you two explore it together."

Jackson looked aghast and said, "I thought you said you loved me!" at the very same time that Casey spluttered, "No way!"

Willa smiled at them both. "It's not that I don't love you, Jackson. The opposite. I don't want you to have any regrets. If you want to be with Casey, I'll step away. I just want you to be happy."

"Willa," Jackson said. "That is the kindest, sweetest thing anyone has ever said to me. But... I love you. I don't want to lose you. I want you here, I swear it."

Casey reached for her hand and looked at her. "Willa, Jax and I haven't messed around together in a long time. I don't even identify as bisexual because I don't think my actions with one person in my entire life ought to label me." He looked at Jackson and took his hand as well. "That isn't to say I don't have feelings for you or that I wouldn't welcome the opportunity to explore this triad, as Willa called it, more deeply. As long as it's the three of us and not two."

"Okay," she said happily raising her hands. "Your reactions put my worries to rest. Forget I said anything. And I do love you, Jackson. I just had to put it out there." She leaned over and kissed him softly as he seemed to relax.

Jackson looked at Willa and then Casey. "I doubt Casey and I would have been together again as sex partners had it not been for you. You're the glue here, and I'll just put it out there too, that if the two of you want to keep this going with all three of us, I'm in. I love you Willa. And, Case, I have to admit finally that I've kind of been a little bit in love with you since we were kids."

"It's true," Willa confirmed. "He told me that a few weeks ago actually. And I think the idea is pretty exciting that we could try this relationship with all of us together."

"Wow." Casey looked from one to the other of them. "How can we do this? You guys practically live together being next-door neighbors. How do I even fit into that?" He looked at Willa and asked, "Um... how often do you want to get together?"

"I guess a lot of that depends on you, Casey. I assume you date women. How do you want to handle that? Jackson told me that you don't have a girlfriend right now, so I guess that helps. How long has it been since you were involved with someone?"

"Oh, um... I guess it's been quite a while since Tamara and I broke up. I've been on a few dates over the last year or so, but nothing more than that. As Jackson said, I've been in and out of the country—not exactly conducive to developing a relationship even if I'd wanted one."

"How did you manage to get all of that wonderful work done on Jackson's house if you were gone so much?" she asked.

"I had it all planned out ahead of time and hired a contractor to do the remodeling. Then as the pieces came in, my assistant took care of things when I couldn't be there myself. Part of why I was gone was to shop for things for his house at the same time I was working with a guy who builds superyachts and mega-yachts. The seaside theme worked well for both projects."

"Wow, it sounds like you have a fun job. How did you get into designing like this?" Willa asked.

He smiled and answered, "When Jax took off to learn how to become a successful nerd at Berkeley, I headed to Pasadena to study at the Art Center College of Design. I'd thought about studying architecture, but really wanted to make sure the final product was beautiful and inviting more than I cared whether the structure had the right kind of beams and girders holding it up. So, I became a designer. I'm not a particularly talented artist, but I love art and surrounding myself with beautiful things, so it was perfect for me." With a chuckle he added, "I also love to shop for treasures."

Nodding slightly, Willa asked, "What happened with Tamara?"

"Ooh, going in for the heavy questions, I see."

Jackson interjected, "She has a habit of that." He smiled contentedly at Willa. "It's probably the author in her."

"So?" she prompted, looking interested.

"We dated for a little over a year, and I was beginning to think she might be 'the one' until I discovered that she was a lying, cheating, manipulative bitch. And that was that."

"Do you mind if I ask what happened to turn you so against her?"

Casey let out a long sigh and explained, "It was the biggest cliché of all time. I came home early from a buying expedition and I found Tamara skinny dipping in my pool—not this one, the one at my last house—with some random surfer she'd picked up at the beach. And when I say 'dipping,' I mean he was sticking his dipstick in her. I tossed her out and threatened to call the police on her when I saw how young the guy was. He swore he was eighteen, but I had my doubts. The whole thing made me sick, and then I heard from common acquaintances that she had a reputation for doing that kind of crap."

"You haven't seen her since?"

With flat eyes, he said, "Nope. I heard she moved to New York. They can have her. I sure as shit got myself tested after that little fiasco, though." He made a face. "At least the test results were all fine."

Willa raised her eyebrows and said, "Okaaay then. Moving on."

"Are you going to be in town next weekend?" asked Jackson.

"Yes. I have to go up to Santa Barbara for a few days, but I'll be back sometime on Friday."

"Why don't you plan to spend it with us in La Jolla then? Sound good?"

Willa grinned and wiggled a little in her chair. "It sounds fantastic to me. Casey?" She looked imploringly at him.

"I'll be there."

"Excellent," both Willa and Jackson said happily.

"I'm curious about your business, Casey," she asked. "How did you get to be so successful so quickly? Do you have some secret for how to find clients?"

Casey burst into laughter. "I do have a secret weapon. It's called 'rich grandfather left millions to his grandkids in his will.' And it's also called 'lots and lots of connections to richer-than-sin family friends.' I can't deny that all of that didn't help me get going. The only thing I had to do was maintain the trust of everyone who took a chance on me when I was just out of school. One success led to another, and I was able to build this house a year ago. I love it here, but I also look at the house as an investment. It's kind of a lot of home for just me. One day I might decide to sell it. We'll see."

Willa got quiet and seemed introspective after what Casey said, so the two guys started talking about football and their predictions for the next season. She tuned them out and got up to walk around the garden surrounding the pool.

Once she was out of earshot, Casey exclaimed softly to Jackson, "She's incredible, isn't she? I can't believe you were lucky enough to meet her. Beautiful, smart, and sexier than anyone has a right to be, but I get the feeling none of that has gone to her head. She's so real, you know?"

"Oh, I do know. She's been through some terrible heart-ache. She lost her parents the day she graduated from Stanford. They died in a car accident—because of coastal fog, I might add." Casey winced and nodded with understanding, remembering her reaction the night before, and Jackson continued, "She also had a book plagiarized that was recently made into a movie and won an Academy Award for the story. That's driving her nuts—for good reason."

"Wow. That's harsh."

"Isn't it? I'd sure like to fix that somehow for her. She just works like a dog on her writing career and tries to keep her troubles to herself. She could sit around and do nothing or shop and get her hair and nails done all the time, but she chooses to work. She also mentors a group of teens who aspire to be writers. I found that out sort of by accident because she's also so humble, she'd never brag about herself." He chuckled then and added, "The funny thing is, she's been using Face-to-Face with the young writers' group for their weekly sessions. Small world, huh?"

"Pfft! Everyone uses Face-to-Face, you dope," Casey scoffed and then they both cracked up. "There's no reason for *you* to be so humble. So, what's your next earth-shattering project you're going to make more billions on, huh?"

As Willa rejoined them at the table, Jackson explained, "I'm working on an anti-hacking program. Firewalls are too easily breached, and I think I can do better. It's still mostly in here, though." He tapped his head. Turning to Willa, he said, "I get the feeling that you're not really with us right now. You're writing in your head, aren't you?"

Laughing, Willa answered, "Guilty. I wasn't aware I was so obvious. I'm sorry. Sometimes inspiration strikes at the weirdest times and I want to spruce up a passage I wrote a few days ago."

Jackson took her hand. "I take it you're ready to head home then and get back to your computer to write it all down."

"Do you guys mind? If you want to stay longer with Casey, I can always take an Uber home." She looked between the two of them.

"It's fine," Jackson assured her. "Or," he turned to Casey and continued, "you could always follow us home and spend more time with us that way. We can work out in my gym or go for a run on the beach or something while Willa writes."

Casey didn't have anything planned for the evening, and the servers had taken care of cleaning up after his party, so he didn't have to think about things very long. "Sure. Sounds great. I have to make a couple of calls, but I'll be able to leave soon. I'll just meet you there. Thanks."

So, it was settled. Jackson and Willa collected their clothes and headed home. Once they were on their way, Jackson asked seriously, "Any regrets?"

Willa's head snapped around as she stared at him. "About Casey and what we're doing?" Jackson nodded, so she continued with a smile, "None at all. That was amazing. Thank you so much for suggesting it." Looking at his face for any signs of regret from Jackson, she asked, "How about you? Are you happy we went through with it? I mean, you must be fairly okay with it if you invited him to meet up with us later."

"I'm fine with it. I just hope it doesn't end up hurting someone. I love what you and I have together, and I feel great about Casey, but I hope this doesn't blow up in our faces. I guess we'll just have to be careful and honest." He blew out a heavy breath then and added, "But, man, that was some seriously heavy stuff we got into with him, and I have no trouble admitting I loved every moment of it."

This admission made Willa grin ear to ear.

Willa went straight to her laptop as soon as they got back, and Jackson headed off to call his parents to check in with them as he liked to do weekly.

Chapter Thirteen

On his drive from Rancho Santa Fe to La Jolla, Casey headed toward the beach and made his way south via the coastal highway through Del Mar instead of navigating Interstate 5. He loved the scenery and preferred the slower driving along the ocean instead of maneuvering through traffic on the freeway. He considered it a lucky day because he spotted a trio of Great Egrets in the San Elijo Lagoon. There was something so graceful and almost magical about those huge, snowy white birds. It took a few more minutes to make the trip along the coast, but he didn't need to hurry, and the day was perfect. Plus, this route gave him plenty of time to think.

He couldn't deny that last night and this morning were the most amazing sexual experiences of his life. Kinkiest too, if he was honest with himself. He'd never even considered being part of a ménage, and this had blown his mind. He'd been melancholy thinking he'd never have that same connection with Jackson again once he realized his buddy was serious about Willa, but he had never dreamed they could be as close as they were last night.

He also hadn't had sex with a woman in a while, so he was definitely looking forward to boinking Willa. Then he amended his thoughts. "Boinking" wasn't what you did with a woman like Willa. With her, you made passionate, beautiful, sexy, sometimes raunchy love. *I can't believe Jackson is cool about it*, he thought. *And she's incredible. I've never seen a woman so invested in enjoying sex in my life. Tamara always had so many rules of what we could and couldn't do and thought blowjobs were beneath her. Fuck, Willa can practically get herself off by giving one! I just hope we all don't end up in one of her books...* He wasn't too crazy about that thought. *I also hope they don't get tired of me too soon. For me, anyway, this is about more than hot sex. It's a chance to have something truly spectacular with two amazing people... if it works. I'll have to be careful.*

♡♡♡

Casey punched in the keyless code at Jackson's house and let himself in. He found his buddy stretched out in a comfortable reclining chair facing the window that overlooked the beach. Jackson was on the phone and looked up at Casey giving him a big smile and a chin lift. He indicated to Casey that he was winding up the call and to have a seat in the chair near him.

"I'll definitely be there, Mom. Don't worry," Jackson said. "Maybe I can get Casey and Willa to come up there with me for the big event."

Casey's ears perked up at that. *What event?* Jackson's family was always big on celebrating things. With a snort, he considered, *Maybe they've finally developed a hairless artichoke. Not likely, though.*

Jackson said goodbye to his mom, promising to give her love to Casey, and he disconnected. "Mom sends her love. My dad's birthday is coming up soon, and she wants me to be there. Interested?"

"Sure. When is it?"

"A week from Tuesday. He supposedly refuses to let her have a party because he doesn't want to feel old, so of course she's going to round up everyone she can find anyway. She knows he secretly wants to celebrate. I'll probably just drive up for a couple of days. I'd love the company, and you can see your parents too at the same time. I wonder if Willa's free. It would be a great opportunity for her to meet them."

"Oh, sorry. I can't do it then. I need to stay here because I have clients who've just bought a second home in Del Mar. They're living in Scottsdale now, but they plan to fly over to go through the place with me the same day as your dad's non-party. I don't think I can reschedule with them because it was tough synchronizing this date with their calendars."

"Bummer. Well, next time maybe." Jackson looked up then to see Willa entering his house looking perplexed. "What's up?" he asked her.

"I don't know," she answered in a troubled voice. "Something's weird with my computer. Would you mind taking a look at it later? I've rebooted it, and that doesn't seem to do anything. I think a recent update somehow messed up Microsoft Office."

Willa started to sit down on the floor next to Jackson and gave a startled squeak when strong hands grasped her around the waist. "You don't need to sit on the floor, Willa. I have a perfectly comfortable lap right here," suggested Casey as he pulled her onto his chair on top of him.

"Oh! Um, okay," she laughed softly. "I'm sorry, Casey. I was so in my own head, I guess I had tunnel vision and didn't see you. But this is nice." She cozied into his arms as he nuzzled her neck. Stealing a look at Jackson, however, she noticed he looked confused and upset.

"Please tell me you've backed up your files recently," he said somberly.

"I did just yesterday. Everything is both in the Cloud *and* on an external drive that's in my desk drawer."

"You keep that external drive safe. It's possible you've been infected with a virus, and I may need to sweep your hard drive completely clean to get rid of it."

"But I have anti-virus software on it," she protested. "How could that be?"

Jackson huffed, "Those programs are only good for the most well-known problems and need to be updated constantly to stay ahead of hackers. Did you do an antivirus scan?"

"No."

"Alright, we can try that first. But don't hold your breath that it will help. Sometimes I suspect those companies of releasing viruses just to stay in business." He took in how comfy Willa looked on Casey's lap and wondered why it pleased him so much. *Shouldn't I be a little jealous?* He felt none of the green-eyed monster. Instead he only saw two people he loved, learning to love each other. "So, Willa, I was just talking to my mom, and I wondered if you could go up to Castroville with me for a little birthday celebration for my dad. Casey, unfortunately, is busy then with clients."

Giving him a beaming smile, she answered, "I'd love to go. When is it?"

When he gave her the date, however, her face fell. "Oh no. I can't leave town then. I have three days of local book signings scheduled. Monday, Tuesday, and Wednesday. Too much advertising has already been done to be able to change them. I'm so sorry."

"Well, that's what happens when the two of you are busy, and in such demand," he said sadly. "I'll have to make the trip by myself this time. At least you'll both be here for each other... if you want to get together."

Casey's eyes lit up as he asked, "You guys wouldn't mind?" He looked first at Jackson and then at Willa, who smiled sweetly back at him.

With a great show of looking put-upon, Jackson droned, "Of course, I'll be lonely and miserable all by myself, but it'll be a great opportunity for the two of you to... um... *bond*." His eyes narrowed at Casey when Casey let out a tiny snicker at Jackson's choice of words.

Turning to Willa, he asked, "Have you been doing research for your books on any porn sites lately?"

She laughed and said, "Once in a while. Why?"

"They're a known source for picking up computer viruses and malware. What about emails? Have you clicked on any that came from an unknown source?"

"I don't think so." She got a faraway look on her face and then amended her statement. "Oh wait. This afternoon when we got back, I went through the ton of emails that had piled up as usual, and something kind of odd did happen."

She had Jackson's full attention as he asked, "What was it?"

"Well, an email came from a blogger who had a weird request." Jackson's eyebrows shot up, and Casey gave her a reassuring squeeze. "She wanted a photo of my book cover in a large jpeg format. Usually, the bloggers just want a smaller one for the web, but I never want to discourage free advertising, so I tried to load the photo into the form they sent."

"What happened then?" asked Casey. Jackson already had a knowing look on his face.

"Nothing. I clicked on the button to upload the photo, and absolutely nothing happened. I thought maybe my image was too big for them after all. So, then I sent them an email asking about it and got an automatic out-of-office response that they'd get back to me on Monday."

Casey also looked less than amused and offered, "Better check any online bank accounts you have, Willa. And change all of your passwords as soon as possible."

She put her hands over her face and groaned, "Oh, ugh," into them. "I feel like a huge dumbass."

"It's not your fault," Jackson assured her. "We'll get this fixed. I'm just glad you had everything backed up externally."

"Yeah, thanks," she sighed. With her tummy growling, Willa asked, "Would you guys like to eat in or go out? I'm famished, and I'm sick of looking at my computer."

Jackson offered his opinion quickly. "I'd rather stay here. I don't feel much like driving anywhere." He noticed the relieved faces of his friends and said, "I'll go get the menus."

"You need a chef," chuckled Casey as Jackson sat back down. "I should loan you Phillipe when I'm out of town. Then you wouldn't have to look at menus. Or cook."

He looked questioningly at Willa who smiled and shrugged. "Cooking isn't exactly one of my skill sets. But I'm good at other things."

She fluttered her eyelashes at him, and he let out a tiny groan. "You certainly are." Narrowing his eyes, Casey asked, "Why would you do research for your books by looking at porn anyway?"

"Oh, you know... to see if certain, um... *positions* are feasible. Most of it is so fake and *not* sexy, it's a waste of time looking at it for any inspiration, but I just want to make sure the characters can get their bodies into particular situations reasonably comfortably. In my early days of writing, I bought Barbie and Ken dolls to experiment with before I thought of watching porn." She saw the incredulous look on the guys' faces and burst out laughing. "What?"

"You pervy doll lady, you," teased Jackson.

"Yeah, well, it didn't work. Their arms and legs only move so far and are really stiff, so after putting them into a few compromising positions that were boring, I threw Ken and Barbie into the donation basket. I needed more flexible dolls, but when I couldn't find any, I turned to porn. At least the actors have real bodies. I guess I would have known that about Ken and Barbie if I'd ever played with them as a kid, but I always thought dolls were boring and a little creepy."

♡♡♡

They all agreed on a seafood feast that would be delivered in forty-five minutes. Jackson went to get everyone a beer, and when he came back, it was to find Willa and Casey embroiled in a passionate liplock. Rather than interrupting them, he set down the beers and watched with pleasure. His feelings still confounded him a little, but he couldn't deny them.

Sensing his return finally, Willa slowly ended the kiss. With half-closed eyes, she then shifted to Jackson's lap and began kissing him just as ardently. After a few moments of that, she disconnected her lips and sighed into Jackson's chest. "You guys are the best. I can't believe how lucky I feel right now."

Casey spoke up then, sounding concerned. "How do you two see this playing out in the future? I'm not sure what level of intimacy and involvement you're expecting from me. And I understand this is a loaded question because we just started our... whatever it is."

Jackson looked at the emotion in Willa's eyes and felt close to positive they were on the same page about this, so he spoke up. "Case, we don't want you to feel as if you're some side play-thing we're going to call up now and then when we want some kinky fun." He laughed then and added, "Unless that's what you'd like." Seeing Casey wince, Jackson continued, "Seriously, I've known you nearly my entire life, and I know you deserve more than that from us."

Nodding, Willa picked up Jackson's train of thought. "If you're willing to give us a go, I think it would be amazing to see how we do as a committed triad—or throuple in the new vernacular. Threesome... whatever you want to call us. Throuple always sounds silly." She chortled softly.

"So, when you say committed," Casey began, "you mean none of us would date anyone outside of the three of us, yeah?"

"Yes," said Willa, and Jackson said at the same time, "Agreed."

Willa went on, "Rest assured, Jackson and I will be careful with your feelings. There's never a guarantee when it comes to relationships, and we're bound to face some challenges, but the fact that the two of you have remained close through thick and thin says a lot about how you already feel about each other. I don't want to jeopardize that any more than you want to disrupt what Jackson and I have built. But if at any time you feel this isn't what you need or want, or you meet someone else, well... we'll be sad, but we'll understand."

After kissing her cheek, Jackson told her, "Well said." Looking at Casey, he went on, "If at some point you feel you'd like more space from us, please say so. But I, for one, am amazed at just how right it feels for the three of us to be together. I hope this feeling lasts and lasts. I know that you and I talked about having families in the future, and a gay lifestyle together wasn't what we envisioned, but this is actually something we can all consider together—just maybe not this soon." He grinned his charming, crooked smile at them.

Both Casey and Willa got thoughtful looks on their faces. Then Willa spoke up, "So, both of you want families and children?"

"I do," answered Casey immediately.

"Definitely," said Jackson. "That's actually why Casey and I decided to keep our experience together secret for so long. We knew ultimately we wanted wives, and we worried that future partners wouldn't understand..." He laughed then and added, "We never counted on the likes of you, Willa. But the question remains, how do you feel about having kids in the future? We might as well clear the air upfront."

"I've always wanted a whole bunch of them, actually. I was so lonely growing up with no siblings, it sounded like fun to have sisters and brothers around all the time. I know that here in California especially there are plenty of examples of polyamorous families. I might do a bit of research into that and see how it works. Your families might be scandalized by us, though."

"Nah," protested Casey. "Mine wouldn't be. My grandfather had his mistress living with his family for years, and if the stories are true, his wife liked having her there. So, my dad certainly grew up in a household that was accepting of alternate lifestyles." He looked at Jackson and asked, "Your family has always seemed a lot more traditional. What do you think they'd say?"

Jackson's face went a bit pink, and he looked at Casey. "I've never told you this, but my parents suspected there was something going on between you and me when we were teens, and they sat me down and told me they loved me and were proud of me, and all they wanted was for me to be fulfilled and happy. I think they were trying to save me the anguish of coming out to them."

Willa chimed in, "What did you tell them?"

Jackson's lips pulled up at one side with a lopsided grin, and he said, "We had a long conversation then about sexuality and being sexually fluid. They know I'm not completely straight, and they also thought labeling me or putting me into some arbitrary category would be counterproductive. They encouraged me to simply follow my heart."

"Your parents sound amazing," said Willa reverently.

"They are. I'm sorry you can't meet them next week, but we'll arrange something soon. Oh, and by the way, they think Casey is wonderful."

Willa smiled and murmured, "So do I."

Chapter Fourteen

After a delicious dinner, they all headed next door to Willa's house so Jackson could take a look at her laptop. She booted it up and showed him what was going on while Casey wandered around and looked at her living area. He couldn't resist.

Leaving Jackson to fret over the mess that he discovered, she found Casey in her living room.

"Something tells me you haven't updated your décor in years," Casey observed. "It's a nice enough look, but it doesn't do much to reflect your style." He looked at her somber face and added, "I'm sorry. I can't help myself sometimes. I don't mean to say you need to change anything. It's your house."

"No, it's okay. I know the house looks dated. I just never got around to changing anything after losing my parents. My mom had a decorator help her spruce things up when I was about eight years old, and then she forgot about it. My dad never cared, and, I must say, it just felt normal to me. I'm always so busy writing, it just never occurred to me to make many changes. I also suspect that subconsciously it makes me feel closer to them, even though I understand that I need to move along with my life." She looked down at her feet and continued, "The only things I got rid of finally were their clothes and personal items that had no sentimental value. I hope it doesn't feel to you like I'm living in a memorial to my dead parents or some weird thing like that. The look of the house is more a factor of neglect than anything else. I don't often have people over the way my parents used to."

"Oh, Willa, I never meant anything of the sort." He reached out and gently took her hand. "It's a great house. It's none of my business how you want to live, but if you ever want to modernize your living space, let me know, and I'll do anything I can to help. I tend to look at interior spaces like a blank canvas, no matter how nice they are. It's a blessing and a curse, I guess."

"Well, you certainly did a spectacular job on Jackson's house. I love the colors, the artwork, and the way everything seems so lush and comfortable."

Casey grinned. "Exactly what I love to hear."

For the next hour, they wandered around looking at the house, and Casey filled Willa's head with hundreds of ideas for how she could update and enhance her living space. He even moved a couple of things around for her so they'd look fresh or be more convenient. By the end of the impromptu tour, she was ready to put him to work. The last room they came to was the bedroom at the end of the hall where Jackson was sitting at a desk, hunched over Willa's computer.

Even looking at him in profile, Willa could see Jackson's furrowed brow and hear the quiet expletives coming from him. She asked in a soft voice, "So... I take it things aren't so good?"

Huffing out a long sigh, Jackson hit the power switch and turned to look at them. "You were infected with a Trojan Horse, and I got it removed and cleaned up the mess it made. I hope I got everything put back the way it's supposed to be, but we'll have to see how it acts next time you try to use it. You should be alright now, but if things start acting weird, let me know immediately. And be sure to back things up all the time. Changing passwords would be a good idea as well, like Casey said."

"That doesn't sound too awful. Thank you so much for fixing it for me, Jackson." She and Casey approached him, and they both placed their hands on his shoulders. "I'd like to show you my appreciation for your hard work," she murmured and bent to run her lips over his ear. "Casey and I need you now."

Casey chuckled and moved his hands to Willa so he could caress her while she caressed Jackson. Within minutes they were all naked and had made their way to the big bed.

Some people would have turned off the bedroom lamps, but the sight of what they were doing to each other was as big a turn-on as the acts themselves. For the next hour, they made love to one another in a rapturous tangle of bodies until they collapsed in a spent heap and went to sleep. It was well after that when Jackson awoke thirsty and got up to get a drink of water and turn off the lamps. He climbed back into bed, reaching for the two people he adored, and snuggled in as closely as he could.

♡♡♡

An hour earlier and many miles away, a man called out, "Okay, babe. I'm in. You wanna check and make sure this is the right person?"

"Yeah. Be right there." A woman appeared by his side and peered at his computer display. What they saw made the man's eyes bulge as she gasped, "Holy motherfucking shit! Is she…? Are they…? They are! Oh… my, my, my." She lightly punched the man's shoulder in her glee. "You're recording this I hope." When he nodded without looking at her she continued, "This is pure gold. If she gives me any crap, we can use this as collateral," she cackled.

The two of them stared spellbound at the screen, not wanting to miss one second of the action, and after a while the man had to rub his junk a few times. He was feeling un-comfortable and constricted, so he finally undid his zipper and freed his stiffie from his tight pants.

The woman twitched and squeezed her thighs and tried not to whimper. *Lucky bitch! Those guys are total hotties!* She side-eyed the actual warm-blooded erection closest to her and decided it stacked up poorly in comparison. *But he has his talents, and getting access to this computer makes up for his shortcomings.*

As soon as the action on the screen ended, they tore at each other's clothes and fucked right there on the floor. The woman's imagination took her to a level of excitement.

Her partner was just glad to get his rocks off.

Chapter Fifteen

On Monday, Willa got back to her writing. She wasn't currently writing an MMF book, but her mind certainly drifted in that direction more often than she was comfortable with. *It's too late in the story to introduce a second man*, she kept telling herself. *I'm almost done with this one.*

True to his word, Casey sent his chef Phillipe to Jackson's house, saying, "It's high time you started living like the billionaire you are, man! Get used to having a chef and then buy a yacht, a few more cars—something!" He laughed at Jackson's pensive expression as he got in his car reluctantly and headed home. He needed to get up to Santa Barbara. *At least I have plenty to think about while I drive.*

Jackson actually loved the idea of a yacht. He'd always been frugal with his earnings, but for once in his life he could afford to splurge on just about anything. So, he took a break from movie research and dipped his toe into yachts. He finally decided that chartering one for whenever and wherever he wanted would be a better idea than owning one of his own. He didn't plan to live on one for any reason. *Casey's the one who knows about yachts*, he thought. *Why am I trying to make a decision like this without him?* Jackson considered pulling him into the planning; but he was already heading out of town. *This is so dumb*, Jackson thought bitterly. *I miss him already. I wonder how Willa feels about our situation with him. We can discuss it over lunch.*

A couple of hours later, Jackson wandered over to Willa's place. He knew he could just send her a text, but that might mean he'd miss out on more of her company. This way he could tell her in person that Phillipe had lunch ready and maybe get a few kisses before they made their way back next door. He let himself in and found Willa scowling at her computer. She looked good enough to eat if you ignored her petulant expression.

"Uh-oh. What's wrong?"

Willa shook her head slightly and looked up with a distracted expression on her lovely face. "Oh, Jackson. Is it lunchtime already? I lost track of time. I'm stuck on a scene in my story, that's all. I sort of wrote myself into a box."

"Why don't you save what you have, and come have something to eat? Maybe that will clear your head. Chef Phillipe has been cooking up a storm and something smells fantastic."

"Okay," Willa sighed. She'd skipped breakfast, opting to take her coffee and get right to work. "I could definitely eat." She pulled a thumb drive out of the drawer, saved her file, and then replaced the little drive back in the desk.

"Is the mouse working correctly now?" asked Jackson as they entered his house.

"Mm... it might still be a little slower than I'm used to, but yes, it's working now."

It turned out that Chef Phillipe had made cold shrimp cocktails, followed by a hearty veggie soup and freshly baked rolls with an interesting herb flavor. He topped off their lunches with frothy cups of coffee and some tiny, light-as-air cookies that were his own delicate creation. He called them "cloud cookies." Willa had no idea what was in them, but they were divine—just sweet enough for the end of the meal, but not filling. The chef encouraged Willa to take a few so she could have a snack while she was writing.

"Jackson, I think our evening run needs to be extra-long tonight if Phillipe is going to be feeding us," she said with a sweet smile. "Thank you, Philippe. Lunch was wonderful. And now I'm curious; what do you have planned for dinner?"

"I plan to make a leg of lamb roast with mint seasoning and some new potatoes. I haven't decided on the vegetable sides yet. Is there anything you dislike?" He looked at Willa and then Jackson. "Mr. Melrose refuses to eat lima beans or Brussels sprouts, no matter how they're prepared."

Willa laughed. "I like just about all vegetables, but I guess I'll have to draw the line at liver and onions." She looked at Jackson who seemed to be considering things. "Jackson? Anything you particularly detest?"

"Hmm... beets. They taste like dirt and just look... wrong. I'm also not a fan of black licorice. I guess we're pretty easy customers, Phillipe. And I agree that lunch was great. Thank you. Is the kitchen alright?"

Phillipe chuckled and answered, "Mr. Melrose consulted with me before he planned your remodel, so I'd only have myself to blame if it weren't perfect."

Jackson grinned. "He didn't tell me that, but it makes sense to go to the expert for advice. Tell me, Phillipe, have you ever tried cooking on a luxury yacht?"

Willa's head snapped around. She gawked at Jackson's smug expression as Phillipe answered, "Oh, yes sir, Mr. Mitchell. I have plenty of experience. I actually love boats."

"Jackson? Any reason you're asking that?" Willa asked.

With his signature crooked grin, Jackson answered, "Casey planted a seed before he left for Santa Barbara. Wouldn't it be fun to spend some time on a yacht?"

Willa blinked a few times in surprise and then said, "Well... yeah!"

She was about to head home to get back to work when Jackson got up to go with her. "I'd like to check on your computer one more time since the mouse still isn't responding as well as it should," he explained.

"Thank you."

"It's nothing. I'd do anything to help your career, you understand, right?"

With a sultry look, Willa asked, "Is there anything I can do to pay you back?"

"Just you being you is enough."

♡×♡×♡

Willa did a load of laundry and puttered around the house while Jackson poked around on her laptop. After an hour of clicking on this and that and running things in safe mode, he became more and more convinced that the Trojan had been removed and the computer was once again safe for use.

"It's always possible that something is still wrong, but I think you're good to go." He tried to appear reassuring but serious as he continued, "It looks to me more as if someone was just having some fun with malware—probably released it to lots of users at once. Or... maybe just to you."

Willa let out a frustrated sigh. "Why would someone target me?"

"It could just be something random, or it could also be because you're a talented, best-selling author, and someone wants to steal your newest book so they can pirate it or say they wrote it. That's just an educated guess, of course." Jackson looked thoughtful for a moment and then asked, "What do you know about that Deb Abbey woman who stole your book before?"

"Well... nothing really. Do you think she's at it again in a sneakier way this time?"

"It's possible," Jackson offered. "But whoever planted this Trojan is extremely talented and appeared to be trying to show off. It's like some of the stuff you see at DEF CON."

Blinking at him, Willa asked, "What on earth is DEF CON?"

"It's billed as the underground hacking conference in Las Vegas that hackers and web security managers attend. They offer lots of speakers and what they call Village presentations about how to keep your business safe. Each Village has a hacking competition that attendees can try to win. The conference is so full of hackers, though, no one will even bring a cell phone through the door for fear of having it attacked. Most of the really great hackers are super sneaky about their identities, but a few are there to show off. DEF CON also has a big Capture the Flag competition for teams of the world's best hackers to compete against each other. All of the name badges that people wear have something electronic about them, but the big Capture the Flag winner gets a special badge they keep for life. It will get them into the conference forever." Jackson smiled as though with a fond memory, "I've gone every year for the past eight years, but it's been going on a lot longer than that. I think the first one was back in '93."

Willa appeared spellbound as she asked, "Wow, that's really something. Sounds like you enjoy it."

"I do," Jackson smiled. "Though I didn't go for fun, not at first."

"Why did you?" Willa asked.

"Because I wanted to make sure I was using cutting edge techniques to combat attacks on my software. If you stay up-to-date and learn to think like a hacker, you can stay pretty safe. It's way better to program safely from the get-go than it is to try to fix problems later. That's a huge problem many large companies have. They're too anxious to get to market and release unsafe products."

Willa pondered this a moment and asked, "Do you know any of the big hackers? Or... you're not one of them, are you?"

Giving her his crooked smile, Jackson answered, "I'm definitely not one of the interfering hackers. I'm what's known as a white hat. I have the skills to hack in anywhere I set my mind to, but I only do it for educational or research purposes. I'm there to learn how to fix the coding problems that let me in. The black hats hack in to steal, control, or otherwise disrupt things. It's a whole different world. I know some of the black hats with big reputations, and I can't claim to be friends with any of them. I've also pissed off a few of them by besting them at their game and winning the coveted Uber Badge, as they call it. They're pretty sensitive about their skills." He looked thoughtful and continued, "This Trojan of yours reminds me of something a couple of them might have created. I'll see if I can find out anything else about a new malware going around."

Willa narrowed her eyes in thought. "My gut tells me that if Deb Abbey had that kind of talent, she wouldn't waste it on looking for books to steal."

"Maybe not," Jackson said. "Though I'd imagine she's under a lot of pressure to write the next big book, and since she had to steal her first idea, she probably doesn't have the talent to do that on her own."

With a frustrated huff, Willa replied, "At least I have a back-up this time. And the book is essentially done now except for one scene. I was mostly polishing up a few things and getting it ready to go to the editor." Shaking her head in annoyance, she went on, "I hate the idea of losing my work again." She wrapped her arms around Jackson and said into his neck, "Thank you for helping."

Chapter Sixteen

Casey came back from Santa Barbara, and they filled him in on what they'd been up to and discussed. This gave them a weekend with the three of them together before Jackson had to leave for Castroville.

And what a weekend they had. Willa was already so comfortable with Jackson, and he had such a strong connection to Casey, it seemed to help forge a deep connection between Willa and Casey as well. What could have been awkward felt right. Willa started to realize she'd been longing for Casey's return from Santa Barbara. He was the missing part of the machine that made things hum. She giggled to herself as she thought of him as the high-octane fuel that helped things move smoothly.

Early on Saturday morning, however, Willa had to leave for a couple of hours. "I have a hair appointment," she explained, then kissed them both goodbye and took off. On her way out the door, she added, "I'm going to do a little shopping before I get back."

As soon as she was out the door, Casey turned to Jackson and said, "She's amazing."

"Agreed."

"Do you actually think we can keep this going, Jax? I'm not messing up what you have with her, am I?"

Jackson barked out a laugh and said, "Considering the number of times she brought you up while you were gone, I'd say we're safe." He took Casey's hand and looked him in the eye. "This is about as perfect as life can be, if you ask me." He saw Casey relax and changed the subject. "How would you feel about taking a vacation? I think we all need to have some fun."

"Fantastic idea," Casey agreed. They had a long conversation about what sounded like the most fun and set to work planning it all out.

And as soon as they put down their phones and closed their laptops, Willa reappeared, looking as radiant and gorgeous as ever.

"Need any help with packages?" asked Jackson, ever the gentleman.

"As a matter of fact, I'd love that. I bought out the boutique. But what's for lunch first? I'm starving. You guys didn't eat yet, did you?"

"Nope," answered Casey. "But Phillipe has something that smells delicious just waiting for us. And Jax and I have something to discuss with you while we enjoy it."

So, they headed to the dining room where Phillipe had outdone himself once again with an exquisite pasta dish.

"We've been doing some research and some planning," began Jackson. "Casey and I have always wanted to head up to either the Bugaboos or the Cariboos in British Columbia to do some heliskiing, and we've found a place that sounds perfect. It's a super-deluxe lodge where we can book a big suite and have either a five- or seven-day guided heliskiing package, depending on how much skiing we're all up for. Can you take the time now?" He looked at her expectantly and so hopefully, she had to smile.

Speechless for a moment, Willa finally answered, "That sounds amazing! When can we go? I can take the time off now that my commitments are all fulfilled. In fact, I'd love to take some time off—with you guys, of course."

The guys' faces split into huge grins, and Jackson answered, "I booked it for next week. It sounds incredible. But this is only part of our trip. Casey also has something to tell you."

"Part of the trip? What are you talking about? More skiing?" she asked.

"We thought," continued Casey, "that we'd ski in Canada for the week since April is the best time of year for it, and then we can pop over to France. You know about the yacht I've been working on recently? The owner was so pleased with the result, he told me I could use it sometime, and it so happens that we can have it for the two weeks after the ski trip if we want it. It's docked right now in Nice." He kept talking, faster and faster as his enthusiasm took over. "We can visit Monte Carlo and the casinos, or we can just float around the Côte d'Azur if you prefer. It's also prime time for that vacation—not too hot and not too cold. I do have to warn you that the crew on the yacht is new, so we're sort of acting as Guinea pigs, breaking them in. The good news is we don't have to pay for anything unless we want to tip them. It's the owner's way of making sure everything is perfect."

Laughing with joy, Willa exclaimed, "When you guys put your heads together, you can certainly accomplish a lot in a few hours."

"We enjoy putting our heads together," Jackson said with a wink.

"What can I do to contribute to this trip?" asked Willa.

"Nothing," said Casey at the same time Jackson said, "You don't have to do a thing."

"Oh, no you don't, you guys. I'm at least paying for the transportation to get us to Canada and France." Willa had a mulish expression on her face. "I may not be a billionaire like Jackson, but I'm not insolvent, you know." Then she cracked up. "This is going to be great!"

So, after they ate, Willa took care of booking car services and private planes for their travels. This was really an adventure to look forward to.

Unfortunately for Chef Phillipe, the yacht's crew already included a Cordon Bleu chef.

Chapter Seventeen

Jackson took off for Castroville on Monday, planning to stop and charge his car somewhere around Bakersfield. He had plenty of audiobooks to keep him entertained along the way, but as soon as he left La Jolla, a loneliness overtook him. It caught him off-guard. *I've always been independent, so how come I feel like I've just lost the use of my right arm or something? Those two have really invaded my brain—and my heart. I'm used to missing Casey now and then, but the two of them together are positively irresistible. I wonder how her book signing is going. I'm sure her fans adore her. And I hope Casey does well with his new clients. I hope this party goes well and I can get back soon. My family is great, but I sure wish Casey and Willa could have joined me on this trip. Oh well, the next couple of weeks will give us plenty of opportunity to make up for lost time.*

His thoughts continued in that vein for much of the trip until he decided to listen to one of Willa's audiobooks. He'd downloaded a few of them and picked one about a skier that sounded good. He figured it would get him in the mood for some snow.

Who'd have figured he'd move next door to not only the woman of his dreams, but one who also loved to ski as much as he and Casey did? They used to beg their parents to let them head up to the various Lake Tahoe ski areas all the time when they were teenagers, and the older they got, the more frequent the trips became. It was during one of their trips during a college break that they had taken the next step in their physical relationship, and it not only excited them, it shook them up. Being so young, they weren't exactly sure what to do about it.

Thinking back to the night they had actual penetrative sex for the first time, Jackson smiled. It was mind-blowing. Neither was a virgin at that point, but this was a whole new level of intimacy. The two of them hadn't seen each other for a few months, and they couldn't contain their excitement at reuniting. The topic of sex came up as soon as they got to their hotel room. Casey shut the door and blurted out, "I want to try fucking you."

Jackson blinked at his friend for a beat and then laughed. "I was going to say the same thing. I even brought lube. But I want to fuck *you*."

Eventually it was decided that they both wanted the same thing, and fair was fair. So, Casey deferred to Jackson—since he'd brought the lube and all—with the caveat that he'd bottom for him if he'd get his chance on top too.

Jackson felt himself starting to get hard as he remembered how strange and wonderful it felt to have Casey inside his body in the most intimate way possible. He'd loved it. But when Casey reversed roles with him, he also loved fucking Casey's tight ass.

He couldn't honestly say whether he preferred having sex with a woman over having it with Casey, but he felt in his heart that they were both lucky to be free enough with themselves to enjoy it all. And now? With Willa *and* Casey? Life was nearly perfect.

Jackson's Tesla took over much of the driving, and he relaxed as he listened to Willa's beautifully crafted story told by a wonderful narrator. She was right, he realized, when she told him that the characters in her book were not autobiographical. The woman in the book was nothing like Willa, and she didn't relate to her boyfriend in a way that felt familiar to him. He recognized Willa's amazing aptitude for story-telling and appreciated her imagination.

Several hours later, he arrived in Castroville and had a quiet dinner with just his parents. He was happy to see them but tired from the drive, which they understood. "I'm going to take a shower and go to bed. Dinner was wonderful, Mom. Please let me know if there is anything I can do around here tomorrow, but now I'm worn out."

In truth, Jackson wasn't as worn out as he was lonely. As soon as he got to his room, he texted Casey and Willa.

Jackson: Arrived safely. Parents are good. Missing you both. Doing OK?

Casey: We just stuffed ourselves at Tony's Jacal and decided to come on up to Rancho for the night since we were close. All is well here.

Willa: We both miss you too.

Jackson then got an idea...

Jackson: Let's do some Face-to-Face, OK? ;)

Casey: Perfect. I'll get my laptop set up in just a sec.

A few minutes later, they were all connected via Face-to-Face, and Willa asked, "Are you somewhere private?"

"I am. I decided to stay out in the guest house instead of up in my old room. Why? Did you have something naughty in mind?" he asked with a leer.

"Take your clothes off, Jackson," she ordered.

"Wow. You're feeling bossy tonight. Is it the margaritas?"

Willa grinned and Casey laughed. "All we had was one beer, Jax. She didn't want me driving around the windy roads tanked on tequila. She's smart. Now take your clothes off like the lady asked."

"You guys too," replied Jackson as he yanked his shirt off over his head. In seconds, his pants were on the bedroom floor.

In a soft, flirty voice, Willa asked, "If you were here, what would you want to do to me, Jackson?"

"I'd be kissing you right now. Slowly and deeply."

Casey, who'd lost his clothes as quickly as Jackson had, got closer to Willa and kissed her, just as Jackson described.

"Turn sideways a little more so I can see you better, Case," ordered Jackson.

Willa's hands went around Casey slowly as she caressed his muscled back and ran a hand through his hair.

Willa hadn't been as quick to lose her shirt, so Casey pulled back a moment and swiftly drew it off over her head. Then he unclasped her bra and dropped it.

"Beautiful," breathed Jackson. "And now I'd be playing with those perfect tits of yours. I'd have my mouth on one and I'd tweak the other with my hand."

Casey obliged and did just that. And he did it with flair. The man was obviously enjoying himself.

Willa purred her approval. "That feels so good."

The sight of this turned Jackson on as usual. Only this time he felt tremendously frustrated and definitely jealous. That feeling surprised him, so he tried to swallow it down. He concentrated on Casey's incredible physique for a while and watched as Willa enjoyed the feel of all those muscles. He knew just what both of his lovers felt like. They were both silky-skinned, with toned bodies, only Casey was much harder than Willa with her soft, feminine curves. Jackson's hands itched to touch both of them.

"I'd love to go down on you now, Willa," he said with a growl. "Lie back so I can watch Casey eat you out. Make her come so hard she screams, Case."

They positioned themselves to accommodate that wish, and with a little readjusting of the laptop on the bed, Jackson was treated to an up-close view of Willa's most feminine parts. She was slick with arousal, and Casey had yet to put his tongue on her.

Jackson lay back on his bed and got comfortable. He groaned, wishing fervently that they were there with him. Grabbing a bottle of lotion from the bedside table, he greased up his hand, wrapped it around his erection, and slowly stroked himself.

"Yes, right there," he heard Willa gasp. "Keep going, don't stop!"

Jackson sped up his strokes and squeezed himself harder. When he saw Willa clench her muscles and let out a long groan, he could tell Casey had brought their woman to a satisfying orgasm. He groaned along with her, enjoying her pleasure. "Willa, I want you to suck Casey's dick for him now," he ordered. *Damn, I wish I were there with them!*

So, Willa and Casey traded places and Willa went to town on Casey's impressive erection like it was her favorite ice cream cone.

"Stroke him with one hand while you suck him, sweetheart," Jackson ordered gruffly. He pretended he could feel those gorgeous lips of hers wrapped around his boner, and his arousal grew and grew—along with his frustration.

Casey lay with his head raised by pillows so he could watch Willa suck him off, and Jackson saw the lust and excitement build and build in his best friend's eyes. Casey's chest began to heave as he got closer and closer to his release.

"Now, grab his balls with the other hand," Jackson said with squinted eyes. Casey looked at Jackson questioningly. This was new. "Okay, now twist them really hard!"

Willa jerked back and turned to stare at the camera at the same time that Casey jolted up and shouted, "What?"

Jackson burst out laughing. "Just kidding. I didn't think she'd do it, man. But you two have no idea how frustrated I'm feeling right now." They both continued to stare at him for a beat until he said, "Willa, go back to what you were doing before Case loses his boner."

Shaking her head with a grin, Willa leaned back over Casey and resumed sucking him off.

Casey leaned back onto the pillow muttering "Very funny. Watch your back, Jax."

"You're not going to do anything. Now shut up and enjoy what Willa's doing to you, you lucky fucker." Jackson kept stroking himself, but he needed something else to get him there. "Willa, stop sucking for a second and put your finger in your mouth. Casey, open your legs for her."

She complied with a knowing look as Jackson then ordered her, "Now suck him some more and slide your wet finger into his ass while you're blowing him." He watched as Casey's eyes closed in bliss. "Now fuck his ass with your finger and keep stroking."

Casey moaned in ecstasy as Willa stroked and sucked. He looked he was about to come when Jackson ordered loudly, "Willa, stop!"

They both turned to stare at him again with incredulous expressions, but Jackson quickly amended his directions. "Trade places again," he said in a strained voice. "Willa, lie back so Casey can fuck you."

They quickly shifted positions, and Casey was about to enter Willa, when Jackson said, "Not so fast. Tease her a little with the head of your dick. Rub it on her clit and then slide in slowly."

Willa let out an impatient huff that morphed into a purr as Casey finally breached her entrance. Ever so slowly he entered and retreated, entered and retreated again, until Willa begged with a moan, "Please, I need you inside me."

"Do it," commanded Jackson, and Casey was deep inside her at last. Both of them exclaimed their relief. Jackson squeezed himself harder and pumped his erection in time with Casey's thrusts.

Jackson watched Casey's toned muscles bulge and relax as he pushed inside and pulled out again, and Willa wrapped her long, slender legs around Casey. Jackson pumped his hand harder. He knew what it felt like to fuck Willa like that; to have her legs wrapped around his hips as he thrust forward... Casey buried his face in Willa's neck as he began to come inside her, keening a long, guttural groan of joy laced with some colorful curses.

Jackson felt everything as though he were there with them. He imagined the feel of Willa clenching around him as he came in her. He spilled all over his hand and belly as he shouted out his release.

With a sweet smile, Willa exclaimed dreamily, "Well, that was fun." She continued to stroke Casey's back in a lazy motion.

"Oh... oops," added Casey with a sheepish look. "We, or rather I, forgot to get a condom. Jackson said to fuck you, and that was all that was on my mind. I'm sorry, Willa. It *sure* felt amazing, though."

"No worries. I have an IUD, and... you're the first man I've slept with without a condom."

Casey tried not to appear too smug when he turned to look at Jackson. "Sorry, man."

"It's fine. I forgot too. As long as everyone's okay with it, it's not a problem. I can't wait to do that with you too now, Willa." *It's not all that fine actually,* Jackson thought bitterly. *She was my girlfriend first. I should have been the first to have her bare.*

"I'll be waiting," she said with a wink.

Instead of getting up to take care of a condom, Casey stayed buried inside Willa. He nestled his face into her neck as the two of them relaxed. Willa closed her eyes in contentment, and Jackson felt another spike of envy. He wanted so badly to be there with them. They looked for all the world like a couple in love, and that knowledge stabbed him in the heart.

Am I a hypocrite? he wondered. *This is what we hoped for—that we'd all be equal partners and all be in love.* Jackson knew he had to tamp down his feeling of possession of both Casey and Willa. Yes, he'd found them first. They were his first, but if this whole arrangement was going to work, they had to be free to fall in love.

It will be alright once I get used to it, Jackson thought. He watched as they murmured lovingly to each other words he couldn't hear and felt another small stab to his heart. *Apparently,* he thought, *I can deal with them being together just fine as long as I'm there with them too. This is way harder from hundreds of miles away.*

After disconnecting, Jackson stewed for the next couple of hours. He recognized his jealousy for what it was and then decided that it truly stemmed more from loneliness for them than any kind of distrust. *Sure, Casey was the first to have sex with Willa without a condom, but it could just as easily have been me eventually anyway. What were we supposed to do? Draw straws? I can be the first with Casey.* That thought cheered him up some, and he felt infinitely better as soon as he realized that they wanted to include him as much as he wanted to be included. *They aren't going to fall in love without me and run off together, for heaven's sake. They both love me. I need to let this go and be happy with them. This jealousy nonsense will only hurt everyone in the long run. I need to trust them and love them the way they deserve.*

Finally, Jackson was able to drift off to sleep.

♡♡♡

Back in Rancho Santa Fe, Willa and Casey were still wound around each other in Casey's bed. Neither seemed to have the gumption to get up, and Casey was still buried inside her. Since there was no condom to dispose of, he relished being able to stay there.

"This is so perfect," he murmured into her neck. "It's like this is how it should always be. Condoms have their purpose, but this feels so much more... real, you know?"

Willa gave him a squeeze with her inner muscles and laughed softly. "I couldn't agree more. I'm a little sorry for Jackson though. You think he's okay?"

"He's so head-over-heels in love with you, he'll be fine. I am too, you know." Casey kissed her then, deeply and sweetly. There was no desperation to his kiss—just a sensual demonstration of how he felt.

When their kiss ended, Willa sighed happily. "I love you too, Casey. It's amazing how quickly this happened, but it's so profound. My feeling for you does nothing to diminish my love for Jackson. If anything, it makes me love him even more. We're all so lucky." She gave him another couple of squeezes as he began to stroke her breast.

"You're making me hard again," he said with a chuckle. "Ohh," he groaned, "Willa..."

That was the end of their conversation for a while as things heated up all over again.

Finally spent, they drifted off to sleep still wrapped in each other's warmth.

Chapter Eighteen

The birthday party for Jackson's dad was enjoyable, but Jackson still felt like he was missing an important part of his life by being there without Willa and Casey. He visited with neighbors, old friends, and extended family members, but as pleased as he was to see his parents doing well and their farm thriving, he couldn't kick his loneliness to the curb.

Once the guests finally left, Jackson's mom took him by the hand and asked, "What's bothering you, son? You seem a million miles away. Is something wrong?"

"No, not wrong, Mom. Maybe I need to explain something to you and Dad, though. Can we all sit and have a drink before we go to bed?"

"Sure, we can. I'll just go round up your father and a bottle of something and we'll meet you in the den, okay?"

"Perfect."

A few minutes later they were all situated in the cozy den with crystal snifters of cognac.

"It was a great party, Mom. I'm sorry if I seemed like I wasn't enjoying myself, because I really was. I'm just missing... someone... very badly."

His mom's eyes lit up and she asked, "Is it that lovely Willa you've mentioned to us? Are you seriously involved with her now?"

"Well, yes, and... yes. But that's not all." Jackson took a bolstering breath and hurried on, "I also miss Casey. They're... um... together."

Jackson's dad piped up sharply, "Wait, what? You mean your girlfriend and your best friend are cheating on you? I'd have expected better than that from Casey!"

"No. It's not like that. That's what I need to explain." Jackson let out a breath and just went for it. "We're *all three* involved. Seriously. Together."

"Um..." began his mom. She seemed to run out of words after that. She just blinked a few times.

"Jackson? How can that be?" asked his dad.

"It's called a triad, Dad. Three people committed as a unit. They would have come with me for the party, but they both had business obligations they had to attend to."

Looking his son square in the eye, Mr. Mitchell said, "I've heard of it, Jackson, but I sure hope you know what you're doing."

Then his mom, who seemed to have finally gathered her wits about her, asked softly, "Are you happy, son?"

A lopsided, somewhat goofy grin changed Jackson's features from worry to joy as he answered, "Happier than I've ever been. I never thought such a thing would be possible. I have Casey *and* Willa and they have each other... and me. It's perfect—except that they aren't here. That part is bugging the shit out of me, quite honestly. Sorry, Mom."

She waved away any concerns about his language.

"What about the future?" asked his dad.

"I guess we'll have to see how it plays out. We've discussed that we all want a family. It just may not be a conventional one. But—this is California for heaven's sake, and no one is going to care."

His dad voiced his concerns, "I'm not worried about what the neighbors might think, but I am worried that you're involved in something that will wind up a disaster."

"Darling, don't be hard on Jackson," said his mom. "We've always suspected he was... um..."

"Sexually fluid?" Jackson prompted.

"That term will do," she said with a nod to her son. Looking back at her husband she continued, "He's just lucky that in this day and age it's acceptable. No relationship comes with guarantees, so let's be happy for them." Turning to face her son, she continued, "We've always been very fond of Casey. He's a good man and he's always been a good friend to you. I hope things work out well for all of you. You just have to promise to bring them both up to see us soon. We need to meet Willa." Then she blushed and went on, "I actually read a few of her books recently, and all I can say is, she's certainly..." She cleared her throat. "Imaginative... and talented."

Relaxing finally now that his parents were informed, Jackson promised, "I'll bring them by as soon as we can all manage it. We're heading up to British Columbia to do some skiing this week, and then we have a yacht chartered out of Monte Carlo that we'll spend a week or two on, depending on how much we like it. I thought we all needed to get away and have some fun. They are both workaholics, but the timing is right for all of us. I can't wait. Maybe we can swing by the farm on our way back."

"That would be marvelous," said his mom with a smile.

"I love you guys. How many other parents would be as accepting, I wonder?"

"We love you too and hope it works out," said his dad.

Chapter Nineteen

T he next few days saw the triad finishing up last-minute business negotiations and getting ready to leave. They rushed around with lists to check off and made calls to everyone who needed to be alerted that they'd be out of the country for a while.

Finally, early on a Thursday morning, the limo driver pulled up to Jackson's house. Considering all of the bulky ski clothes and cumbersome equipment they needed for the Canadian part of the trip, they had an awful lot of baggage. But—they managed. Willa wanted to double-check every last thing she'd packed, but Casey told her, "Don't worry. They have stores where we're going. If you've forgotten something or need something different, you can pick it up there."

Jackson leaned in close so the driver who was loading the car couldn't hear him and said, "I *didn't* pack any condoms." He gave them both a cheeky wink as Willa tried to not blush.

And finally, they were on their way.

The private plane Willa booked for them just had one attendant—a handsome young man who introduced himself as Spencer. He showed them around the exquisite interior of the plane and went through the safety spiel. Soon they were cruising through the sky, sipping mimosas and eating eggs Benedict.

By having their own charter, they were able to avoid the hassle of changing planes in Vancouver, and it made the trip go by quickly. They began swapping ski stories about their favorite places and heroic feats of skiing brilliance as well as some other stories from past trips.

"We were at Heavenly Valley when we were about nineteen," began Casey. "During winter break. Jackson and I decided to go off the beaten path a bit and ski some trees."

"You're *not* telling Willa that story," chided Jackson with a grimace.

Casey smirked and continued, not stopping for a second. "Have you ever noticed that small scar on Jackson's thigh?"

"Oh, I have, now that you mention it." Turning to Jackson, she asked, "Did you hurt yourself skiing?"

Jackson glowered and didn't answer, so Casey filled in the blanks. "He got too close to a tree stump and snagged his pantleg on it. He was going so fast, he couldn't stop, but the pants gave way, and he scraped his leg. Once he picked himself up out of the pile of snow he fell into, he had to ski down to the bottom of the mountain with his tighty whities hanging out for all to see and enjoy."

"I've never worn tighty whities in my life," grumbled Jackson, but then he shook his head, and his eyes twinkled with humor. "My butt was so cold by the time we got back I couldn't even feel anything. I now have a new appreciation for the phrase 'freezing your ass off.' The worst part was I had my ski lift pass attached to the pants—which were the only snow pants I owned—and I couldn't afford to go buy another ticket for the rest of the day after I got bandaged up and changed into jeans. It was a sad, lost opportunity because the next day we had to leave." Looking at Casey he added, "The rest of the trip was great, though."

Casey gazed into Jackson's eyes and smiled fondly.

"What's been your favorite place to ski, Willa?" asked Jackson.

Without even stopping to think about it, Willa answered, "Taos, New Mexico."

"Huh," said Jackson. "I thought you stuck mostly to Colorado with your friend from Boulder. Taos... so you like it steep?"

With a mischievous grin, Willa responded, "I do. I also loved the food and probably gained five pounds that week after going out to dinner every night and eating about a thousand sopapillas. You know how hungry you get after skiing all day? I had to go on a diet when I got home." She sighed. "We decided to try New Mexico on a lark that one time and were delighted we'd done it. What a blast. And yes, it's definitely meant for those who like steep slopes."

The plane landed smoothly at a private airstrip in the Cariboo Mountains, and a luxury SUV limo waited for them on the tarmac. Looking around at the scenery, Willa smiled broadly, "It's fantastic up here." They had all donned jackets, hats, and winter gloves before exiting the plane, but she still exclaimed, "Whew! It's cold!" She stomped her booted feet a couple of times and zipped her jacket up higher. The sky had that gray look to it that seemed to warn that more snow was coming.

They were all happy with the heated seats in the limo. Their jeans weren't doing much to beat the cold.

A couple of hours later, after driving through spectacular mountain passes, they arrived at their lodge, a charming alpine establishment that looked homey and opulent at the same time.

The proprietor welcomed them and offered keys to what he called their "newest and most luxurious suite." It turned out to be a separate house that was basically its own mini estate. "You are most welcome to have dinner either by yourselves or in the dining room with the other guests," the manager said. "Just let us know about thirty minutes before you want your meal if you want it delivered. Breakfast and lunch are buffet-style in the dining room where our guests typically meet up with their guides for the day and plan their itinerary." He gave them the hours for the dining room and then handed them pamphlets explaining the ski terrain and safety precautions for the helicopter rides. "The guide who has been assigned to you is named Lorne. He's young and enthusiastic with a great sense of humor, but he knows his stuff. He grew up near here, so you won't go wrong with him, I assure you. Oh, and your unit has its own sauna and private outdoor hot tub. Our guests definitely enjoy those amenities after a long day on the slopes. We also have several licensed masseuses on staff for those tired muscles."

Their bags were already in their suite by the time they got there, so they quickly unpacked and sat down to enjoy some of the delicious snacks and fresh fruit left by the management. After that, they decided to bundle up and take a walk into the nearby town to explore before dinner.

As they walked through the snow to town, Casey asked, "So, how do you both feel about eating at the house instead of in the dining room tonight? I think it's likely people will gawk at us."

"Screw that," answered Jackson immediately. "Let them gawk. More likely than not, they'll just think we're three people who like to ski together. But even if they figure out we're together, I don't care. Besides, we'll be here all week, and we won't be able to hide from them."

"How do you feel about it, Willa? Do you worry you'll be recognized from your book covers?"

Willa looked at Casey and then at Jackson. She had a pensive expression. After a moment she said, "If someone recognizes me, they already have an open mind, so that doesn't worry me at all. If anyone else thinks we're up to no good, it's their problem, not ours. I say we eat with everyone in the dining room tonight and act friendly to the other guests. They can make up their own stories about what they think, and I don't give a darn. Are you okay with it, Casey?"

"Yeah, I'm cool. I just want to make sure we're on the same page. Also, it's not like we're dining in some fancy la-di-dah private club. The guests here will no doubt be on the younger side."

"And considering what they're here to do, they're probably pretty adventurous," Jackson added.

With that decided, they wandered through the small, and surprisingly sophisticated, town. They admired local and indigenous artwork at a gallery. Casey couldn't resist purchasing a few pieces that he had sent back to his business, saying, "I know just where these would look great. I'll call my clients about them as soon as we get back."

They looked at some hand-carved scrimshaw that was interesting, but not anything that particularly grabbed them, so they moved on. The town also boasted no less than three very busy ski shops and a bakery that smelled like heaven. Finally, they found their way into a cozy, colorful tavern and ordered Irish coffees to warm up.

"Are you guys here to do some heliskiing?" their waitress asked. When they all smiled and nodded, she added, "Awesome. The rest of the week is going to be sunny and around four or five degrees. Perfect conditions."

"Still sounds pretty cold to me," grumbled Casey.

"Celsius," clarified Jackson. "You're in Canada, remember?"

"Oh... yeah. Duh. Sounds nice!" He winked at the waitress who smiled seductively at him and sashayed away to get their order.

After their hot drinks, they meandered back to the lodge, stopping to let the front desk know they'd be having dinner in the dining room, and the proprietor assured them their table would be ready. As they exited through the back door and headed to their cottage, snowflakes were beginning to fall.

Looking at the sky, Jackson mused, "I wonder how deep the powder is on these slopes. This is going to be so great."

♡♡♡

Dinner was magnificent. The dining room was intimate; they were close to the rest of the guests, but the acoustics were designed so that they couldn't overhear anyone else's conversations. There was a roaring fire warming the room, and the décor was decidedly mountain chic. Willa thought she could hear Casey's wheels spinning as he took in ideas for decorating this kind of space.

They did garner some curious looks from a few of the other guests. Trying their best to ignore it, the two men got rather mulish looks on their faces when a couple who'd finished their dinner approached them. Right away, the woman told them, "We're sorry to bother you while you're eating, but I had to know, you're Willa Camden, aren't you?"

"I am," answered Willa warmly.

"I have to tell you that I've read every one of your books and they changed our lives." She looked a bit embarrassed, but continued, "I used to be so closed off to the idea of, um, certain things, but after reading your books, I learned to relax and enjoy... things... with my husband. So, I want to thank you for saving our marriage."

Her husband, although red in the face, said, "I know romance writers sometimes get criticism for not writing more serious stuff, but you're doing a service to readers everywhere. Thank you."

"No, thank you! I'm thrilled to hear I could provide some helpful entertainment." Willa addressed the man, "Do you also read the books?"

"We read them to each other," explained the wife. "Especially... certain parts." She blushed even more. "Anyway, we didn't mean to disturb you, but I wanted to say hello and thank you. Enjoy your stay here; it's really a terrific place. And, well... have fun skiing." She took her husband's hand and they left. Just as they reached the doorway, the husband dropped his wife's hand and grabbed her butt. They could hear her giggling her way into the lobby.

They all looked at each other and tried not to snort.

"That was nice," Willa said. Her eyes were glowing from the couple's complements. "They were private people, you can tell, but they thought to come and talk to me."

The next person to stop by their table that evening was their guide Lorne. He introduced himself and said, "I didn't want to wait until breakfast to meet you all in case you had lots of questions." Just as advertised, he was a handsome, jovial young man who seemed to have a ready answer for everything and filled them with confidence. By the time they were done talking with him, they were all chomping at the bit to get out there and ski some deep powder.

Chapter Twenty

The snow was really coming down when they left the main building that night, but by morning, the sun blazed in the clear sky, making the world look magical and pristine. They were just finishing up their breakfasts when Lorne appeared like an excited puppy.

"Nearly ready to go? It's going to be an awesome day!" he announced happily.

Willa had never been in a helicopter before. Her first impression was that it was noisy, and the view was unbelievable. When the pilot took them over the crest of a mountain and immediately dropped their altitude, Willa's stomach dipped. It felt as if she were in a falling elevator. "Whoa!" she laughed. She grabbed Jackson's arm, and he looked at her with amusement.

"You'll get used to it," Lorne said cheerfully. "Stefan is an amazing pilot, but he loves to show off a little for the guests."

Willa thought she could do with a little less of a show.

Soon Stefan dropped them off at the top of a mountain that was so white and perfect, it looked like heaven. There was an open bowl for them to ski down above the tree line.

"We'll start with this and see how you all navigate the powder," said Lorne as they exited the helicopter and stepped into their ski bindings. "It's deep here, but there aren't any obstacles to get in the way. It's the best place to warm up, in my opinion."

He spaced them out evenly so they could ski down almost side-by-side. Then he pointed to an area way below them and explained, "Stefan will meet us there with the chopper."

The hours that followed were some of the most exhilarating of Willa's life. They were waist-deep in fluffy powder and, except for them, the world felt completely silent. She and the three men slalomed their way down mountain after mountain, whooping and laughing with complete abandon. Feathery snow flew around them as they glided through it, covering their bodies with white.

Each wore a tracking device just in case of an avalanche, and they all respected the possibility of danger, but they were having so much fun, it was impossible to worry.

At first, they skied conservatively, getting the feel of navigating through such deep snow, but as they grew accustomed to it, they sped up. Willa seemed to be the speed demon of the bunch and routinely left the others a few paces behind. Lorne had to make sure she knew where she was going so she didn't get too far out in front and wind up lost.

After three glorious hours, they headed back to the lodge for lunch.

"Our Willa's a monster on skis!" exclaimed Casey when they sat down to lunch. "She's bruising my ego," he laughed.

"Show me where it hurts, and I'll kiss it," she said with a cheeky grin.

Jackson piped up with a snort, "Your ego needed a little adjustment, if you ask me." Then he gave Casey a blinding smile that told him clearly that he was only kidding. "Our Willa is pretty amazing, but we knew that already." He kissed her cheek.

Excitedly, Willa told them, "Lorne says he has a steeper slope in mind for us for this afternoon. Are you guys ready for it?"

Casey snorted, and Jackson gave her an amused look. "Maybe we were hanging back just to watch you ski, my lovely snow goddess. Ever think of that?"

"Yeah, right," she chuckled. "Maybe we ought to have a race this afternoon. Loser has to... hmm..." She got a pensive look and continued in a hushed voice, "Nah, the *winner* gets to be in the middle tonight. You guys game?" She wiggled her eyebrows at them with a lascivious grin.

"I'm in," agreed Casey at the same time Jackson said, "Sounds like fun! No one will be a loser this way."

♡♡♡

When they saw the slope that Lorne had in mind for them, however, all thoughts of racing flew out of their heads.

"That sucker is *steep!*" exclaimed Casey with his eyes wide. "And it's narrow. There's no way to race each other down that."

Lorne burst out laughing and said, "We'll go one at a time, and I'll use the GoPro to shoot all of you coming down. This is definitely not the place to race, but you all did so well this morning, I thought you might need more of a challenge. Is everyone cool with this?"

They all agreed to give it a go. Once again, the helicopter touched down and let them out to put on their skis. Stefan conferred with Lorne about the next meeting spot and took off.

"I'll meet you all right down there where the slope levels out a bit. We can catch our breath and then ski some trees if you like," Lorne explained as he pointed out where he planned to stop. "Wait for me to turn around so I can film each of your runs." And he sped away through the snow.

Watching Lorne ski was a sight to behold. He was so comfortable and powerful as he created a wake of sparkling snow that blew around him in the bright sunlight. He checked his speed a few times, making giant slalom turns, and then finally came to a stop. He turned to face back up the mountain and waved with one of his poles.

Ladies first," said Jackson. Willa took off like a flash. Though her skiing was less powerful than Lorne's, Willa was more graceful. Where Lorne seemed to attack the snow, she appeared to dance through it with her own built-in sense of rhythm. She kept her movements spare as she carved out a beautiful, even zigzag pattern down the mountainside. She made more turns than Lorne had and still made excellent time getting to him.

Next came Casey who had an aggressive style. He tended to keep his weight well forward and his hands rather high. His speed checks were erratic and choppy, but he whooped and shouted his entire way down. The man was clearly enjoying himself.

Jackson was the final skier. He stayed to the right of the other ski tracks, carving his own way through the virgin powder. Tall and strong, Jackson attacked the slope like everything in his life. He studied it, and then he conquered it. When he reached the others, his smile was as blinding as the snow surrounding them. "That was *great*," he exclaimed.

"Best day ever," Casey agreed.

"I bet the video will look amazing. Anyone need a breather?" asked Lorne. When everyone shook their head, he continued, "We'll be making tracks over there." He indicated an area to the left of them where the trees were sparse. "Check your speed, and we'll be going down single file. It's not as steep as what you just did, but there's a fun little drop-off at the end of the grove of trees, so I hope you're all comfortable with a little ski-jumping. It'll seem like it comes out of nowhere, so stay loose." Seeing their happy smiles, he ordered, "Leave some space between yourself and the skier in front of you because we won't always be able to see one another as we get close to the bottom. Let's go!"

They took off in the same order as before. At first, Willa had to consciously make herself slow down so she didn't overtake Lorne. He was more deliberate and careful now than he had been on the earlier slopes. Willa knew it had to do with the trees around them; Lorne was skiing through them with care.

Willa, too, had a healthy respect for the danger of crashing into a tree. Many a skier had broken bones smacking into one. Some had even died.

Before long, Willa got a sense of Lorne's rhythm and speed, which left her free to focus on the path between the trees. She navigated carefully, following the tracks Lorne had made in the silky powder. Suddenly, Lorne disappeared from her view altogether. Within seconds, she realized why.

The path between the trees stopped at an outcropping of a snow-covered boulder with a sheer face. Gravity pulled her to the edge, and suddenly she was flying through the air. The jump was a lot higher off the ground than she'd anticipated, but the thrill she felt as she sailed through the air was exhilarating. She landed smoothly and gracefully and skied over to Lorne to watch the others.

Casey burst through the trees next and let out an ear-splitting whoop as he took to the air. Not as graceful as Willa, however, he landed on his butt—laughing his head off. He got up quickly and moved out of the way for Jackson.

"You okay?" asked Willa.

"Perfectly fine. You didn't just see that," he laughed.

Jackson didn't appear for a while, and Willa had a moment of fear that he'd crashed into a tree somewhere above them. But then she thought she saw a flash of movement way above them in the trees. She scanned the tree line, but lost sight of

Jackson as he made his way to the drop-off. Visible again, he took off into the air and had time to raise his arms and spread his legs in an abbreviated aerial split before pulling his feet together and making a solid landing. He skied over to them looking satisfied.

"Always the overachiever," snorted Casey as he reached over and gave Jackson a friendly pop on the arm.

"Eh. At least I didn't try to do a backflip."

"Why did you take so long to ski down? I was getting worried," asked Willa.

Jackson let out a snort. "I've skied with Casey for years, and when Lorne said we'd be jumping, I thought I'd give my buddy here time to get out of the way after he crashed and burned." Looking back up the slope he added, "And judging from the crater over there, I was right."

With a put-on sneer Casey replied, "Ha-ha," and then he joined Jackson laughing. "I haven't quite mastered the 'stay loose' technique. Somehow I always end up on my ass."

After two more spectacular runs, they decided to call it a day. Their muscles were tired, and a glass of wine in the hot tub was beginning to sound like heaven. Stefan picked them up and dropped them back at the resort, wishing them a pleasant evening.

The rest of the week in Canada was fantastic. Each day was sunny and warm enough to be comfortable, and they traveled farther and farther from the lodge each day to try out new mountainsides.

"I don't know how I could ever buy another lift ticket after this," announced Jackson one afternoon. "This is the best way to ski in the world. When we get to my house in Aspen, it might feel like we're slumming after this experience."

Casey laughed and said, "I seriously doubt that. When it's done, that house is going to feel like a palace. And you can always charter a helicopter there too, you know."

"Maybe I'll buy one," Jackson mused. "Nah, on second thought I'll leave flying to the pros."

"When is the house going to be done?" asked Willa.

"Probably in August. We can all go stay there for as long as you like. It's gorgeous there in the summer too. I know how much you love the beach, but it's a great change of pace. Pretty soon I'll have to start hiring a staff."

Willa raised her eyebrows at him.

Smiling, Jackson added, "Hey, it's a lot of work being ridiculously rich, and I'm still getting the feel of it."

♡♡♡

Some of the guests liked to settle in the comfortable, opulent sitting room off the lobby after the dinner service was over. They congregated around the fire and swapped ski stories and anecdotes. There was plenty of laughter to go around. The various guides loaded their GoPro videos onto a large screen that ran continuously, and they all had a ball pointing out their runs to each other.

Willa, Jackson, and Casey joined the group several nights in a row. They usually sat together on a comfy couch, and although they didn't really display out-and-out PDA, they looked pretty snuggly. Willa tended to sit in the middle, but if she picked a side, she alternated which of the guys she sat next to. Then someone would get up to get them drinks, and the configuration would change.

Finally, on their fifth night there, the woman who'd approached Willa on the first night apparently couldn't stand the suspense any longer and asked Willa outright, "Pardon my nosiness, but are you a couple with one of these guys? And if so, which one? You seem pretty cozy with both of them."

Willa smiled politely and said, "We're all together."

"Oh! So, you have two men?"

Casey piped up then and said, "She does, but we also have each other. What Willa means is that we're a triad."

The woman gave a tiny gasp and asked, "Like in a couple of your books? Wow."

Looking at Casey and Jackson and then at the woman, Willa responded, "Sort of like that. I wrote the books before any of this happened, and this is real life rather than fiction, but it works for us. We've never been happier."

"Wow," breathed the woman once more. Then she locked her attention onto her husband.

He looked back at her wide, questioning eyes, raised his eyebrows, then laughed. "Not a chance."

Jackson chuckled. "It's not for everyone, but as Willa said, it works beautifully for us."

Word spread quickly after that. They got a lot of curious looks from some of the other guests. A few of them got flirty, which made Willa wonder if these folks thought the three of them were down for an orgy or something. Fortunately, no one was rude enough to propose anything outright.

Flirtatious guests aside, most of the other resort-goers seemed unfazed by their arrangement, so the three of them relaxed and got more and more demonstrative with each other. Willa found it to be a relief to be able to express her feelings openly. She often hugged her guys or gave them quick kisses around other people. Jackson and Casey never went so far as to kiss publicly, but one might sling an arm around the other's shoulders for a while.

The nights in their suite were the best. They headed to their private hot tub as soon as they pulled off their ski gear. It felt so decadent to sip a glass of wine, champagne, or beer, and stretch out their muscles in the steaming, bubbling water. Invariably, they would start smooching and make their way to bed. By the time they had to get ready for dinner, they all had happy, relaxed faces.

After dinner and visiting with the other guests, they would head back to bed and start the fun all over again. It was a two-bedroom suite, both with large king beds, but they picked their favorite room right away and all three of them stayed in it together.

They'd realized early on that Casey tended to move around while he slept, and Willa always needed to get up to pee in the middle of the night, so after much trial and error, it just worked out that Jackson, the quiet one who rarely moved a muscle, slept in the middle. A king bed worked pretty well for them, but Jackson had already decided to have a special, extra-large one built for the Aspen and La Jolla houses. He'd also changed the plan for the master suite's closet. It would be expanded to service three wardrobes. And he requested, much to the Aspen builder's confusion, to have three sinks in the monstrous en-suite bathroom. The shower was already enormous enough to provide enough room for all of them.

Casey was thrilled when he heard about Jackson's plans and responded, "Thank you, Jax. That does a lot to make me feel... well... permanent."

Jackson leaned his forehead against Casey's and answered in a soft voice, "As you should."

Willa took in their exchange with a fond expression. Casey really had become a complete and essential member of their relationship. She could barely remember what it had been like to just be a couple with Jackson now that Casey was so en-meshed with them.

By the end of the week in Canada, they were exhausted in the best way possible. Their bodies had taken on some in-credibly difficult skiing situations, and they'd all done it with style. They had very few spills and had wonderful videos to take home and watch. And their nights together were incredible. Each of them expressed their love for one another over and over as they explored their bodies in intimate ways. Their hearts were filled with warmth and affection.

The night before they were due to leave, Casey brought up a question that he'd been pondering. "I think we ought to do something special for Stefan and Lorne. They've made this a wonderful adventure for us."

"Agreed," said Jackson as Willa nodded.

What they finally came up with was to write both of them generous checks. To say that the two Canadians were grateful and surprised is putting it mildly. Stefan blinked at the figure before whispering his thanks, and Lorne threw his arms around each of them, treating them in turn to a massive bear hug. He had tears in his eyes when they all said their goodbyes.

"I hope you come back again," he told them. "You're some of the nicest people I've ever taken out in these mountains, and you're all amazing skiers. Enjoy the rest of your travels."

And off they went in their SUV limo to catch the private jet that would fly them to Nice, France. Some warm sunshine and perhaps some sunbathing sounded pretty good after their week in the snow.

Chapter Twenty-One

The transcontinental and transatlantic flight was a long one, but they amused themselves by dining on exquisite cuisine and relaxing. They all read for a while after lunch and then opted to take a nap in the luxuriously appointed stateroom. The nap, of course, began energetically with some mile-high fun before they collapsed and slept for a few hours. A mouth-watering aroma woke them, and they were treated to an amazing dinner.

"This is the best way to travel," sighed Willa. "It's way better than first class."

With all of the time zone changes, it was morning in Nice when they arrived.

Another helicopter met them at the private airstrip and took them directly to a mega-yacht. The yacht was anchored off the coast of the French Riviera, and they could see the coastline and other boats, but it was still quite private.

The yacht owner—a silver fox named Cyril who had the courtly manners of an English peer from the nineteenth century—met them and proudly took them on a tour, explaining things as they went. The 330-foot yacht boasted a swimming pool with a waterfall, jogging track, and four large staterooms with their own terraces, plus a magnificent master suite. There was a large gym and spa with a professional massage therapist and fitness trainer, a cinema room, a gorgeous dining salon, a library with Wi-Fi and an array of computers, and several comfortable sitting areas. Willa, who'd been taking photos with her phone all through the tour, was thrilled when they were shown to the underwater observatory that boasted a fully stocked bar and bartender.

Casey's amazing skills were evident everywhere. Willa thought that he'd outdone himself; the décor was breathtaking. It seemed opulent and elegant without any extras that detracted from the sleek lines of the boat's design. It was colorful and tasteful.

Looking pleased with himself, Casey remained mostly silent as they meandered through the incredible space. Jackson and Willa complimented his sense of style over and over as they remarked on the special touches he'd added.

Cyril introduced them to the crew as they made their way through the various levels. All-in-all, it took thirty people to pilot, maintain, serve, and otherwise entertain the guests. The tour did not include the crew's quarters, being mindful of their privacy.

Cyril explained to Jackson and Willa, "It takes a lot of people to keep a boat of this size running smoothly, but we are only allowed up to twelve passengers at a time. Once you go over twelve, you become a passenger ship in the eyes of the International Maritime Organization, and you need to comply with a whole new set of regulations." He smiled proudly and continued, "Besides, it's more fun to have a few close friends instead of a huge crowd. We all appreciate our privacy, don't we?" He winked at Willa, causing her to stifle a giggle.

The captain was a no-nonsense kind of man in a sharp uniform, and the rest of the crew were all attired in spotless, professional blue-and-white outfits that bore the name of the yacht: Dream Come True. Everyone was inviting and cordial, but respectfully reserved toward Cyril's guests.

"Before I take my leave, I need to tell you, Jackson, that there was a message that came for you today. The chief steward can give you the information. Now," he addressed Casey, "if there is anything you find that is not one hundred percent to your liking, or there is anything at all amiss with the staff, I trust you will report back to me immediately." He took Willa's hand and brought it to his lips in a very old-fashioned manner. "You grace my yacht with your beauty and elegance, and I trust you and your gentlemen will all have the time of your lives aboard my new toy. Thank you all for taking the crew on this test voyage for me. My pilot will take me ashore now. Should you need his services with the helicopter, the captain will assist you in reaching him. He is on-call twenty-four-seven."

After everyone expressed their profound thanks, Cyril remembered something else. "If you all decide to go to the Grand Casino in Monte Carlo, be sure not to take cameras. They are not allowed inside for fear of anyone taking photos. They haven't banned phones yet, however, so they aren't exactly up to speed." Then their host gave them all a cheery salute, climbed into the helicopter, and flew away.

After the long journey and their strenuous activities in the mountains, the trio was happy to relax. They explored the observatory, lounged on the deck, and enjoyed a sample of the chef's cooking.

"I really have to do something active today," Willa said on their second morning. "I don't want another experience like when I got fat from too much good food at Taos. These crepes are amazing, but they'll go straight to my hips. Anyone care to join me later for a run around the track?"

After that, the three began a routine of exercising, swimming, and sunbathing for a few days. They found that the yacht had a below-deck garage full of watersport vehicles that they could take out right at water level, so they spent a lot of time trying them out. Willa discovered she loved whooshing around the clear blue water of the Mediterranean on a jetboard, marveling at how different the sea looked compared to the Pacific Ocean she was so used to.

Casey and Jackson got the biggest kick out of showing off on the flyboard waterjets. They could zoom up to twenty or thirty feet in the air, hover around and be goofy laughing their head off, and then dive down and propel themselves underwater.

"Come on, Willa. This is amazing. You need to take one out too. You feel like you're flying," Casey coaxed gleefully.

"I prefer the *surface* of the water, but you guys have fun," she laughed.

After several days of quiet enjoyment on the yacht, they began to crave something new. They decided to head into Nice. They asked a crewman to take them aboard a skiff into the harbor, where they were met by a car service.

Casey served as their guide and showed them all over the city. Naturally, his idea of sightseeing was to go to upscale shops and antique dealers. Jackson and Willa loved watching him get excited about his finds and didn't mind a bit that they weren't wading through crowds at the typical tourist sights.

Late in the morning, they entered one of the local art galleries. Casey gasped, "Whoa!" and sped to the back of the exhibit. Willa and Jackson followed him to where a spotlight illuminated a glistening marble sculpture of a nude man and a woman embracing. "Look at this piece!" Casey said enthusiastically. "It's an original Guillaume Routrez. I've been trying to locate one for years, and this one is *gorgeous*. I can't believe my luck." With wide eyes, he explained, "The sculptor came from Arles, and he died just a few years ago at the age of a hundred and one. This is an incredible find!" Casey was practically hyperventilating as he handed over his credit card and made arrangements to have the piece insured and shipped to California. As soon as he finished the transaction, he grabbed first Willa and then Jackson, laying happy smooches on both of them.

"Remember when I told you how infectious his enthusiasm can be?" Jackson asked. "This is what I was talking about. I've been on buying expeditions with him before, and it's pretty entertaining to see him uncover treasures and sometimes bargain for the best price. He used to drag me around to estate sales even back when we were kids. I'd look at old bicycles and cast-off computers, and he'd be digging around for an under-appreciated painting or a filthy old antique that the owners didn't realize was worth a small fortune."

"You loved it," Casey scoffed with a smile.

Jackson chuckled. "I did. Until I had to help you drag the stuff home." He turned to look at Willa. "By the time we left for college, he had made himself a small fortune selling things to collectors."

Willa smiled at both of them and remarked, "Pretty enterprising for a kid. That's impressive."

Eventually, they were all ready for some lunch. Casey had sent home a variety of pieces besides the sculpture of his dreams, and he looked like a satisfied cat. "Okay, come on, I know just the place to hit for some food." He took them to a delightful and understated seaside bistro where they spent the next two hours relaxing, eating, and sipping wine. The fresh seafood was magnificent.

As they finished eating, Willa said, "Jackson, I've been meaning to ask you—did you ever get your message from the steward? And how did someone know to reach you aboard the yacht?"

"I did get it, and it's nothing to worry about. I've been doing some research and left information about where we'd be staying with one of my contacts. My phone had been off while we were flying to France, and that's apparently when he called. I also had a voicemail from him." Abruptly, he changed the subject, turned to Casey, and asked, "Where to after this, fearless leader?"

"I'm done buying art for now. Why don't we go buy some beautiful things for Willa?"

Willa chuckled, "You guys don't need to do anything like that."

"Oh, but it sounds like fun," Casey protested. "Aren't you getting tired of her same old bikinis, Jax? She needs a few new ones, if you ask me. And if we want to head to the casino," he looked at Willa, "do you have anything suitable to wear? Some people like to dress up."

"I brought a nice cocktail dress—just in case," she answered.

Jackson asked, "The red one? I have such fond memories of that dress." He leered at her when she nodded—her blush giving away her memory of what he'd done to her at Casey's party in that very dress. "I think the occasion of being here in the south of France, loving every moment we all have together, warrants a new dress." He turned to Casey and ordered, "Lead the way. We have more shopping to do!"

After settling the bill, they all piled into their waiting car. In just a few minutes they were dropped off at a boutique that was so exclusive they had to ring a bell to be allowed in. Casey answered the shopkeeper's questions in rapid French that left Willa and Jackson slack-jawed. But the door buzzed, and they all entered an exquisite space where they were greeted by an elegant woman.

For the next hour, Willa tried on every imaginable style of dress. Some were classic and sleek, and others were positively scandalous. A couple of them were so revealing with side slits up to here and plunging décolleté down to there, she couldn't wear any undergarments. The men decided those were great, and Willa looked spectacular in them, but they were for their eyes only. Having other men leer at her made them uncomfortable.

They finally narrowed it down. An off-the-shoulder black dress that revealed her excellent cleavage and did a magnificent job of showing off her shapely legs, plus a teal blue shift dress covered in tiny crystals. The fabric skimmed her curves in an alluring way, and the sparkles brought attention to her beautiful figure. The blue also brought out her dazzling eyes.

They ended up buying the two dresses, incredibly beautiful and ridiculously expensive shoes for both outfits, and a half dozen or so tiny but costly bikinis without bothering to see if they even fit. They were about to pay for everything when Jackson remembered one of his favorite ultra-revealing dresses, and told the saleswoman to add that one to their purchase as well. The shopkeeper was practically salivating when she gave them the final tally. She seemed relieved when no one batted an eye at the exorbitant cost of the clothes. She wished them well and asked them three times to be sure to come back again. "Mademoiselle is extremely well-suited to our designs," she assured them needlessly. "Or, pardon, is it Madame?"

Willa looked confused by the question, so Casey stepped in to set things straight. "Mademoiselle is fine, thank you." He turned to Willa and explained, "French authorities have tried to stop people from using the honorific 'Mademoiselle' because they decided years ago that a woman's marital status is her own business, but in private speech it's still widely used. She just means you're not wearing a wedding band, so she assumed you weren't married. If you were fifteen years older, and she called you Mademoiselle, it would be a compliment. It would mean that you looked as young as a lady in her twenties."

"So complicated," Willa chuckled.

"It gets even more complicated in other French-speaking countries. In Canada, for instance, 'Mademoiselle' is considered an insult. The Belgians just try to ignore it completely, apparently. And... some younger French women—even married ones—bristle at being called Madame because they think the person addressing them is saying they look old. I guess it's like Americans calling a young woman 'ma'am.'"

Willa visibly shuddered and then laughed. "Thanks for the etiquette lesson."

Laden with their purchases, they were soon back aboard Dream Come True. Casey went off to locate the captain and found him making arrangements for their visit to Monte Carlo.

The captain informed Casey that he'd have to arrange for a slip to dock at, but assured him that it would be no problem. The marina was used to superyachts and even mega-yachts like Dream Come True.

Chapter Twenty-Two

Casey made his way back to the enormous master suite, admiring his work around the yacht as he went. He could hear Jackson and Willa talking and laughing as he entered the master bedroom area.

"Another one!" ordered Jackson cheerily. "I haven't decided which is my favorite yet." His head whipped around as he saw Casey and met his questioning look with a sexy smolder. "Willa's been trying on bikinis for me. You've missed the show." He turned back to Willa and continued, "You'll have to start over now so Casey and I can vote." His look was that of amused innocence.

Willa was, at that point, attired in a tiny yellow and blue striped confection that was barely there. In fact, the bottom half was actually a thong, and it made her tanned and toned bottom look amazing. Casey had specifically chosen this little number, and he felt himself getting hard just standing there looking at her. "Yes," he said. "Please go back to what you were doing. I'd love to see them all on you... and off of you too."

With a sultry smile, Willa slowly peeled off the top and then the bottom and stepped into a shiny black ensemble held together with complicated laces. Casey thought she looked a little like a sexy dominatrix. He plopped down next to Jackson on a pillowy loveseat. They were very cozy with their bodies touching one another. Jackson put his arm around Casey as they made themselves comfortable.

Willa began making a big production of doing a mini-striptease with plenty of booty shaking each time she changed outfits. She also smirked knowingly at their evident arousal. Jackson eventually unzipped his pants to get some room for his... excitement. "It was getting hot in there," he mock-complained. "Ahh, that's better."

Casey winked at him and did the same as he peered at Jackson's wood with approval. "Yeah. Free balling's the way to go."

Willa strutted around showing off her favorite bikini and wiggled her butt at them a few times. Finally, she ordered them. "Kiss each other. You know that gets to me."

"Fine, but you only get to watch if you put on the naughty-girl dress we picked out for you," Jackson told her. "The one that's not all there."

"Okay." She gave him a saucy wink. "I hung it in the closet." Willa turned and sashayed away, swinging her delicious hips as she left.

In no time, she was back wearing the dress and a pair of sky-high heels. Jackson and Casey, however, were already kissing and fondling each other. Since she didn't have anything on under the dress, Willa could already feel dampness on her thighs. Watching her two men love on each other always did that to her. She approached them quietly to stand in front of them.

Slowly they pulled away from each other's kiss and took in the sight of her. Casey exclaimed to Jackson, "Doesn't she look like one of the beautiful celebrities who show up at the Oscars in a scandalous barely-there dress to get attention? She looks amazing."

"If you ask me, not one of those actresses has anything on our Willa." Jackson sighed, "So gorgeous." Locking eyes on Willa, he added, "You have the most perfect tits in the world, and those legs... wow." He turned back to Casey. "We were smart to get this dress for her, but we can never let her go out in public like this. She'd cause a riot." That made them all laugh.

As they sat back to enjoy Willa's beauty, they kept their hands busy stroking each other.

Casey then reached out his free hand and slipped his fingers under the slit of the dress. He caressed Willa's leg, moving right into the promised land. "You're soaked," he observed with a grin. "Feel this, Jax. It's like our little bit of heaven right here."

Jackson obliged, and Willa gasped and had to grab their shoulders as she felt not one, but two large fingers plunge into her. Her eyes rolled back and she let out a moan. The men stroked in and out of her in unison, making her writhe with their touch. She clamped her muscles down on their fingers and could barely stand up.

"You like this, don't you?" Casey asked softly. It was obvious she did. "Would you want us both in there together?"

"What?" she breathed. "You mean...?"

"Yes, beautiful. Jax and I talked about it, and we want to fuck you at the same time. Can you do that for us? It would be like we're all making love to each other at once."

"Oh... that would be... amazing. Right now?" She focused on their handsome faces and realized they both stared at her with lust in their eyes.

Jackson said, "Let's take off this beautiful dress so we don't ruin it." He stood and unzipped the dress, letting it pool at Willa's feet. He then gently picked it up and placed it on a nearby chair.

Casey took that opportunity to chuck his pants a few feet away. He sat back on the loveseat the long way and said to Willa, "Come here." Willa's eyes glistened as she went to stand in front of him. "Turn around," Casey said, "I need you to sit down on my dick."

Willa stepped out of the shoes and complied by turning so her ass faced Casey. His hands moved to her hips and he helped to guide her warm pussy down over him. They both let out moans of pleasure as she took him all the way in.

"That's it. Ahh, you feel so good," Casey breathed out.

Jackson removed his pants the rest of the way and knelt down beside the loveseat. Looking at his most beloved people in the world, he thought to himself, *I can't believe I ever harbored any jealousy about seeing these two together. It's the hottest thing I can imagine.*

Smiling crookedly, Jackson whispered as if in awe, "I can't imagine anything better than this."

Leaning in carefully, he began to lick Willa and Casey where their bodies were joined. He probed around her opening with his tongue, lapping at Casey's cock at the same time and then retreated to suck on Willa's clit. He played with both of them alternately with his tongue and his fingers, eventually sliding his index finger inside Willa where he could massage her and stroke Casey simultaneously.

"God, this is sexy," exclaimed Jackson. "I love this." He added another finger very carefully and felt how vicelike Willa was around his hand. It was going to be a very tight squeeze.

"This feels incredible," Casey rasped as he bucked up into Willa. "I feel everything so much more with your fingers on me, Jax. But I also want your dick. Do you need some lube? It's in the drawer next to the bed."

Jackson withdrew and cursed himself for not thinking of that before things got so heated up. Within seconds, however, he was back at their sides. Casey was manipulating Willa's clit as they bounced and moaned against each other. Jackson paused for just a moment to appreciate their beauty, thinking what a lucky man he was. Then he whipped his shirt off over his head and proceeded to lube up his dick.

"You seem pretty close to coming, Willa. Go ahead and let it go. It'll help you relax," he coaxed. "I don't want this to hurt." Once again, he leaned in and took over for Casey on her clit. He felt as if anticipation and arousal were about to make him explode as he sucked her into his mouth and heard her shattering moan. Giving her a few more soft licks, he pulled back and placed one knee on the far side of his partners on the loveseat. He pushed his finger inside Willa again, feeling less resistance this time. He added a second finger then and rubbed them along Casey's shaft, making him sigh with pleasure.

Finally satisfied that Willa was ready, he positioned himself carefully and began to push his erection in alongside Casey's. He'd always loved the feel of jacking off their two dicks together, captured side-by-side in both of their hands, but this was way, way better. Willa's warmth and heat surrounded the two of them as Jackson thrust all the way in.

Immediately, she gasped and shuddered with a second orgasm. Jackson wrapped his arms around her as he and Casey matched each other's rhythm, stroking in and out, in and out.

"I won't last much longer, Jax," Casey warned in a strangled voice. "This is the best thing I've ever felt in my life." No sooner did he say that when his movement became less languid and far jerkier.

Keeping his gaze on the crazed look in Casey's eyes, Jackson locked onto Willa's mouth, thrusting his tongue inside her like he was mouth-fucking her.

Casey slammed his eyes closed and began to curse a blue streak as he often did when he came, and Jackson smiled around his probing tongue. He knew they shouldn't, but Casey's orgasms often struck his funny bone. Jackson let go as well and came just seconds after Casey did with a long and enthusiastic groan. He held onto Willa for dear life as the three of them collapsed together, filling the loveseat with their warm, sated bodies.

"That was absolutely amazing. I want to do it again and again," Willa declared into Jackson's shoulder. "But let's all go take a shower first, okay? Also, I'm starving. Can we have the chef make us dinner? All of this dressing and undressing made me hungry."

Casey mumbled into Willa's hair, "Sure, that's what did it."

They all cracked up.

Jackson sobered quickly and announced, "I love you both so much."

"Me too," agreed Casey as he affectionately squeezed Willa and Jackson's arms.

Willa sighed, "Absolutely. It couldn't possibly get any better than this."

Squirming a little, Casey asked, "Can we get up now? It's getting hard to breathe down here. I love you both, but you two are heavy."

Chapter Twenty-Three

The next morning, they raised anchor and cruised eastward along the southern coast of France. Like every other day, the sun was bright, and the coastline stunning. The three of them watched as they passed by the Nice Castle, quaint houses, and breathtaking villas.

As they pulled into the harbor, the three of them got an up-close and personal view of the elaborate techniques it took to park a mega-yacht. There were already several men awaiting them dockside, ready to tie up the boat as it moved carefully into position. The boat slowly backed into the slip assigned to it. Dream Come True pulled in only a couple of feet away from the dock, attesting to the skill of the boat's pilot. It was impressive to see something so enormous maneuvering around with such precision.

Anxious to check out Monaco, the three of them disembarked after conferring with the chef and letting him know they would be dining ashore for the rest of the day. He seemed crestfallen, so they agreed to have him provide them with a late-night snack when they got back from the casino. That cheered him up considerably.

"That man certainly loves to cook," laughed Willa as they piled into their waiting car. "Speaking of which, what has Phillipe been doing while we've been gone, Casey?"

"He went home to see his parents in Quebec, and then he was planning to go to some cooking extravaganza conference in New York for a few days." Casey smiled thoughtfully. "It's wonderful to have a passion that keeps you interested in learning."

"I'm just glad there are people who are passionate about cooking so I don't have to be," laughed Willa. She took both their hands, and they spent the next couple of hours wandering around like that. A few people did double-takes, but mostly they were ignored or merely admired for their collective beauty. A few women looked enviously at Willa, and when she caught their looks, she winked at them, smiling like a Madonna.

As usual, Casey managed to locate a few treasures he needed to send home. They found a place where they wanted to have dinner and made reservations for later. Eventually, they made their way back to the yacht to shower and change for dinner and a night at the casino.

♡♡♡

This set up a pattern for the next two days. They took in the considerable sights of Monte Carlo during the day, visiting museums, galleries, and some high-end shops. After dinner at one of the local restaurants, they would head to the Grand Casino. Just the sight of the building itself was impressive with its beautiful architecture and grand fountain in front. Inside, the feel of the place was totally different from any Las Vegas or Reno casino. There was no neon or glitziness; instead the space glowed with stately opulence, though it might have been a tiny bit frayed around the edges. Everywhere they looked, there was marble and crystal—all gleaming and majestic, but there were no tuxedos in evidence like in the James Bond movies. The ceilings were adorned with beautiful frescoes and mosaics where everything competed for attention, and there were plenty of folks rubbernecking at it all. Another pleasant difference to the Nevada casinos, however, was the total lack of bells and whistles going off. The slot machines were silent, and the atmosphere subdued throughout.

They tried out a few different casino games and discovered that Jackson was happiest with blackjack. He would do his best to count cards surreptitiously until he'd won a tidy sum, but when the dealer changed decks, he would get up from the table and move on. Once he started over at a new table, he invariably lost for a while before getting a good sense of the deck.

Willa and Casey loved to watch Jackson while he was playing—he was so laser-focused, it seemed as if they could sense his impressive brain calculating the odds. They always stood a comfortable distance away—so as not to look as if they were helping him cheat somehow—and whispered to each other about how hot and brainy he looked and how much they loved him. It was hard to not get turned on by each other as well, though, as they whispered teasing things in each other's ear. They were hard-pressed to keep their hands from straying into impolite territory once they got worked up.

Casey preferred poker, fancying himself a good reader of the other players' tells. He did well at it too, but he'd sometimes bet on a lousy hand, thinking he could bluff. He couldn't. The other gamblers in the private games were far too adept at reading his tells, and his face was just too expressive.

Willa loved the excitement and immediacy of the roulette wheel, but none of them particularly cared for playing in the grand hall among all the gawking tourists. The private rooms that charged an entry fee suited them better; they felt less on display. However, after two nights of gambling for a couple of hours, they'd had their fill. Each of them had set a budget before playing, so they wouldn't leave feeling like broke chumps.

Their winnings, after all was said and done, were unimpressive, but they'd had fun and enjoyed the experience of gambling in the famous Monte Carlo.

"I don't know about you two, but I'm starting to feel ready to head home," declared Jackson after their trip back to Dream Come True. The chef had once again set out a lovely dessert buffet for them to enjoy with after-dinner drinks in the master suite, and they were savoring their cognacs and sweets as they looked at the reflection of lights on the water. They'd kicked off their shoes and were relaxing on a comfortable couch. "Before you both say anything about it, though, I have to tell you something." Willa and Casey gave him their attention as he continued, "Don't look so worried, this is something wonderful actually."

"Okay..." prompted Casey. Willa still looked a little nervous.

Taking a deep breath, Jackson began, "Before we left for the Cariboos, you both know I was researching some options for future investments." Willa relaxed then and nodded at him as Casey grinned. "I don't know much at all about this business, but I feel that with my monetary support and our collective talents, we could create something together that is lasting and amazing."

"Something like what, Jax?"

"I put out a bunch of feelers and queries to movie studios." Willa gasped at him then and he quickly continued. "Remember the message I got from the chief steward when we got to Nice? It was from one of the studios, and they were interested in what I had to say. I think they had to check into my background a little to decide whether I was a wannabe or a nut. I must have passed inspection because I heard from them again this evening while you two were gambling."

"So, you want me to star in a movie? I do look remarkably like a young Robert Redford, if I say so myself," laughed Casey. "Or maybe I'm more the Chris Hemsworth type—more muscles than Redford. Remember when I was the scarecrow in our sixth-grade production of 'The Wizard of Oz?' I was great!"

"Case."

"What?"

"You're not starring in a movie," Jackson laughed. "You were pretty convincing, though, wishing you had a brain."

Willa tried to cover a snort as Casey let out a huge and very fake sigh, asking, "Well, what then?"

"I've explained to them that I'm very close with a best-selling author whose books have a huge following. I figured out which one of your books has been your biggest moneymaker so far..."

"You did?" Willa asked.

Jackson looked slightly sheepish. "Sorry to do it behind your back, but I didn't want to get your hopes up until this thing had a real chance. Anyway, I suggested that if their studio were willing to make a movie from the book, I would be a very generous backer."

Willa seemed to be vibrating with excitement. Her eyes were as round as saucers as she stared at Jackson.

He continued, "I also said I had a lead on another potential backer who has extremely good sense when it comes to entertainment and what people like to see." He skewered Casey with an expectant look, and Casey's eyes crinkled up with one of his biggest smiles ever.

"Jackson," was all Willa could say. Then her eyes filled up and brimmed with happy tears and she flapped her hands in front of herself as though to erase something. She took a big gulp of air and choked out, "This is the sweetest thing I have ever heard."

"I agree," said Casey. "And I think it's a fantastic idea. What do we do next? Oh, and also... can we wait one more day before we leave?"

"There's no huge rush, but we do have a meeting in Los Angeles in three days, so we ought to be back in time to get over jet lag a little. Why do we need to stay one more day though?"

Casey looked smug and reached into his pocket. He whipped out an envelope and announced, "I was just about to tell you that I scored three loge seats for tomorrow's tennis finals at the Monte Carlo Masters tournament. I thought you both might enjoy some spectator sport for a change. Surprise."

With a profoundly admiring look, Jackson demanded, "How on earth did you get those on such short notice? I thought they sold out like a year in advance or something."

With his trademark grin, Casey answered, "Apparently our chief steward is a very resourceful guy, and when money is no object..."

"Casey, that's great," Willa gushed. "I've never been to the finals of a major tournament, but I've always wanted to." She beamed at both of them. "I'm so lucky to have the two of you."

And so, the three of them hobnobbed with the international elite the next day in a row of seats behind the baseline. They all agreed that the steward had worked magic for them, and it was so much better watching from one end of the court rather than swiveling their heads back and forth all through the match.

Their favorite man won—not that they'd have really cared either way because the entertainment factor was off the charts. The match had been a nail-biter to the very end, and the fans all felt as if they'd gotten their money's worth by watching it.

"That was fantastic, Case. Thanks again for getting us the tickets. This was the perfect way to end the trip," Jackson said, clapping him on the back affectionately.

Later that night, after dolling out generous tips to the entire crew with their personal thanks, they boarded the private jet. By the time they reached the San Diego airport, they were all well-rested and satisfied.

"I have butterflies just thinking about our meeting, Jackson. This is so exciting!" Willa announced.

"I need to report back to Cyril and let him know he hired a terrific staff for Dream Come True." Casey looked pensive and added, "Do you think maybe he'd like to invest in a movie too?"

Jackson's eyebrows shot up and he grinned. "Not a bad idea. Be sure to mention it to him. Good thinking."

Chapter Twenty-Four

The morning they were due to leave for LA for their meeting with the studio executives, Willa got a call from her agent.

"We have a problem," she said instead of *hi* or *hello*.

"Good morning, Sheila. I was just about to call you. What's the matter?"

"The publisher is going apeshit. There is a pirated, I assume, copy of your new book flooding the online bookstores as we speak. And hardbacks are showing up at the brick-and-mortar stores as well. Tell me you didn't do something weird, Willa."

"What are you talking about?"

"A book that is identical to yours and has the same title—only it completely lacks any editing other than possibly a spellcheck program—is showing up everywhere—e-books, paperbacks, and hardcover. And there are ads for it all over the place. They've done a huge advertising campaign for it suddenly. Some woman named Deb Abbey's name is listed as the author. How could this have happened?"

The room spun for a moment, and Willa braced her head in her hands. Her stomach roiled. "Oh no. Not her again," Willa breathed out in a defeated voice.

"What do you mean 'again?' What are you talking about, Willa?"

"Back when I was at Stanford, I wrote a book in my spare time, and she got hold of it... it's a long story. Anyway, several years later she won the Oscar for best original screenplay from the book she stole from me. Now she's gotten hold of this one, too? This is unbelievable. I think she must have hacked my computer before we went on vacation. The only other copy of it is with the editor."

"Why didn't you sue her ass after the first time she stole from you?"

"I didn't have any proof that the book was mine. I gave it to her on a thumb drive. She told me she was going to shop around for a publisher for me. She was supposedly representing me. Then my computer was ruined in a car crash, and I had no other copies. No one would have believed a college student's word that a literary agent had ripped me off. I told myself she just couldn't find a publisher for me because the book wasn't any good, and I eventually lost touch with her." Willa took a deep breath and continued. "Also... I had some pretty heavy stuff going on in my life back then because my parents had both just died in the same accident that ruined the laptop." Her voice began to crack.

"Okay, I'm awfully sorry, Willa, and I can see why you might not have pursued a lawsuit right away, but after she won the Academy Award? Why didn't you go after her then? When was this?"

"Just this past February."

"Are you shitting me? You're Willa Freakin' Camden! You're a New York Times, USA Today, Wall Street Journal, and international bestselling author, and who is she? A conniving thief! We need to hire a team of lawyers and get to the bottom of this right away. I can't believe you've let that slide, Willa!" Sheila's voice was getting louder and louder, making Willa wince. "So, now she probably wanted to cash in on her success. I bet she stole your book so she could release something right away and make a fortune before everyone forgets about her. She obviously knows how great your work is. God, what a manipulative, scheming *bitch*. She's probably cooked up some stupid story about how she wrote it and you're the one trying to steal it because she's all famous and important now. Listen, Willa, I'm going to get our legal team on this right away, so I'll be in touch. Keep your phone handy, okay?"

"I can get my own lawyer, Sheila. My dad's partners would probably be willing to represent me."

"Do they know about copyright and intellectual property law? You ought to have a specialist for this."

"I'm not sure actually. Maybe you should handle it after all." Willa found herself feeling overwhelmed. "Thank you."

"No shit. This is my job, Willa."

"Well, there *is* something good I need to tell you, though."

"Thank the lord. I need some good news this morning." Willa could hear Sheila take a gulp of something—probably coffee, but she wouldn't have blamed her if it was something stronger. "So, spill."

"Jackson, my boyfriend, got us a meeting for later today with Baxter Brothers Studios. They're interested in possibly making a movie from my book *Lost and Found*. We're heading up to Hollywood to meet with them. Jackson has backing for the movie already. I'm pretty excited to see where, if anywhere, this goes."

"Well, shit. With a mover-and-shaker boyfriend like that, you probably don't need me as your agent. Where's all the money coming from?"

"I do so need you, Sheila. This is just a fluke thing and something he's been researching. The money is coming from him and my... um... other boyfriend Casey, and possibly from one other guy. They're all pretty... okay *really* well-off."

"Willa, I don't know what's up with you lately. You go from living like a nun, as far as I can tell, to suddenly swimming in rich men? Two boyfriends? Do they both know you're seeing someone else? How can they invest together with you in the middle?"

Willa let out a tiny snort. "I'm not always the one in the middle." She paused to let that sink in for a second. "We're a triad, Sheila. It means..."

"I know what it means. Christ on a cracker, Willa!" There was a pause on the line and another audible gulp, and then Sheila continued over Willa's soft giggles, "You never cease to amaze me. I would feel a lot better if you had an attorney with you at this meeting today as well, but it's kind of short notice. Just promise me you'll have a lawyer look over everything before you agree to sign, okay?"

"I promise. And we'll figure out this business with Deb too. What a disaster." She paused and Sheila could hear Willa say something to someone else and then came back to the phone, "I have to go now, Sheila. Our driver is here. I'll talk to you later."

♡♡♡

The studio execs were two smarmy old brothers who eyed Willa with lust. Casey immediately got his back up when he saw one of them talking to her chest. Willa seemed unfazed by him, however, and Casey finally relaxed. *If they can make her dream come true, I guess they can ogle her tits a little. As long as they keep their hands to themselves. I guess this is how it's done in Tinseltown.*

Bernie Baxter, the younger of the two, explained, "It's a wonderful book, Willa, but since you're lacking a screenplay thus far and have no experience writing one, we'd like to hire a screenwriter we recently worked with very successfully to assist you. You may have heard of her—she won an Oscar for the movie we produced with her. As a matter of fact, the subject matter and general feel of your book is similar enough to that story, and it was so successful, that was one of the reasons we were interested in talking to you in more detail." He eyed Willa who'd suddenly put her hands over her face and hung her head. "Is there something wrong?"

"Deb Abbey," Willa muttered. "Of all people. I can't believe it."

"You're familiar with Deb? She's a big talent, I assure you. That story was magnificent." Bernie looked questioningly at everyone. "What's the problem?"

Jackson jumped in and explained in a voice that sounded like a knife fight, "Deb Abbey is a *thief*. Willa was the one who wrote the book that Deb stole from her several years ago. It's all plagiarized material. I don't know what she told you, but Willa wrote that story. The book was stolen from her. There was *nothing* original in what that woman showed you."

Bernie's eyes bulged and his face went pink. "That's some accusation for a respected member of the entertainment community. I hope you have some proof of that allegation, otherwise I'll ask you to get lost!"

Uncovering her face and looking Bernie right in the eye, Willa asked, "Were you aware of any changes made from the screenplay she brought you to what you ultimately used when the movie was shot?"

"Yes, of course. We had to shorten things and combine a few storylines for the sake of the movie. That's standard procedure. The first draft of the screenplay needed revisions, and we had our people work with Deb on that."

With steel in her voice, Willa addressed him. "I'm not doubting your practices, Mr. Baxter. My point is, that was an unpublished *book* that was turned *into* a screenplay. My book.

I have personal knowledge of what was included in the original story before it was adapted and then abbreviated. Would most people know that? I watched the movie, and I can give you several examples."

Bernie's mouth dropped open for a second, and then he urged her in a nasty tone, "Try me."

"The main character in the book had a little dog named Scooter. It was a Papillon. There was no dog in the movie."

"Yes, well, we had to cut out the dog because the actress was allergic..."

"Not in my book, she wasn't. Scooter went with her every-where. He was her purse dog. And the original name of the town was Marbury, not Cadbury."

Bernie blinked a few times. "We were afraid people might think it sounded too much like Mayberry."

"Cadbury sounds like something out of *Willy Wonka*—not much of an improvement unless you're selling chocolate," Willa muttered.

He glowered at her. "Wait just a minute. These are things you might have read on some film trivia site. They aren't ex-actly secrets."

"Don't you have people in your PR department who post things like that to drum up interest in the movie? I didn't see anything of the sort, although I looked for information about the movie online. Can you tell me who posted those particular details and where?"

Shaking with anger, he retorted, "Now look, young lady, I'm not in charge of every last piddly little detail of the marketing and promotion of our movies."

"I understand, sir. What if I told you that the priest who married them in the end was named Father Flanagan, not Father O'Connor like in the movie. Who would even care about something like that enough to put it in a blog or on some trivia website? It's boring!"

"Well, we figured the name Father Flanagan was too recognizable..."

"I agree," she said softly. "And I probably would have changed it myself before the book was published. Unfortunately, it was *stolen from me before I had the chance!*"

"You keep claiming it was *stolen* from you." Bernie's face had turned a terrible scarlet color at that point, and he blustered at them pointing his finger in Willa's face, "You listen to me! I don't make appointments with many people who aren't respected for their contributions to this industry. I made an exception because of the known quality of your books, and the considerable monetary backing you brought with you. But if you think you can come into *my* office under false pretenses and accuse *us* of stealing your book to make a movie, I will ask you all to leave immediately. I'll call security to escort you out if I have to, and I seriously hope you have no crazy ideas about suing the studio for plagiarizing a book you *claim* that you wrote. I'd like to see some proof of that!"

Skewering him with a death glare, Willa explained, "We did not come here with that intention at all, Mr. Baxter. It was our understanding that you were interested in making a movie from *Lost and Found.* I never in a million years thought you would suggest that I need to work in any capacity with Deb Abbey or, as she introduced herself to me over five years ago, Deborah Abrams. She told me she was a literary agent and then disappeared with my book. Honestly, I had put the whole thing behind me and moved on with my life. It was only when I watched the Academy Awards that I became aware of the extent of her subterfuge." He started to interrupt her when she glared at him and put up her hand. "And just this morning I became aware that she has stolen a *second* book from me— probably by hacking into my computer. Did you know that today she released a new book that *I just wrote*? I can show you proof of that. My version is currently being edited, but hers is an editorial massacre that was never polished. When I get going with my ideas, I'm not always the most careful, so I'm sure the book is full of typos. She wanted, apparently, to capitalize on her recent success at the Oscars, and she knew the quickest way to get a book out would be to steal one and rush it to the bookstores. Again, I can prove this clearly. But why don't you talk to her and see what bullshit she has to say about it, huh?"

Throughout this exchange, Jackson and Casey's attention went back and forth between the two squabblers. The men's expressions went from anger to admiration laced with humor as they enjoyed watching Willa stand up for herself against a self-important Hollywood mogul.

Before Bernie had a chance to reply, Casey's phone rang. He pulled it from his pocket and saw that it was Cyril getting back to him after he'd left a message. "Excuse me, everyone. I need to take this. It's from our other backer, and he's calling from Dubai." Casey actually had no idea where in the world Cyril was, but it sounded good at the moment. He stood and walked toward the door, cheerfully greeting his friend, "Cyril! I'm stoked to hear from you. We have lots to talk about investment-wise. Hang on a sec so I can go somewhere private, though."

Willa looked at Bernie Baxter and saw that his eyes were squinting at Casey's retreating back in a calculating way. He finally snapped to attention and addressed Jackson. "He's not talking to Cyril Mayfair, is he?"

"I'm certain he is, yes," answered Jackson. "Why?"

"Who *are* you people? Mayfair's one of the richest men on earth! Your friend knows him?"

Willa, who was still steamed at the jerk, snapped at him, "We all know Cyril. We were just guests on his new yacht until a couple of days ago. *He's* a lovely man." She made it clear with her emphasis that not everyone was so lovely, and by that she meant Bernie. She swore she could see dollar signs in his beady eyes.

"Well," Bernie began in an oily, placating tone as he plastered on an overly whitened and very fake smile. "Maybe I acted a little out of order, and perhaps you do have a claim that's legitimate regarding your book, Willa."

In a voice that could chip ice, Willa said, "It's *Ms. Camden.*"

"Uh, yes, right. Ms. Camden, I'd like to hope we can somehow put this behind us and work together making a wonderful movie." Clearly the idea of having anything to do with Cyril Mayfair and his considerable fortune was giving Bernie a riches-induced boner. Just the name-dropping alone would keep him happy for years.

"No. Thank you for your time." Willa turned to Jackson and said, "Let's go find Casey and get out of here. If we're ever going to make a movie, I'd prefer to do it elsewhere. This awful place reminds me too much of that bitch Deb Abbey." She turned to Bernie then and flattened him with a glare. "I have no proof that you weren't instrumental in the theft of either of my books, but rest assured that you'll be hearing from our legal team. I don't trust anyone who's associated with that woman."

She and Jackson stood to go as Bernie spluttered at them nonsensically, saying something about how they ought to not be so hasty leaving. His brother remained silent, but his face was a livid shade of purple and he seemed to be shaking in an odd way.

Bernie stammered, "I'm sure we can work something out. It's probably all a silly misunderstanding." When they headed to the door, his voice took on a desperate tone as he implored, "You'll need our expertise! Don't you want to make this movie?" Neither Willa nor Jackson answered him with so much as a pitying look, but they flinched when they heard Bernie bellow at his brother, "Conrad, *stop that!* It's probably your fault they left!"

As they entered the elevator, she said, "I hope you're not mad. I really appreciate all of the effort you exerted to get a meeting with them, but those guys make my skin crawl. The one guy who said nothing at all looked like he was trying to be sneaky about rubbing one out behind the desk while he ogled my boobs, and Bernie was just plain horrible."

Choking back a snort, Jackson answered, "It's fine, really. I completely understand. I should have realized they were the people who'd produced the movie with Deb, so I'm sorry I subjected you to them. Anyway, there are other studios. They were just the first one to get back to me. We'll have to look harder for a good fit." Giving her a hug, he said, "You were magnificent in there."

They stopped speaking as soon as the doors opened. Harried-looking people bustled on and off the elevator as it descended in fits and spurts to the ground floor.

They found Casey talking cheerfully to Cyril out in front of the massive building. He looked up at them with his beaming smile. "Cyril, apparently they've just cut their meeting short. I think we all need to have this conversation on speakerphone, so let us get into the car where we can all talk, yeah?"

As they made their way to the car, Casey explained, "Cyril loves the idea of investing in a movie made from Willa's book."

"Well, that's some good news finally," she muttered and tried to look happier.

Soon they were all seated comfortably in the spacious limo with Cyril on speaker.

Willa spoke up first, saying, "Cyril, we can't thank you enough for the experience we had on your yacht." She chuckled, "It really was a Dream Come True."

"I'm so glad you all availed yourselves of the considerable entertainment aboard. Now that the crew's been broken in, my wife and I plan to spend a month or so cruising around the Greek Isles." It was easy to hear the smile in Cyril's voice. "And speaking of my lovely wife, she was a little put out with me that I let you all get away before she met her favorite author. She is appeased now, however, thinking that there might be a movie forthcoming."

A woman's voice piped up from the background and said, "Let me say hello to her too, Cyril." He put his phone on speaker as well, and she said more clearly, "Willa? I want you to know I'm an avid fan of your work. I've absolutely devoured every last one of your books."

Giving Jackson and Casey a wide-eyed look, Willa answered, "Thank you, Mrs. Mayfair. I'm flattered."

"Call me Beatrice, please. And if my husband is going to go into business with you and your lovely men, I hope I can meet all of you soon. I've met Casey already, of course. He's a doll."

As Casey rolled his eyes and Jackson smirked, Willa answered, "That would be wonderful, Beatrice. As soon as I can, I'll make sure you have a signed copy of my newest book too."

"Thank you, Willa." She sounded genuinely pleased. "I'll let you all get back to your conversation now. I just wanted to say hello. Bye now."

They could hear Cyril's voice then saying, "She really does love the books. She says they make her feel good." He let out a hearty chuckle. "But—back to business. I'm sorry you wasted any of your time on those Baxter brothers. They're nothing but a couple of manipulative, cheating blowhards, if you ask me. Pardon my language."

Willa, Jackson, and Casey looked questioningly at each other.

"If Beatrice is sold on your books, and I believe *Lost and Found* was one of her favorites to boot, I'd love to invest in the project with you. You may not know, however, that I have an affiliation with an indie studio that I think would suit you

—and the subject matter—in a more beneficial and enjoyable way. It's called Twenty-First Century Wolves. Don't let the name fool you—they don't just make wildlife documentaries, though if they did, I'm sure they would be top-drawer. They are a couple of brilliant young filmmakers who are always looking for the next great story. Their time is due for a major success, if you ask me, and Willa's book just may be the catalyst that makes everyone involved a star."

Chapter Twenty-Five

Over the next couple of weeks, Willa spent a lot of time talking with lawyers—an activity that drove her to tension headaches—and the two "brilliant young filmmakers" who were a lot more fun. Cyril's guys turned out to be consummate and creative businessmen with a great eye for talent and a knack for promotion. One of them was Cyril's nephew, but he assured them that it wouldn't stop him from voicing independent opinions. With Cyril's generous backing, Twenty-First Century Wolves had already begun to make a name for itself in the film industry. As Cyril had said, they were on the road to stardom, and he hoped Willa's book would be just the ticket to get them there.

Plus, when they spoke to Willa, they kept their eyes on her face.

That was a refreshing change.

After tossing around many ideas about the book and the basic story, the filmmakers left it up to Willa to select her own scriptwriter to help her convert the book into a screenplay. They wanted her to be comfortable with the process.

So, Willa considered the writers she knew and researched what they'd been up to lately. Eventually she settled on two women she liked. Calls to them narrowed the decision down immediately, however, because one of them was going to have a baby at any moment and thought her time would be too limited.

"Call me for the next one?" she implored Willa. "I'd love the opportunity to work with you, but it's just not in the cards for me right now."

Willa understood and called her other friend Janie Arden, a writer she'd met in college. Her research indicated that Janie was making some inroads in the movie industry.

"Willa! It's great to hear from you," Janie greeted her. "When are you going to have another book out? I've read all of them so far."

After a bit of chitchat and reminiscing, Willa got down to business. "Janie, we're going to make a movie out of my book *Lost and Found*, and I need some help creating a screenplay. I hoped I could count on you to partner with me on this project, and I really hope you're not too busy to take this on." She could hear Janie gasp as she continued, "I have backing and a studio lined up. They'll be managing the major details, but I need to convert the novel into a usable script for them. I have the bare bones ideas already, but scriptwriting's not exactly my talent."

"Willa! That's the best news I've had in months. I'm just finishing up this boring project and I'll be free in about four or five days. Working with you sounds awesome. Thank you so much for considering me for the job. I'm flattered."

They discussed some details, and Willa emailed Janie a contract after making plans for them to meet in a week via Face-to-Face. Janie lived up in Paso Robles, and although they discussed getting together in-person, Janie didn't relish the idea of leaving her dogs, and Willa didn't want to leave her men. Face-to-Face was a godsend for people who needed to conference remotely.

Janie promised, "I'll look over the book again before we talk. Thanks, again."

♡♡♡

Even though the meetings with them stressed Willa, the law-yers, Charles and Mckenna, were quite optimistic about Willa's chances for a successful case against Deb. Deb's claims that the books were her own were "as flimsy as toilet paper," as Charles put it. Their sources also indicated that Deb's person-ality and likability were "just about as appealing as a slug." They felt that if the case went to trial, Willa had a great chance of winning.

"I do want to warn you that we can't predict how a jury might react to you as a person," Mckenna said kindly. "Some-times an attractive, successful young woman becomes the bad guy just because people tend to be jealous."

Charles nodded in agreement. "We'll want to take steps to make sure that you come across as professional and likable."

Willa thought she could probably do that, but the whole thing made her nervous.

The police were granted a search warrant and they con-fiscated a laptop from Deb. She was charged with felony com-puter crimes under California penal code 502, grand theft of intellectual property, and fraud. Once she was arraigned, how-ever, she only stayed in lockup for a couple of hours before making bail.

Through sources he didn't name, Cyril learned that the Baxter brothers had put up the bail money. He thought it likely that they were hoping to avoid any scandal that would cast a poor light on their studio. They also hired her the best criminal defense lawyer in California and, since they had the press in their pocket, so far there was no hint of scandal spread around anywhere in the entertainment news. A juicy story about stealing a manuscript from a well-known author and making it into an Academy Award-winning movie was the stuff of dreams to the entertainment paparazzi, so the Baxters were being extremely careful to make sure the news didn't break.

Willa's lawyer Charles let her know that Deb resided in Pasadena with her boyfriend Ryker Davies, a self-proclaimed entrepreneur whose business dealings were unclear. Ryker only answered he was "in tech" when asked. As much as Deb came across as sneaky, Charles reported that Ryker was a viper —silent, calculating, and dangerous.

Jackson was certain he'd seen Ryker at DEF CON in Las Vegas. He was one of the black hat hackers who was arrogant enough to show off, and his skill was unparalleled. "Wouldn't you just know that a woman with Deb's moral compass would be attracted to a guy like that?" he asked Willa. Jackson shared everything he knew about Ryker with the lawyers, but his knowledge was terribly limited. He was able to tell them that "Ryker is a hacker on the level of international stardom, unfortunately. I've been working on a new program that will hopefully shield computers from the likes of him."

♡♡♡

Deb's fancy defense lawyer ordered her to act like a model citizen and stay out of trouble while he built his case. Unfortunately for her, she was much too emotionally unstrung and pig-headed to follow his advice. Deb was both a pathological liar and a megalomaniac who was convinced of her rights to Willa's material. And she seemed to have no qualms about stealing Willa's work.

Her attorney was familiar with the criminal mind, but he was still shocked by Deb's thinking when they spoke. Deb reasoned, in her own mind, that she'd discovered the first book, and that gave her the claim to it. She argued with her lawyer that, "That child wouldn't have known what to do with the manuscript on her own."

Even though he tried to get to the bottom of things, he was still baffled. Her justification for why it was fine for her to publish Willa's newest book was far less clear, and she tended to ramble and rave when asked about it.

Her lawyer knew he had his work cut out with this one. He was used to having guilty-as-sin clients, though, and promised to do his best.

♡♡♡

Shortly after the police raid on Deb's house, Willa received a shocking email.

From: yourworstfuckingenemy@hotmail.com

To: WillatheBitchCamden<WillaC@WillaCamden.com>

You better drop your claims about book theft, bitch, unless you want a graphic video of you screwing two men at the SAME TIME to spread all over the internet. Drop this action immediately and say you were mistaken, or the video goes live. You have two days to comply or at 12:01 am on Monday, you and your actions will be world news. Imagine how you'll feel when everyone sees how freaky you all are! The Monday morning water cooler discussions will be a riot. Tick tock. Get busy retracting your claims. Now!

Kissy Kisses,
The Real Talent

P.S. Don't be stupid. I have more than one copy of the video. It's great spank bank material. ;) Extras are hidden where you'll never find them.

Willa gasped as she read this. Remembering how strange her computer had been acting, she didn't doubt that Deb and Ryker had the video as they claimed. Clearly, she left the lid open on her laptop and they had hacked in just in time to see intimate moments between Willa, Casey, and Jackson.

Stomach aching, Willa grabbed her computer and went to find her men. They were working out in the gym over at Jackson's house while she worked on ideas for a new book.

"Hey, guys. I'm afraid I have some bad news." The expression on her face made Jackson's smile evaporate. He immediately set down his weights. Casey also climbed out of the ab crunch machine, and they both went to her with concern written on their faces.

With a pained look, Willa showed the men her email.

"Oh no," Jackson moaned.

"Fuck me," Casey wailed.

Grabbing a towel and wiping off his face, Jackson said in a flat voice, "Okay, look. I'm going to go take a quick shower. We can discuss this in a few minutes. I need to clear my head a little."

"Yeah, me too," Casey muttered. Both men turned to leave the gym.

"I'll meet you both in the living room." Willa followed them out and headed the other direction. No one said another word.

Chapter Twenty-Six

When the men returned, they found Willa standing by the bay window staring out at the ocean. She had tear tracks streaking her cheeks. When she turned to look at them, she asked plaintively, "What have I done to you both? I'm so sorry that you're now embroiled in my mess. You must hate me." She buried her face in her hands and sobbed.

"No, sweetheart, no," Jackson protested softly at the same time as Casey drew her into a hug and buried his face in her neck, whispering, "We could never hate you. This isn't your fault. We'll figure out how to handle it; it's not the end of the world."

♡♡♡

In Pasadena at roughly the same time, Deb and Ryker were watching the video of Willa and her men for the umpteenth time. Just as Ryker was getting really turned on, Deb cackled gleefully in a nasty tone, "I can't wait until that bitch reads the email I sent her about this!"

Grabbing her roughly by the shoulders, Ryker bellowed, "You *what?*" He gave her a nasty shake. "What are you thinking? You know they can trace that right back to you with no trouble, don't you?"

"Relax, and let go of me." She tried unsuccessfully to shrug him loose. "I made up a new Hotmail account, sent the email and then deleted the account. No one will be able to trace that." She hissed at him, "How stupid do you think I am?"

With a face full of purple rage, Ryker slapped her across the face, hollering, "Apparently you're a lot dumber than I ever believed. They won't give a shit about your stupid email account, but anyone with half a brain can trace the message back to your IP address... or *mine* actually since I assume you used one of *my* computers. Ever think of that? No! Apparently, you think it's more important to gloat. I can't fucking believe this!" He turned away from Deb, who'd crumbled onto the floor in a sobbing heap, and his eye caught something on the video he'd never noticed before. He'd always been focused on watching Willa and didn't pay much attention to the men.

"Holy *fuck!*" he cried. "It's him! This is really, really bad, Deb." He glanced at her sniveling at his feet. "Get up off the floor, you idiot. I didn't hit you that hard."

Sniffling and wiping her nose on her arm, Deb stood up and stared at the video, wondering what he meant. It looked the same as ever to her. "What?" she asked in a pitiful tone. "What's so important? And for your information," she poked him in the shoulder for good measure, "when that bitch Willa sees my email, she'll retract her claims that I stole anything from her. She won't want her kinky sex life exposed with these two guys all over her and each other. It was a brilliant plan. Admit it."

Ryker ignored her and stopped the video. He ran it back a bit and then scrolled through it frame by frame until he got to a spot where one of the men was facing the camera. "Look! Do you see that man? I've never paid any attention to his face before because it's usually out of the shot, but right there you can see that it's Jackson Mitchell!"

"So?" All Deb thought about him was that Jackson was incredibly handsome, and it made her hate Willa all the more.

"He's the asshole who stole the Uber Badge right out from under me at DEF CON. I was *this* close to winning when that know-it-all blocked my attack! He deserves to go down—the self-righteous prick."

"You really give a shit about a glorified video game?" she sneered at him.

Ryker's face whipped around and he glared at her. "Don't you ever compare what I do to a video game again, or you'll be sorry. You enjoy living in a nice place like this, don't you? You enjoy having me find things for you like books to pirate, don't you? It's my hacking skills that do all of this for you, you ungrateful bitch!" Spittle flew in her face as he continued his tirade. "And now you've jeopardized everything because you wanted her to know we have the goods on her and those two guys. Shit, I wonder who the other one is..." He turned the video back on, but Casey's face was not familiar to him. He knew that didn't mean much. "Did you know that the guy you've probably just pissed off is a *major* player in the technology world? He's a fucking billionaire and a genius, Deb. You are so screwed. Just don't expect to take me down with you. As a matter of fact..." He stomped away muttering and headed for the closet. He grabbed some clothes and crammed them haphazardly into a bag that he tossed at her feet.

Deb looked appalled and whispered, "What's that for?"

"Get out of here."

"What? Where am I supposed to go?" she cried.

"Your problem, not mine. Now leave. You're more trouble than you're worth. I don't want the cops sniffing around here anymore because of you." He glared at her for a moment and then went back to his computer, ignoring her.

Ryker had been hacking into the computers of large companies for years, syphoning off amounts of money that were small enough to go unnoticed or chalked up to accounting errors. He was clever enough to cover his tracks, and he did it so often and to so many different places that he made a decent living. But lately it was becoming harder and harder to breach some of his best sources. His best "clients" were starting to teach their coders to write safe material that didn't leave gaping holes for hackers to penetrate. The practice pissed him off, and he was perpetually in a bad mood.

Crying and screaming didn't seem to faze Ryker, so a few minutes later, after snatching her prized Oscar off of the mantel, Deb tried—and failed—to exit the house with some dignity. She slammed the door of her car and called Bernie Baxter, tears streaming down her face. "The bastard threw me out, Bernie! I don't know where to go! What can I do now? I can't leave the area, or I'll get arrested again. Can you put me up for a while? Please?" Even though Bernie had rescinded his offer to make another movie with her, she figured he still adored her.

Bernie Baxter, who knew just how annoying Deb could be even on a good day, told her placatingly, "Just sit tight a second. I can't put you up here because I have... um... company coming from out of town. But I'll find you a hotel and I'll call you back." Avoiding a scandal was one thing, but spending time listening to that voice of hers grate on his last nerve was quite another. With an irritated sigh, Bernie pulled up accommodation information on his phone.

Deb rallied a little while she waited. She had dreams of room service and spa treatments at the Beverly Wilshire on Bernie's tab. He obviously owed her a lot after her brilliant movie won an Oscar, and he was loaded. Her breathing slowed and she mustered a small smile when he called her back. The smile disappeared immediately, however, when he directed her to the Pasadena Parade Inn.

"That place is a dump, and you know it, Bernie. What gives?"

In a no-nonsense tone, he replied, "You're way too much trouble lately, so take it or leave it. They're holding the room for you until six, so you better skedaddle over there. It's the only room available in the area tonight according to Pricecheck. Oh, and they take credit cards. I hope you have one on you."

"They probably have roaches!"

"Well, then maybe you can make friends with them." He hung up and blocked her number.

Deb stared at her phone in shock. So much for loyalty in Hollywood.

She checked into her ugly room before they gave it to someone else and then proceeded to call around for something better. Apparently, Bernie had been right about the lack of rooms. She couldn't find anything. That made her feel less awful about Bernie's failure to put her up in the lap of luxury like she clearly deserved, but not by much. The motel was noisy and uncomfortable, and the orange and brown décor made her feel queasy. She spent the night worrying about bedbugs and vowing to herself that she'd get back in Ryker's good graces as soon as he cooled down. She knew just what to say.

♡♡♡

Ryker wasn't all that fond of Deb, but he was so socially awkward, having her around for regular and fairly enthusiastic sex was important. He'd cooled down a little—enough at least to open the door when she rang his bell at nine-thirty the next morning.

"Whaddya want?" he asked scratching his stomach and yawning. Deb could tell he hadn't slept well. He also apparently hadn't showered by the looks of him. His hair was greasy, and he smelled like a pair of dirty sweat socks. There was a bit of cereal decorating his beard that she had to ignore as she looked plaintively into his eyes.

"Ryker, baby, I'm so sorry for messing up. I missed you terribly last night." Her lower lip stuck out like a petulant toddler who'd been deprived of a favorite toy. "I promise to make it up to you if you let me come back."

Squinting at Deb suspiciously, he asked, "What does that mean—you'll make it up to me?"

Deb batted her eyes and whispered, "You know, baby. I'll let you do that *thing* you've always wanted to do."

Ryker's squint relaxed and his eyes opened up with a much greedier look. "You're going to have to be a little more specific."

Blushing and looking at her feet, Deb said barely audibly, "You know... I'll let you, um... *do the... backdoor thing.*"

Ryker grabbed her wrist and pulled her inside as he muttered, "You better be telling the truth."

♡♡♡

Half an hour later, Deb lay on the bed whimpering. She was amazed that anyone enjoyed that activity, but she'd gotten a good look—actually several looks—at what Willa's men were packing, and she finally reasoned to herself that if Willa seemed to enjoy it, she could definitely put up with Ryker's crummy little dick. What she didn't realize was that Ryker had plenty of enthusiasm for backdoor entry but completely lacked the skill for how to do it without just barging in. It was excruciating, and she'd hated it. Still—she needed a place to live, and she had no other options. There certainly weren't any movie deals coming her way like she'd expected, and she'd gone through all she'd earned on the last one long ago. Just having all of those hardcover books printed and shipped to bookstores by the vanity publisher had set her way back. And now no one could even buy them because the books had been confiscated by the cops until her trial. *What a crappy deal.*

Ryker, on the other hand, was so pleased with his experience, he ignored Deb's lack of excitement. Feeling like the king of the world, he announced, "Fuck the Monday morning deadline, babe. We're letting that video loose right now. I hate that Mitchell guy, and he has it coming for keeping me from winning what I deserved at DEF CON. He won't know what hit him."

An hour later, Deb lay in the tub relaxing when she heard Ryker cackling gleefully from the other room. She hauled herself into a standing position and dried off. After putting on a robe, she went to find him. "What's so funny?" she asked.

Laughing so hard he was wiping his eyes, Ryker explained, "I got back into Willa's computer from this one the cops didn't confiscate and attached the video to everyone she's ever sent an email to or received from. It went out to all of them just now, and when it hits the receiver's inbox, it will attach to all of their addresses as well, and on and on. I also faked the original IP address so that it looks like it started in Brazil. God, I'm good. Now *this* is brilliant, right?" He didn't wait for a reply, but strutted away singing loudly and off-key, "We will, we will mock *you!*" And then he laughed maniacally.

Thinking Ryker sounded more like Alvin and the Chipmunks than Freddie Mercury, Deb sat down on the bed with a plunk and winced. She hoped to hell Ryker's game improved with experience. She planned to go buy some lube later and kicked herself for not showing up with it in the first place. She'd been too anxious to get out of that motel and back home where she belonged. Then she thought about the video hitting all of those inboxes and spreading like wildfire, and she forgot her sore butt. She started cackling like Ryker just thinking about how Willa and those two guys must be feeling. It felt like divine justice somehow. Willa didn't deserve all of the looks, all of the success, and all of the handsome men. *Those things should have been mine.*

She remembered back when she'd first met Willa. The girl had been incredibly talented, that was obvious after hearing one beautifully creative sentence from her manuscript, but she'd also been so naïve and trusting, it tickled Deb to remember how she'd tricked her. She had been so gorgeous with those perfect tits and those big blue eyes. Of course, it never occurred to Willa that someone might not have her best interests at heart. *Stupid bitch.* It pissed her off. *Well,* she thought to herself, *the mighty have fallen now.*

Chapter Twenty-Seven

After a long night of reassurances to each other about their mutual trust and love, Willa, Casey, and Jackson were exhausted. They were still in bed trying to catch up on a little sleep when all their phones began to ring and vibrate with calls and ping with text message alerts. It sounded like a cell phone symphony as all three devices sounded off.

"What the fuck?" Casey muttered groggily. He was closest to his phone, so he reached over and picked it up. The incoming call was from his dad, but the text message alert kept chiming and chiming. He ignored his dad for the moment and took a look at the most recent text. It was from his assistant telling him that not only had he been attacked by a virus that was sending out a video, the video was quite graphic and compromising. Casey scrolled through more texts, and they all said variations of the same thing. He did notice, however, that none of the messages were damning to him in any way. One even explained that the other two people in the video were identified by name, but that Casey was not. They all seemed to want to warn him more than anything and let him know they'd also apparently been infected by a virus.

Casey opened up his email and confirmed that a message was sent supposedly from Willa while he knew for a fact that she was sleeping. He opened it and saw what the fuss was about. "Just turn off your phones," he told the others. "It's already happened. The video is going out allegedly from Willa's email account, and it's replicating." He turned to Jackson and asked, "Is there anything you can do to stop this?"

"I'll see what I can figure out," Jackson answered, shaking his head in disgust and sadness. "What a mess."

"I'm calling the lawyers," said Willa. Her hands shook with anger as she punched in the numbers.

♡♡♡

A couple of hours later, one of the lawyers called Willa back. "The FBI now needs to be alerted because of the severity of the cyber threat and subsequent attack. By threatening you and two other individuals via the internet, and by distributing damaging material, the perpetrator has committed a serious felony." He paused and let that sink in and then went on, "You need to fill out a form and send it immediately to the Internet Crime Complaint Center, also known as the IC3, and the FBI will be in touch as soon as possible. I could file it on your behalf, Ms. Camden, but I think it will be faster if you do it. You have at your disposal all of the information they'll request. I'll alert them that the suspected perpetrator of this attack has already been charged with grand theft of your intellectual property." He gave her the specifics on where to download the form.

Jackson's computer was the only one that was not infected. Although Willa was on his safe-senders list, and the email was delivered to his inbox, he had an experimental program installed that removed and destroyed harmful attachments before they could invade his system. It was one of the things he'd been working so hard on, so despite the horrible circumstances, he was happy that the protection had worked. It also safeguarded his information from being hacked, but—just to be extra safe—he also checked his online banking accounts and saw that nothing untoward had happened. Nevertheless, he created complicated new passwords for everything. That kind of information could never be too safe.

"I'm going to load my new program onto your laptops just to add some more protection," Jackson told Willa and Casey. "I just worked out some of the bugs yesterday, and I didn't want to install it until I'd checked to make sure it worked. I'm sorry now that I didn't take the chance."

"You didn't know we'd be attacked by a cyber-criminal," Willa pointed out. She knew none of them needed more re-criminations or blame. They were already reeling from having their privacy invaded and their personal business splattered all over the internet. Casey hadn't stopped pacing around the house all day as he spoke to his dad, several clients, and business associates.

Until now, they hadn't managed to come up with a plan other than calling the authorities. But after practically pacing a hole in Jackson's floor, Casey announced, "I have an idea that I'd like you both to consider. Let's sit down and have a talk, yeah?" He was the only one not sitting down actually, so he took a chair and faced them, asking, "What if we do nothing?"

"We have to do something!" Jackson retorted.

"I've already done what I can," Willa added. "The FBI is going to be involved now as well."

Jackson looked mighty perturbed when he asked Casey, "Since when are you the pacifist? You've always been the one to go on attack at the drop of a hat."

"Maybe I've matured." Casey regarded them calmly and said, "What you've both done so far is fine, but I'm thinking about a statement, a retaliation, or a claim that the video is a fake." They both started to speak, but he held up his hand politely. "It's my strong opinion that we should just do nothing and let it blow over. We don't owe anyone an explanation for our lifestyle. This is California, for heaven's sake. Even my dad wasn't really upset—he just wanted me to be aware of the problem and he wanted to know if he could help me in any way. Most of the messages I've gotten are equally supportive. I bet if you look at the ones you're getting, you'll be pleasantly surprised."

Willa's brow furrowed as she opened the messages on her phone. *Could Casey be right? Am I not going to be vilified and called every horrible name in the book?* She scrolled through a few of them from people she knew well, and Casey was correct. They were mostly messages offering support and expressing remorse that her private life was invaded.

Feeling bolstered by the friendly messages, Willa continued to scroll and got to people she didn't know. She assumed they were contacts of her contacts. These messages were more caustic, thanking her for sending them a virus—like she could have prevented it somehow? The thought was ridiculous. Here and there she had some rather disgusting proposals and suggestions. A few made her cringe, and she was furious that the original sender had posted her name and phone number with the video. She felt like she'd been lauded on the wall of a public bathroom stall for all the world to see—as in, "For a good time call Willa Camden! (858)555-2170." *Still, it could have been a lot worse. Well... maybe.*

Willa and Jackson silently considered Casey's suggestion for several minutes. Finally, Jackson broke the silence and announced, "We're all getting new phones. I've ordered them, and they'll be here soon. We can distribute the new numbers to the people we trust and leave the old ones alone until all of this is cleaned up. The FBI may need them anyway."

"Okay. Thanks, Jackson," Willa said. "I think Casey is right, though. I vote for no public acknowledgment whatsoever of this breach of our privacy. I doubt seriously it will hurt my career anyway." She finally broke a smile and laughed softly. "Some of my readers might think this is how I do research."

Casey nodded thoughtfully and added, "Hey, I work in the design business, and half the people I run into assume I'm gay anyway, so this isn't exactly going to spoil my rep. It'll just make me more... colorful!" They both laughed at that with him.

"Yeah, you're a regular rainbow," chuckled Jackson. "I guess you're both right. My immediate reaction is to fight back somehow and tell the world to butt out of our business while I try—and, realistically, fail—to erase every possible copy of this video. But I have to face the reality that it's out there. No one knows who I am anyway unless they're in tech, and I might turn out to be some kind of folk hero in those circles. A nerd in a three-way! Who knew?"

Right after Jackson made this statement, the buzzer for the front gate sounded. He answered the intercom, "May I help you?"

"Express delivery for a Mr. Mitchell," the voice said.

"I'll buzz you in. Please bring it to the front door."

The young delivery man did a doubletake as he offered the package to Jackson, and then he craned his neck and stood on his tiptoes, staring into the house. "Hey, there she is! And you're one of the guys with the chick who likes to do..."

Stepping forward hastily, Jackson forced the guy backward and away from the door. He snarled, "Don't say another word, and I'm sorry that you just lost your chance for any kind of tip. Now shut up and get out of here."

"Jeez, man. Don't get your tighties in a twist," the little weasel sniggered at him. He winked at Jackson with a leer and left.

Sighing, Jackson slammed the door and turned to Casey and Willa. "Why does everyone assume I wear tighty whities, anyway? Sorry about that, Willa. Why don't we all pack up and head out to Casey's house for a while. Now that that idiot knows where to find us, he'll probably tell all of his sleazy friends. No telling who else is going to show up. Case's house is a lot more private, and it helps that all the addresses for Rancho Santa Fe are P.O. boxes." He dropped the package of phones on the table near them and headed for the kitchen to see whether Phillipe had started work on dinner yet. It turned out that he had, so they decided to all head out to Rancho Santa Fe after an early supper. It gave them more time to pack anyway. Jackson figured he just wouldn't answer the intercom if any strangers showed up.

Unfortunately, a small group of gawkers laughed and stared up at the two houses from the beach below. There were a few cameras in the mix that looked like paparazzi as well. Jackson was quite relieved he had one-way glass installed facing the water. It was still over an hour before sundown, and they all had a clear view of his huge window, but they couldn't see through it.

"New plan," he announced to Willa and Casey. "I'm calling the driver to drive you two out to Case's place, but I want you to wait until I see if there are any gawkers out front. I'm pretty sure if we leave by car we'll be followed, so I'll go first and lead them in the wrong direction. Then I'll lose them and meet you back at the Ranch." He snickered. "I've always wanted to say that."

Smiling and then quickly sobering, Willa asked, "How are you going to lose them?"

Looking satisfied, Jackson gave her his signature crooked grin and answered, "That's why they invented Ludicrous Mode."

"Jackson, please don't do anything dangerous or stupid," she pleaded.

Holding her close and kissing her forehead, Jackson tried to reassure her, "Don't worry. It'll be fine."

After dinner, as the sun was finally setting magnificently over the Pacific, they loaded their suitcases into the Tesla and Jackson headed out. Within minutes, he phoned Casey from the car. "It's not too bad. One jerk is following me, but I didn't see anyone else. He probably thinks we're all in the car, but who knows what he thinks he's going to get out of tailing me. Anyway, I told the driver to pull into the garage to get you guys, but leave as quickly as possible before anyone else shows up, okay?"

"Yeah, we're on it. Willa and I will see you at my place. Be careful, Jax."

Trying to drive as though he had no care in the world, Jackson turned south and headed up to the top of Mt. Soledad by way of Via Capri—the steepest climb in the entire town. It was the wrong direction to get to Rancho Santa Fe, which was north of La Jolla. He thought a few times that he'd lost his tail because the car following him was having a difficult time making it up the mountain, but when Jackson started down La Jolla Scenic Drive after cresting the top, the unknown idiot was back on his tail again. It was far too residential and curvy to try any Ludicrous shenanigans, so Jackson kept to the speed limit, took a left turn onto Soledad Mountain Road, and headed down toward Pacific Beach. Finally, he reached the commercial section of the beach town and turned right onto one of the main drags. After he merged onto Grand Avenue, he encountered a lot of congested traffic. He figured if the other driver were around, he'd soon be lost in the mix. Just to be careful, though, Jackson finally pulled into a small parking lot of a liquor store and parked around behind the building.

As he waited, he called Casey again. "All clear for you guys?"

"Yeah, we're fine, but Willa forgot her laptop, of all things, so we're going to have to go back."

"Don't worry about it, Case. Take her to your place, and I'll stop back home and get it. I'm just sitting around for a minute until I'm sure the jerk who followed me is gone. I'm just in PB, so I'm not far away. And tell Willa I didn't have to resort to Ludicrous Mode to lose the tail."

"Okay. She says to tell you thank you for getting the laptop and that she thinks she left it on the dresser in the bedroom. We'll see you soon."

Twenty minutes later, it was fully dark as Jackson pulled up to his house and entered through the electronic gate. He hopped out quickly to run in and get Willa's laptop, but he made a colossal error of judgment. In his haste, he neglected to close either the garage door or his car door. As soon as Jackson entered his house, a man stepped out of the shadows, entered the garage, stuck his head inside the car, and snapped a quick photo of the VIN number of the Tesla. The man ran like hell as soon as he accomplished that and hid in the bushes again. He narrowly missed seeing Jackson come back out of the house again with the computer in his hands. Jackson didn't see anyone around and didn't think a thing about the door being left open for a minute at best—especially since the outer gate was closed. The intruder let a couple of minutes pass before he climbed over the fence, scratching himself pretty badly in the process.

Chapter Twenty-Eight

Ryker could not believe his luck. He'd shown up at Jackson's house not really knowing what he would find or how he could cause Jackson some trouble, but when he saw that Tesla arrive, he followed it in through the gate on foot, slipping through at the last minute, crouching low. Then he dashed into the bushes where he waited until Jackson got out of the car. The fact that Jackson had left the garage and car doors open too was a gift. Ryker had previously thought maybe he'd do something easy like cut off the asshole's cable so Jackson couldn't use the internet or something like that, so he was rooting around the landscaping to see if he could find anything like a cable box. This scenario, however, was a split-second decision that could lead to a lot more fun. It was more than worth the drive down from Pasadena. Now he just had to face all the traffic on the way home.

Once he finally got back to his house, he was crabby, hungry and tired. He barely looked at Deb who tried to look perky and happy to have him back. He headed straight to the kitchen where he made himself an enormous sandwich and grabbed a bottle of beer. He ignored Deb's questions and observations and went to mess around with his computer while he ate. The only thing he said to her was, "Clean up the kitchen," as he walked away.

♡♡♡

For the next several days, Ryker stayed close to his computer, totally engrossed in some project he didn't share with Deb. He seemed to swear a lot and mutter things too low for her to hear.

Deb, however, made sure that Ryker's house stayed neat, she looked her best, and his nights were satisfying—at least to him. She'd messed up royally when she accepted a lump sum payment for her magnificent screenplay. She'd been thrilled with the sound of a hundred grand, and was so anxious for the cash, she stupidly signed away her rights to any kind of future royalties from the movie. It took three long years to make the movie, and she'd gone through that money pretty quickly with her terrible spending habits. Now she wanted to kick herself sideways to Sunday for not being smarter about it, which was what prompted her to "discover" another book from Willa with Ryker's assistance. Then she spent a fortune getting books printed up and sent all over the country. It had seemed like her best option at the time—capitalize on the Oscar win and take as many sales as possible. But with the seizure of her books, she was nearly tapped-out financially, so she really needed Ryker to be happy enough with her to let her stay.

At least Bernie was paying her lawyer. That would have proved impossible. But she had faith the creepy shyster would get her off. She knew her rights. Maybe Willa wrote the first draft, but Deb was the one who made it great. *She* found that book after sifting through piles and piles of shitty manuscripts. *She* was the one who had the brains to see its potential. And *she* was the one who hired a ghostwriter to turn the book into a screenplay. Thank goodness she'd given the writer a fake name and paid her in cash.

It didn't surprise Deb at all to see Willa's writing career blossom. She watched from a distance as the pretty young woman's fame grew. Sure, she had talent. It made Deb burn with jealousy to the point of irrationality to admit it, but it was true.

While Ryker played around doing God-knows-what on his computer all day, Deb went through her beauty regimen with religious intent, and when she was all done making herself look as good as possible, she searched porn sites, looking for something that Ryker might enjoy besides screwing her in the ass. She sort of wished she had the money for a boob job because her girls weren't quite as perky as Willa's—a fact that Ryker had pointed out a few times while watching that video. Willa's tits were apparently magic or some crap.

Meanwhile, Ryker was seriously up to no good on his computer. He tried and tried to hack into Jackson's computer, and found that the guy had put up a wall that was apparently impenetrable. This pissed Ryker off so badly, he resorted to his other plan—one with more Machiavellian intent. After days and days of tinkering, he finally had it where he wanted. Unfortunately for him, now he had to wait. And wait.

Chapter Twenty-Nine

Willa, Casey, and Jackson thought things were going pretty well. They had plenty of privacy out at Casey's gated estate, and they were far from the prying eyes of the gawkers on the beach. Phillipe had made a run back to Jackson's house to get a couple of items that he'd forgotten and reported back that the beach was still full of voyeurs. Jackson, Willa, and Casey tried not to be discouraged by the loss of their private beach havens. They figured if nothing happened there for enough time, people would lose interest eventually and they'd be able to go back. They all missed their evening runs on the beach.

Willa didn't have many reasons to leave the confines of the estate, and she was content to write and talk on the phone when she needed to communicate. Jackson was also pretty comfortable, since all he really needed were his computers. Unfortunately, Casey's business needed to be done in-person. After a few days in hiding, he knew he had to go back to work.

When he got to his office the first time, his out-and-proud lesbian assistant told him, "Apparently, your identity has been disclosed after all, stud. I've been making appointments for you left and right to meet with about a bazillion Hollywood types who are 'just dying' to have you work on their houses and yachts. Somehow word also got out that you worked for Cyril Mayfair on his little dinghy. Here's a list of your appointments." She handed him a folder. "From what I gather, they all embrace your commitment to the LGBXYZ blah, blah, blah lifestyle or some crapola and want to show their support. They also know you're damned talented."

"I'm not trying to further some cause; I'm just living my life," he protested. Then he laughed when he saw the prominent names on the list and added, "But I'm not averse to cashing in on this good fortune. Casey Melrose... Designer to the Stars." They both cracked up. "I guess I'm cool at last."

Casey made several trips up to places like Malibu, Beverly Hills, and Bel Air over the next couple of weeks. Jackson insisted that it would be a great idea for Casey to take their driver so he would arrive safe and relaxed at his appointments. Casey had no problem with that idea. The driver and the new limo hadn't had much of a workout lately anyway.

After Casey made several trips north, Jackson got a call from his brother Miles.

"Hey, good to hear from you, Miles. How's it going?"

Miles answered, "We're good, Jax. I just wanted to see how you're holding up. I'm sorry to hear about your sudden movie fame, but... um... wow."

"We're all fine, really. I'd sure rather be known for something more professional than who I'm sleeping with, but it's bound to blow over when someone else's private life is invaded and it entertains the masses."

Miles sighed. "Yeah, I guess. Listen, I'm flying down to LA tomorrow to meet with some markets about carrying some of our products, and I'll be done with my appointments by around three. Any chance you could drive up and meet me? I'd love to catch up, especially since I had to miss Dad's party. It's been too long. I'll spend one night, and then I need to get back up here."

"Hey, that sounds great actually. Casey mentioned he has a luncheon appointment up there at one. We'll take the limo and drop him off, and I'll book you a suite at the Hotel Bel-Air.

I can check-in for you, have lunch, and meet you there, then Casey can Uber over to us when he's done. Maybe Willa can make it if she's not too busy, and you can meet her."

"That would be great. Be sure to tell her—and Casey too for that matter— that I haven't watched that video, though, okay? I don't want them to feel awkward. Also, thank you, but you don't need to book me some fancy suite."

"It's my pleasure to do it, Miles. Besides, this way we'll have somewhere comfortable to wait for you."

"Well, if you insist," Miles answered laughing. "Don't let me stop you."

♡X♡

Over dinner that night, the three of them discussed their plans. Willa was excited to meet Jackson's brother. She knew how strongly he felt about his family. "Can we all go up to Castroville sometime soon?" she asked. "I'd love to meet the rest of your families."

Both men agreed happily, and Casey said he'd look for a break in his schedule so they could arrange it.

Later that night, they headed for bed and Willa announced, "I have an absolute craving to be in the middle this time. Does that work for you two?" She began slowly removing her clothes as she looked at her men with a tiny grin and a gleam in her eye.

"It works for me for sure," laughed Jackson as he approached Willa and wrapped his arms around her.

"Oh, it *so* works for me," answered Casey who stepped behind Willa and kissed her neck while he stroked her butt cheeks. "Mmm. You're so soft." Immediately he began to yank off his clothes as he eyed that delicious ass. He was already so hard, it almost hurt. "Get your damn clothes off, Jax! Our lady here is waiting." He hurried to the bedside table to grab some lube while Jackson peeled off his clothes.

Jackson leaned back onto the bed, pulling Willa down on top of him. As she straddled him, he leaned up and nibbled on her tits, watching with lust as the nipples responded to him. Then he lay back and scooted Willa up over his face. He began kissing, laving, and sucking her clit so hard, she was a quivering mess. In minutes, she came all over him, shouting his name and groaning.

"I guess I needed that," she laughed breathlessly. "Casey? Where are you?" she asked and turned around to see him lubing up his dick. He looked ready to explode.

"God, that's sexy to watch. You two are so beautiful," he moaned as he pulled and stroked himself. "I *really* need to fuck you now."

"Please," answered Willa. "Do it."

She scooted down Jackson's body and impaled herself on his erection, causing him to let out a happy sigh. He seized her around the hips and thrust up into her several times. Then Casey moved in behind her and said, "Slow down, cowboy. The lady wants some DP action. You don't want to end this too soon."

Jackson growled, "Get busy, Case!" Then he laughed and slowed his pace.

Casey stroked Willa softly and then slid one lubed finger into her crack. She moaned in appreciation as he gently massaged her anus. Then, slowly and carefully, he breached her opening, adding a bit more lubrication. Once he could easily insert two fingers and Willa was thrusting back onto his hand, he pulled his hand away and carefully guided his dick into her as she hissed, "Yesssss! That's what I need." She leaned forward and locked onto Jackson's mouth, kissing him deeply and aggressively.

It was a tight squeeze, but Casey reached around Willa and manipulated her clit while he and Jackson found each other deep inside her. They rubbed their dicks together on either side of her thin membrane, making Willa pant and moan. It was almost too much to handle. The sensations they all felt were pure overload.

Soon Willa shuddered as another spasm of delight ripped through her. Her muscles pulsated, squeezing their erections, and Casey began his profane muttering as he swore and grimaced in ecstasy. Jackson thrust up into Willa one last time with a mighty shout and filled her with his love.

It was definitely a night they would remember for a long time.

❤❤❤

The next morning, they were just heading out to the limo when Willa got a text from The La Jolla Romance Readers Book Club reminding her of their afternoon meeting. Apparently, the ladies were terribly excited to have her speak to them about a book of Willa's they'd read that month.

"Oh, no. I'm so sorry, Jackson. It's a good thing she reminded me because I completely forgot about this appointment. They contacted me a couple of months ago knowing I was local and asked if I'd come chat with them after their discussion about my book. I agreed to do it, and I can't let them down now. I'll meet your brother soon, though, hopefully—especially if we're going to go up there."

"I understand. We'll drive one of our cars up to LA then and leave the limo and driver for you then," he said.

"There's no need for that. Can't I just take your car since mine's still in La Jolla? I only need to drive over to University Town Center for the appointment. It's not that far. You guys will be a lot more comfortable in the limo. It would be a waste for me to take the driver."

In fact, Casey had already loaded up his iPad, a stack of notebooks, photos, and fabric samples into the limo, so he was ready to go. They'd be late if they didn't get moving. Scowling a little, Jackson asked, "Are you sure you'll be okay on your own?"

"Of course, I will. It'll be fun talking to the ladies. Where's the key?"

"Look in the ceramic bowl on top of the dresser. It's the little fob that's a replica of the car."

Willa kissed him sweetly and said, "I know what it looks like, and I love you for caring so much. Now go have fun with Casey and enjoy your visit with your brother. See you tonight."

Casey and Jackson both kissed her goodbye then, and off they went.

Willa sighed happily as she watched the limo pull out and thought of her lovely men. A strong gust of wind kicked up suddenly, whipping her in the face with her hair, so she pushed it out of her eyes absently and went back indoors to get some writing done for a while. Passing through the kitchen, she grabbed some coffee and let Phillipe know there had been a change of plans. "Would you mind making me a salad or something later for a light lunch?"

"My pleasure, Ms. Camden. I have some salmon I can marinate and grill, and I'll make a bed of some lovely fresh greens, if that sounds good."

"Perfect. How about in an hour?"

♡♡♡

Willa went off to write, but her mind kept drifting to her up-coming appointment. She knew at some point she'd have to face the outside world. She'd been in the safe haven of Casey's quiet estate for long enough now. But even though she'd put on a brave face for Jackson's benefit, she worried that the book club might be full of gossipy women who were interested in more than her book. *Put on your big girl pants, Willa, and face the world. You have nothing to be ashamed of. Your privacy was violated in the worst way, but you're lucky enough to have the love of two incredible men. Anyone who wants to look down on you has a problem, not you.*

Finally, she relaxed enough to get back into her story. This one was a bit of a tear-jerker, so writing it was exhausting. She was definitely ready for a break when Phillipe came to tell her that her lunch was prepared.

When Phillipe started to leave her alone, Willa decided she'd rather have some company and asked him to join her. He looked pleased and went to pour himself a cold drink. Willa realized she knew little to nothing about the young man other than he could cook circles around anyone she'd ever known.

"Tell me about yourself, Phillipe. I know your family is in Quebec, and that's about it."

Phillipe's eyes lit up with pleasure, and he announced, "I just got engaged!"

"Wonderful, congratulations! Who's the lucky... um...?"

"Girl," he laughed. "I know in this day and age you never know." He reached into his pocket and pulled out his wallet.

Pulling out a photo, he showed it to Willa as he smiled down at the photo. It was of a dark-haired, dark-eyed young woman who was extremely pretty. "This is my Gabrielle. We both grew up in Saint-Félicien, and we knew each other a little, but we didn't start dating until a year ago when I discovered she was also in San Diego. Imagine that! She works at the zoo as a primate curator."

"Wow, that's amazing."

They talked for a while about possible wedding plans and when the couple would tie the knot. The conversation took Willa's mind completely off her worries. By the time lunch was over, she was relaxed and feeling energized. She headed back to her writing and got into it with no hesitation.

Finally, it was time to leave, so she grabbed the little car fob and headed for the garage. She started the car up and told it to take her to University Town Center. Willa wasn't all that familiar with the winding roads of Rancho Santa Fe and didn't want to get lost before she even got to the freeway. The book club meeting wasn't exactly in the mall—just close by, but it was the area around Casey's place that tended to confuse her. She had always been driven by someone else when she came and went from the estate.

Willa wound around some sharp turns and smiled when she saw some young women riding their horses along a bridlepath. She knew the area was crisscrossed with trails for riders. She thought how pretty the horses were and didn't notice at first that she was getting terribly warm in the car. As she passed by the riders on her right, she realized finally that her bottom was uncomfortably warm. *Stupid heated seats! Why are these turned on when it's so warm outside today?* She tried to adjust the temperature and turn off the seat warmer, but nothing happened. Willa then tried to roll down the window to get some fresh air, but it wouldn't budge. Her bottom was so uncomfortable, she decided she needed some advice and called Jackson via the car's system.

"Hi sweetheart," she heard Jackson say, but quickly interrupted him.

"I need to know how to turn off this damn seat heater. I'm burning up and the window is stuck closed!"

There was a moment of silence as Jackson processed this strange bit of news. "There isn't any reason for that." He put her on speaker so he could open the car app. "The car is always temperature controlled. I'll see if I can send it a message from my phone and cool things down for you. But, Willa, can you please turn down the radio? It's awfully loud."

"I never turned it on!" she hollered. "Oh, thank heaven. It's cooling down in here finally. I thought I was about to faint. But now the radio is going crazy. You know I hate this kind of music. I'd never want to listen to this crap and certainly not at this volume!"

Jackson tried to kill the radio, but all he apparently managed to do was get it to change channels, and now Willa's ears were being bombarded by a weather report in Spanish—also at top volume.

"Oh, Jackson! Stop! The air-conditioning is on so hard now it's making my eyes water. This isn't funny!"

"I'm not doing anything, I swear. I'd never do that to you, and certainly not when you're driving. I'm trying to send a signal from my phone to fix it."

Miles sat and stared at his younger brother as Jackson's face went red and he looked like he was about to explode. Miles had always wondered about those cars that were too self-sufficient. He thought they might be big trouble someday. Hopefully, this wasn't the day, but poor Jackson sure looked upset.

"Is the car steering alright?" Jackson asked in a shaky voice.

"I think so." A small pause, and then Willa said with her teeth chattering, "Y-y-y-es, I seem to b-be able to d-d-drive it well enough... Oh no! Now it's slowing down on its own! At least the air just stopped freezing me, though."

"I think you may want to pull over somewhere and park it, Willa. Can you call a rideshare to get you to your meeting?"

Willa looked at her surroundings and answered, "There's nowhere to park here. It's all private property, and there isn't any room to leave a car. The road is too narrow and curvy. Oooh! It's speeding up, Jackson. Now I'm really scared. What can I do?!" She let out a squeal as the car careened around a curve, going way too fast for comfort. "Jackson! Help me!"

Frantically, he tried to calm her down by saying, "The car's collision avoidance feature will protect you from crashing into anything, but as soon as you can, pull over and get out. I'm trying to send an override message to the car so it will stop acting crazy. I didn't think Teslas would ever do this." Jackson was full-on sweating now. The thought of Willa scared to death in his car was killing him, especially since it was supposed to be the safest thing on the road.

I never should have agreed to take the driver. From now on Willa gets driven by a professional everywhere. This is so fucked up! If I need to hire a fleet of chauffeurs to keep her safe, I'll do it. Or I'll have her flown around by helicopter if I have to! "Where are you now, Willa?"

"I'm on Via de la Valle now, so at least the area is familiar to me. The car keeps lurching so badly, it's making me sick to my stomach. It's getting hot again too. And now the windshield wipers are going, and the sprayer keeps shooting out liquid. This car is possessed!"

Jackson was yanking at his hair and cursing a blue streak, and Miles thought to himself that he was glad they had someplace private to meet. He'd just ordered room service for a late lunch for himself because he was famished after his back-to-back meetings, and they were sitting in the luxury suite Jackson had reserved for him. He knew they'd like some privacy in case Jackson wanted to talk about Willa and Casey, but he never in a million years thought something like this would derail their time together.

"I'm by the golf course now, but there still isn't any place I can see that's good to pull over unless I want to land in a ditch. The road's too narrow here. Maybe I can stop at the polo grounds or the Tack and Feed store. They have a parking lot there. I just hope I don't hit anyone getting into it. Oh, it's so hot again, and I can barely see through the windshield."

"Yeah, okay. Try slowing down enough to get into the parking lot. Good thinking. Stay calm." Jackson felt like a blithering idiot saying that. Willa had to be terrified. He was terrified for her. He felt a comforting hand reach behind him and massage his tense back as he sat hunched over. Miles had always been a great brother.

Willa looked at the radio volume readout and hollered at it, "Oh, *shut up!* Sorry, not you, Jackson! I'm just so sick of this noise; I was yelling at the car."

"I understand. Are you close to the parking lot now?"

"Almost. It's up ahead... but... oh no! The car is speeding up! I can't slow it down, Jackson. Help! It won't let me do anything." Willa sounded close to tears.

Chapter Thirty

Across town, in Pasadena, Ryker sat in front of his computer laughing his ass off. He'd waited for what felt like an eternity for Jackson to take that stupid, expensive car of his out for a spin. Finally, the jerk was driving it, and Ryker felt omnipotent. This was *fun*.

Hearing Ryker's distinctive laughter, Deb went to investigate the cause. Ryker was beside himself, slapping his leg in glee. Stomping into the room, Deb asked, "What the hell?" She didn't like being left out of the joke and hoped it didn't have anything to do with her.

Ryker's attention shifted from his computer screen to Deb's pissed-off expression. He pointed to a bunch of lines of numbers and letters on his computer screen that meant absolutely nothing to her and declared, "I'm just having a little fun with Mr. High and Mighty who thinks he's so damn smart. That'll teach him to block my DEF CON attacks now. He who laughs last laughs best, ya know?"

"Ryker! Aren't we in enough trouble? Why are you trying to make things worse?"

Glaring at her, Ryker growled, "I'm just messing around—just a harmless prank. No one will ever know this was from me anyway. I'm completely protected." He thought so, anyway. Realizing he hadn't done anything for a minute, he looked at the screen and realized that Jackson had managed to slow the car down a little. *Well, that's no good! Take this, you big know-it-all!*

Ryker sped the car back up again and drove it forward as fast as it would go. Since a Tesla Model S Performance can make it up to sixty miles-per-hour in just over two seconds, the lurch was impressive.

Cackling like a crazy man, Ryker said, "I think it's about time for Mr. Big-Brains Mitchell to have a fun little drive on the freeway. Five is just ahead, so let's see just what this jalopy of his will do in Ludicrous mode."

Playing with the car like a video game, Ryker zoomed the Tesla onto Interstate Five and wove it in and out of already swiftly moving traffic. He laughed and laughed as he imagined what his unsuspecting passenger must be feeling. "Not so much fun when someone else takes over control, is it, asshole?" he shouted at the computer screen.

"I'm not so sure this is a good idea, Ryker," Deb whined at him. "What if a highway patrolman tries to pull him over?"

"There isn't a cruiser on the freeway that can catch up to him! Don't be such a dolt." Suddenly feeling like trying something else, Ryker cut the car's speed and decided to take it off the freeway and head toward the coast and Torrey Pines Road. He vaguely remembered it from when he'd driven down there for a convention once, but all he knew for sure was that there was some annual tournament at the Torrey Pines Golf Course.

What Ryker's map didn't show him was elevation, and he forgot that in this area, Torrey Pines Road had a long uphill climb.

The upward slope didn't bother the Tesla, though. And he gleefully accelerated the car up to one hundred twenty miles-per-hour before he lost interest in this game. He knew it could go way faster than that, but it was more fun to goof around with the controls, he decided. For a while he started and stopped the car at random interludes, making it jerk and lurch. "This is probably a great workout for your brakes, isn't it?" he asked. He had a crude aerial view of the terrain and knew where the car was by tracking its progress. To Ryker, the car looked like a green dot on his computer screen.

Up ahead of the car, he could see a large open area on the map and decided to do a little off-roading for some extra grins. He zoomed way in on the map and saw that there was a stretch of what looked like a road through the middle of an area that was oddly devoid of trees and bushes. *A big parking lot, maybe?* The map showed the name Black's Beach along the coast there. *Oh, yeah... I think that's the nude beach I've heard of. Cool! This'll be fun.* It looked to him like a perfect area for some tricks, and maybe he could shake up some nudists at the same time. The thought made him giggle.

Chapter Thirty-One

As Willa struggled to control the Tesla, Jackson and Miles decided the best thing they could do was take Miles' rental car and get the heck down there as soon as possible.

Jackson called Casey.

Fighting to keep his voice calm, Jackson announced, "Sorry to interrupt your meeting, but we have an emergency situation, Case. I'm sending the driver back to you, and you need to get back home as soon as possible."

"What is it?"

"Willa took the Tesla, and it's gone rogue on her. She's terrified, and I'm worried that a certain someone might have hacked the car somehow. She's been careening all over the place, and now she's on her way into La Jolla via Torrey Pines Road. Since that's not how she'd normally get to where she's going, I suspect some serious foul play."

"What the fuck?" was all Casey could say.

"I don't know, but I'm calling the police and I'm tracking the car. I've tried to override the controls and slow her down so she can get out somewhere, but so far that's been impossible. Miles and I are heading out right this minute, and I suggest you do too. No matter what happens, she's going to need us, Case."

"I'm on my way—or I will be as soon as I see the driver. Keep me posted, yeah?"

"You bet. And Case?"

"Huh?"

"If you've ever been a praying kind of guy, this is the time to do it. Hopefully this is just a sick prank, and the person controlling the car will cut it out when he gets tired of the game. I just hope we can get to her before anything worse happens. See you soon."

"Wait! Can we just get a helicopter to fly us back?" Casey asked desperately.

"We could try, but I'm pretty sure it would take us a few hours to charter one. If the traffic isn't too bad yet, we'll be home in less time than it would take to get one. But it's on my shopping list for the future, that's for sure. Case, I need to get back to Willa. If I can, I'll patch you in on the call, but the car has been cutting out the phone intermittently, so we'll have to see."

Miles grabbed his suitcase, and the two of them dashed out the door, only to nearly collide with the room service waiter bringing Miles' meal. The poor waiter looked shocked by their wild facial expressions and stood gaping as Jackson reached for his wallet. He grabbed a few fifty-dollar bills and shoved them into the guy's hand. "Oh, sorry! Look, we have to get out of here. Eat the meal yourself, and use the room if you want. We won't be back."

They left the dumbfounded young man staring at the wad of cash in his fist. "Thank you, sir!" he yelled as the brothers rushed out of sight. "Rich people are crazy," he muttered to himself and wheeled the cart in through the open door. For sure he would eat the meal; it smelled delicious. He was due a short break now anyway, so he pocketed the bills and made himself comfortable.

Once they made it to Miles' rental car, Jackson called the car again. Completely distraught by now, he yelled into his phone, "Willa! Willa?! What's going on? Talk to me, please!"

"I can't control anything! I'm going up Torrey Pines right now, and the car is going way too fast. Where are the cops when you need one? I don't know what to do! Oh. Well. How weird. Now the car has slowed way down. A guy on a bike just passed me actually."

"Can you get out?"

"I'm trying, but it slows way down and then suddenly lurches ahead really fast. I just don't have any control, and I'm afraid I'd get halfway out of the car, and it would speed up again, and I'd get hurt. Oh, here we go again! I just zoomed past the cyclist. This is so scary. I should have gotten out when it was going slowly." Willa's voice was quivering, and Jackson knew in his heart she was trying not to cry.

"We'll figure something out, Willa. I'm going to patch Casey in too so you can talk to him while I call the police and try to get you some help. I'll also call the Tesla people. Maybe they can override it somehow. Hang on."

He heard Casey try to soothe Willa as soon as he was added to the call, and then Jackson called 911. He had to explain that he was in the wrong city for them to help locally, and really needed help in La Jolla. After a frustrating sequence of connections and misunderstandings, he finally got his point across to a dispatcher who sounded mildly skeptical about a car taking its passenger captive and driving itself, but she promised to send a squad car to the area to look for her.

"I'm telling the truth, lady!" Jackson bellowed at her. "This is a dangerous situation and the car needs to be stopped somehow before anyone gets ki... seriously hurt!"

"We'll do our best, sir. Calm down, please."

"I can't calm down! Okay, look, I need to call the Tesla Company, so I have to go. *Please* get someone over to that area to stop her!" Jackson disconnected and called the Tesla helpline.

He heard recorded music. He was put on hold before even talking to anyone.

After a few frustrating minutes of hearing crappy music, Jackson gave up. He reconnected to the call with Willa and Casey, and things sounded bad. Really, really bad.

Willa was full-on sobbing now, and Casey wasn't a lot better. Jackson could hardly make out what she was saying, but finally got the gist that she was being flung around in what sounded like maybe a figure-eight pattern at top speed. She had lost complete control over the speed and the steering, but she could finally get the windows down.

"I'm going to try to jump out, and hope the car doesn't run over me or break my neck in the process," she sobbed. "I love you guys, and I hope I see you again. Alive."

"Willa!" Casey hollered. "Aren't you safer in the car?"

"NO! I'm *not*. The car keeps getting closer to the cliff!"

Cliff? "Where are you, Willa?" Jackson asked, although he had a horrible idea of just where she was.

"I'm at the gliderport! It's deserted, so I'm not going to hit anyone, but the car keeps getting closer and closer to the edge! Oh, God, help me! Oh, no!"

"Willa, wait! I think whoever is controlling the car must see where you are, and he's not going to drive it over the cliff with you in it. He's just playing a game. It will either stop or swerve. I'm afraid if you jump, you'll be seriously hurt!"

They could barely understand her panicked voice as she shouted, "It's *not* slowing down!"

There were some clicking noises. Then they heard Willa scream bloody murder—followed by a series of horrible crunching noises, and finally, everything went silent.

"Willa!" screamed Casey into his phone.

"Willa!" cried Jackson simultaneously. "Oh no, it can't be. *It can't be!*"

Chapter Thirty-Two

Ryker, meanwhile, was still cackling about the wild chase he was treating Jackson to. "You like speed, asshole? Try this!" he'd say and put the car into hyper speed for a few seconds. "Too much for you, sissy?" and Ryker would abruptly put on the breaks, squealing the tires and making the car fish-tail all over the road.

Inside the car, Willa bounced around, hitting her head against the window now and then as she careened sideways, and nearly vomiting when the car abruptly stopped speeding and came to a crawl. She never stayed slow enough to bail out, unfortunately. She was scared to undo her seatbelt for fear of what would happen, but by the time she worked up the courage to take the risk, she was off speeding again.

To Ryker, this was the most entertainment he'd had in ages. He cackled gleefully and glowered at Deb the few times she suggested, "Enough's enough Ryk. Why don't you call it quits and leave the guy alone?"

He ignored her question. This was way too much fun.

When the car got to the big open area, Ryker played games with it, making figure eights and zigzag patterns at top speed. The patterns grew larger and larger until he hit the edge of what he thought was Blacks' Beach. All of a sudden, he lost control of the steering and the speed, and the car looked as if it were bumping up and down for a few seconds, and then all progress stopped.

"Huh. Look at that. It must have gotten stuck in the sand or something," he told Deb.

"What sand? I thought you said he was up on Torrey Pines. There's no sand up there."

"Yeah, there is. Look at the map. It says right there, 'Black's Beach.'" Just as Deb read what Ryker pointed to, the screen went blank.

Deb's eyes bugged out as she gasped in horror at what Ryker had just done. "You *idiot!*" she cried as she shoved his arm. "Black's Beach is at sea level! That's not the edge of the sand! It's a huge, steep drop-off! You probably just killed him. Is that what you wanted? The car went over the cliff. You're a murderer!"

"No way, you lying piece of shit! It's just stuck in the sand." Ryker's face didn't look as confident as his words sounded.

Deb couldn't stand it. "Google Black's Beach and get a picture of it then, you'll see what I'm talking about. Black's is below a huge cliff that people climb down to get to it. It's really steep." She did a fast search on her phone and shoved it into Ryker's face. "*See?* It says right here that it's *three hundred and fifty feet high*. I wonder how many other people you killed when that car *landed* on them!"

"Holy fucking... I gotta get outta here!" Ryker ran to the closet and began stuffing random items into a gym bag.

"I thought you said no one could trace this back to you. That's what you assured me anyway. Were you lying?"

"No one *should* be able to, but if I've killed a bunch of people that might just inspire them to work a little harder at it than if it was just me playing around with someone's car for a while."

"So, when the cops show up, what am I supposed to tell them? That you murdered a bunch of naked people with a car you hijacked *for fun* and then ran away to Timbuktu?" she shouted at him. "Wouldn't you be better off destroying that computer and claiming you're innocent?" She stepped into his space and yelled, "Use your brain, Ryker!"

"I can't just *destroy* it. It has all of my... work on it."

"Then I'll do it for you, you big idiot." Deb reached for the can of grape soda sitting next to Ryker's laptop, and as he watched incredulously, she poured the contents all over the keyboard.

"Nice try, you scheming shrew. Did you happen to notice the cover over the keys? That system is waterproof. It's made for heavy use and for people who work in harsh conditions. All you did was make it sticky, you dumb bitch. Get out of here and get something to wipe it off with. Some paper towels or something. I'm gonna pack."

"Like you were going to go on some *mission* with that computer? Who are you kidding?" she scoffed. "You need the emergency room for a hangnail, you big baby. Harsh conditions, my ass."

"Hey, living with a klutz like you has its disadvantages. The sturdy protections just saved all of my work. So, who's laughing now, huh?"

They went round and round like this for the better part of an hour, both slinging insults at top volume, and neither making any headway.

Eventually the doorbell rang, and Ryker ran and hid in the closet. "Don't answer that!" he shouted.

The doorbell rang again and outside a man called, "FBI! We know you're in there. We could hear you yelling all the way to the street. Now open the door or we'll smash it in. We have a warrant for your arrests."

Deb marched stoically to the front door, and three uniformed and armed men showed their IDs and barged in. One of them immediately handcuffed Deb, while the other two went to search for Ryker. They found him pounding the crap out of his beloved laptop with a shoe. It wasn't doing anything to the basically bullet-proof case, especially since the shoe he grabbed was a sneaker.

He looked at their amused faces and asked, "What does the FBI have to do with this? There's no federal crime here."

Clapping handcuffs onto him, one of the agents said, "Buddy, we've been surveilling this house for days, and you are under arrest for the federal felony of internet crimes. You've used the internet to threaten or cause harm to another individual, and you're in deep trouble. We have all of your online information on our computers already, so smashing up this little toy won't do jack shit for you."

Ryker knew that murder wasn't a federal crime, but he wasn't about to bring that to their attention. He wasn't *that* stupid. He did wonder how many people had died, though, and the idea was starting to make him queasy.

Chapter Thirty-Three

The police who'd been dispatched to the Torrey Pines Road area drove around aimlessly looking for anyone who was speeding or seemed to be having car difficulties. They got to the top of the hill and looked around and still saw nothing. "Wow," one of the cops said to the other, "it's so damn windy; this area is completely deserted. Usually, the gliderport area is full of cars and people going out hang gliding and whatnot. I guess it closed early because of the winds."

"Nature is being difficult today. The beaches are also closed because of a terrible riptide. I guess that goes along with this wind, but what do I know?"

"Well, I don't see anything out of the ordinary. Why don't you call in our 10-42? I'm getting hungry; it's time to go off-duty."

As the squad car left the area, a wisp of smoke drifted up over the edge of the cliff, but they were long gone and missed it. The smoke quickly dispersed in the wind.

Chapter Thirty-Four

Jackson called 911 again. This time he knew exactly where Willa was. He could barely force the words out.

Miles tried to drive faster without causing his own wreck, but he was completely at a loss as to what to say to Jackson.

Casey called Phillipe and asked him to please get over to the gliderport immediately and see if he could find out anything. Since Phillipe was the closest, it made sense.

Phillipe was already running for his van before Casey was even done telling him what was going on. "I'm on my way, Mr. Melrose. I'll let you know the instant I know anything. You can count on me."

Phillipe drove like a bat out of hell getting over to the coast. His insides were churning. Casey had sounded terrified. *He* was terrified for all of them too. He'd been around the three of them enough to know how strong their commitment and love were. It wasn't an average relationship, by any means, but it worked for them. Phillipe had a genuine fondness for his employers and couldn't fathom what would happen if Willa had gotten hurt... or worse. He stepped on the gas a little more and looked in his rearview mirror for police. The trouble was, the sun was starting to set, and visibility was becoming worse. Also, he noticed a lot of debris—sticks, leaves, and the occasional piece of trash blowing around in the fierce wind.

As he drew closer to his destination, he began to hear sirens and hoped they weren't coming from behind him to give him a speeding ticket. He slowed down as he saw flashing lights bearing down on him, and he pulled to the side, swearing colorfully at his bad luck. Much to his relief, however, he watched several vehicles fly by him at top speed. Feeling as if his heart were about to explode, it was beating so hard, he called Casey back and reported, "The authorities just zoomed by me, I assume to get to the site. There was an ambulance, a fire truck, and some cops. I'm right behind them."

Phillipe pulled into the area behind the emergency vehicles and tried to assess the situation without getting in the way. All he could see was that the fire truck was pouring water over the cliff, and there was a lot of smoke billowing everywhere. He politely approached one of the police officers who stood looking over the edge and asked, "Do you know what happened to the driver? She's one of my employers—a friend."

"Sorry, sir. From the looks of things, no one could have survived that crash. It's hard to see, but the car is in pieces, and the lithium batteries in it are about to start a brush fire if they don't get it out right away."

Phillipe's heart dropped, and he began babbling, "But her boyfriend was on the phone with her, and he told me she was trying to jump out through the window. He's on his way home right now from LA. Please, you need to look for her! She could still be alive somewhere down there!"

The officer gave him a sad look, but went to speak to her partner. Within seconds, they had a high beam light scanning the area near the crashed car.

Phillipe was shaking like a leaf but felt compelled to climb down the cliffside to look for her himself. He asked the officer, "Isn't there a path around here that leads down to the beach?"

"It's a little south of here," she answered, "but don't get any ideas. That fire is no joke. Those lithium batteries are tough to extinguish, and they've been known to reignite and even explode once the fire is out."

Phillipe wasn't listening. He was jogging south to look for the trail. He knew he had to do something. Poor Willa! The sun hadn't completely set yet, but with the smoke and the fading light, it was very difficult to see, and it was getting worse by the minute. All he had was a key fob light, but he figured he'd wait until he really needed that. And there it was—the head of the trail!

Ever so carefully Phillipe made his way down the rocky path, thinking to himself, *Those crazy sunbathers sure work hard to get to their nude beach.* At least the path seemed to be traversing back toward where the car went over the rim, so he thought if he were really, really lucky...

"Hey! Over here! I see her! HELP!" Phillipe shined his tiny light ahead of him as he scrambled off the path and back up the cliff. He gave up when he realized he needed both hands to keep from plunging to his death. "Help, she's over here!" His foot lost traction then, and he skidded backward, scraping his knee.

Finally, someone heard him over the noise of the firetruck and trained the high-powered light in his direction—and *right* into his eyes, blinding him. He gestured wildly to get them to scan the area ahead of him instead, yelling, "Over there!" Whoever had the light got the picture and started to pan the area much closer to the top of the cliff this time.

And there she was! Not moving, Phillipe noticed. Hanging limply over a rock outcropping in an awkward position with her face covered in blood. Her foot seemed to be stuck between a couple of smaller boulders above her. *Maybe that's what kept her from falling further?* He couldn't see a lot of her body from his angle. He also realized how difficult it would have been to see her from the top of the cliff, considering the shape of the hillside and the random clusters of brush.

Phillipe doubled his efforts to climb up to where Willa lay. Hot tears streaked down his face when he thought about how sweet and happy she'd been just a few hours ago while they discussed his good news.

Oh, God. I can't bear the idea that Casey and Jackson might lose her. It will kill them! It'll kill me, and I'm not even in love with her. Ouch! Climbing in this terrain was ill-advised and treacherous.

Finally, Phillipe was forced to admit to himself that he couldn't get to Willa from where he was. His heart sank. But just then a fireman yelled, "Get back to the path carefully. We're sending down climbers and a stretcher. Please stay out of their way, sir. We'll take it from here."

Relieved to hear that, Phillipe retraced his steps and slid on his butt a bit until he reached better footing on the path. His hands were scratched, and his knee was bloody where his jeans were torn, but he barely noticed. Once it was safe enough, he ran back up to where the firemen were deploying rescuers.

When the men reached Willa, he hollered to them, "Is she alive?" *Please, God. Please, God, let her be alive. She didn't look alive to me, and there was all that blood. Oh, God.* Phillipe made the sign of the cross.

"We have a pulse. It's weak, but it's there," one of the men shouted back to him.

"Oh, *Dieu merci*." He immediately phoned Casey.

"What's happening, Philippe?"

"She's alive! She got out of the car, but she still fell quite a long way and hit some rocks. The rescue guys are bringing her up now."

"How did she get out? Did she say what happened?"

"Uh, no. She's kind of... um... "

"What, Phillipe? Are you crying? What's wrong with her. Tell me!"

"She's unconscious actually. And, Mr. Melrose, if I'm really honest, she doesn't look so good. There's a lot of blood."

Casey didn't answer. Phillipe thought he could hear him crying on the other end of the line. He asked softly, "Shall I call Mr. Mitchell, or do you want to?"

"Um... I'll do it. Is there anything else you can tell me? Anything?"

"Well, they're hauling her up over the edge of the cliff now on a stretcher, so I guess that's good news. I'll find out what they're planning to do with her if you want to hold on a second." There was even more blood than he'd thought. This was definitely bad.

"Yes, please," Casey said in a strangled voice.

A moment went by as Phillipe conferred with the firemen, and he watched as they loaded Willa into the waiting ambulance. He still thought she looked more dead than alive, but he certainly didn't want to report that to Casey.

Casey could hear the sounds of a conversation, but there was so much extraneous noise and hollering, it was impossible to understand the words. Finally, Phillipe returned to the phone and reported, "They're taking her to the ER at Scripps Memorial. I gave them her name and address, but I don't know anything else to tell them like her birthdate or social security number. They said the hospital may be able to access her medical records with just her name though. Anyway, I'll be right behind them and see if I can find out anything before you get there. How far away are you?"

"Oh, maybe another fifteen minutes or so from the hospital. We'll see you there. Thanks, Phillipe, for everything, and please, call us by our first names from now on."

"Yes sir. Um, Casey. I need to go now."

♡♡♡

Casey and Jackson arrived within seconds of each other and met in the parking lot. After wordlessly giving each other a bolstering hug, they entered the ER. They found Phillipe pacing around the waiting room looking pale and shell-shocked. The poor guy was shaking.

"Oh, there you are," he sighed. "They won't tell me anything other than they're running tests. I'm not her family, and they have all these laws about privacy. I'm so sorry I can't give you more information. They did say they'd come back with an update as soon as they can though—like if they're admitting her or whatever." Then he scoffed, "Like she's in any condition to go home." He shook his head sadly.

Miles arrived then after parking the rental car, greeted Casey somberly, and met Phillipe for the first time. He told everyone, "I'm not sure it's my place to be here right now. I'm going to give you all some space and track down something to eat. I hope this isn't insensitive, but I ate breakfast at five this morning and haven't had anything since. I'll come back and find you soon. I hope Willa's okay." He hugged his brother and went off to find a cafeteria.

Just then, a couple of police officers arrived. One of them was the woman Phillipe had spoken to at the accident site. She made a beeline to Phillipe and said, "Excellent work back there, sir. I don't always endorse the idea of private citizens becoming involved, but you probably saved that woman's life by finding her so quickly."

Casey and Jackson both blinked at Phillipe, and he explained briefly and humbly what had happened.

"I guess that explains the cuts and scratches," Jackson pointed out. "We can't thank you enough, Phillipe."

Casey gave his chef a bro hug, clapping him on the back and whispering, "Thanks, man."

The other officer addressed Casey and Jackson then and said, "One of you is the owner of the car and the one who called in the emergency?"

"I did. It's my car," answered Jackson.

They had a lot of questions for Jackson, so they all found seats and tried to relax. After grilling him for about an hour about his suspicions regarding the hacker who'd taken control of the car, and his relationship to the suspected perpetrator, a tired-looking nurse marched into the waiting room.

Looking around, she called out, "Is there a Casey Jackson here? Or a Jackson Casey?"

The two men jumped to their feet and grabbed for each other's hand.

"That's us. I mean we're Casey and Jackson. How's Willa?" Jackson demanded.

"She's semi-conscious off and on, and she keeps repeating Casey and Jackson, so we assumed that was one person. Are you family?" she asked.

"Boyfriends," Casey explained.

Looking at their clasped hands, the nurse rolled her eyes and clarified in a bored tone that clearly expressed that she thought he was thick in the head, "I mean your relationship to Ms. Camden."

Looking her straight in the eye, Jackson enunciated clearly, "We are her boyfriends. She lives with us. We're her only family."

"Okay, well whatever. She seems to want to see you, so follow me if you're done here." She looked pointedly at the police. They stood up and said they'd be in touch again if they needed more information. It was obvious the two men needed to see Willa *now*.

"Charming woman," the policewoman whispered to her partner as Jackson and Casey made their way out of the waiting room.

At the last minute before the door closed, Casey swung around and said, "Come on, Philippe!"

Phillipe stood a little straighter and thanked the police officers, then quickly followed the others down the hall.

All three of them finally looked cautiously optimistic. At least Willa had said *something*.

Chapter Thirty-Five

There was no sugar-coating it. Willa looked awful. Her arm was in a sling, her head was bandaged, and she had her ankle in a splint. She had an oxygen cannula in her nose, and she was hooked to an IV. Everything about her that normally glowed with vitality had faded.

"She's in and out of consciousness, but go ahead and talk to her if you want. The doctor should be in soon with some information. Use the call button if you need anything." The nurse left without offering any more information.

"Oh, sweetheart, I'm so sorry to have let this happen to you," Jackson moaned as he sat with a plunk in a chair. He scooted closer to the bed and clasped her free hand. A tear rolled down his face unchecked.

"Hey, don't blame yourself," Casey reassured him. "I'm sure Willa won't hold you accountable for what some crazy lunatic did with your car. She understands." He rubbed Jackson's back and tried to find a place on Willa to look at that wasn't a mess. It was difficult. "Hey, Willa. Can you hear us?" he asked softly. "We're here now. Jax and I got here as soon as we could." His voice cracked as he continued, "We both love you so much. I hope you're not in too much pain."

Willa's eyes fluttered, and all three men stopped breathing. But nothing else happened.

"Willa, can you hear us?" Jackson asked. "Try to open your beautiful eyes so we can see that you're going to be alright."

Nothing. Not even a flutter this time.

"I wonder if she's unconscious or on pain meds," mused Phillipe.

They continued to speak to her gently and lovingly for about half an hour when the drape was pulled aside. Expecting a nurse or a doctor, they were mildly surprised to see Miles join them. "Any news yet?" he asked. "They told me to come back here, but that's all anyone would say."

Jackson said in a flat voice, "Not a word."

A good forty minutes later, a doctor arrived and surveyed the crowd as he introduced himself, "I'm Dr. Nugent. Is she talking to you yet?"

All heads turned to Willa to see that her eyelids were slightly open finally.

"Willa?" asked Casey and Jackson simultaneously.

This time her eyes opened fully, and she attempted to smile at them. "Hi," she croaked. "I... hurt." Her eyes closed again.

Jackson regarded the doctor and demanded, "Aren't you giving her anything for pain? Is she going to be alright? What all is wrong with her?"

"Don't worry. We're giving her what we can, but there are limits to what we can prescribe." He checked the IV, picked up her chart, and made a note. Then he stepped up to Willa and bent over her. He lifted her eyelid and pointed a small light at her pupil. She seemed to shrink from him, but he repeated the movement with her other eye. "I need her consent to discuss her medical condition with you. We don't have any signed forms allowing you access to her private information. I'm sorry."

Willa opened her eyes again and looked straight at the doctor. "S'okay," she slurred. "Tell 'em everything you tell me." The words seemed to have caused her so much effort, she drifted off again.

"Yes, well, fine. She only has a mild concussion, and that's good, despite a big gash on the back of her head we stitched up. She had a dislocated shoulder that we fixed. She'll be sore and will want to wear a sling for a few days. Her ankle has a nasty sprain, but surprisingly isn't broken. All in all, I'd say she has some strong bones. It's a wonder she didn't break anything. Her ribs are badly bruised, and that will cause considerable discomfort for a while. But..." He paused. "Ms. Camden, can you hear me?" he asked a little more loudly than he'd been speaking.

"Yeah," she mumbled.

Dr. Nugent got a serious look on his face and added, "There was a lot of blood on your clothing, and at first, we suspected a miscarriage, but the baby is fine."

"*Baby?*" Casey and Jackson cried simultaneously as Willa's eyes flew open.

Phillipe just stood and stared, and then he had the presence of mind to say, "I'll be leaving now. This is your business. I'm glad to see she's okay." No one paid a lot of attention to him as he quietly took his leave.

Miles also said, "I'll be in the waiting room," and he gave Jackson's arm a squeeze before he followed Phillipe out.

That left Jackson and Casey staring at Willa in awe. Slowly their faces split into huge grins.

"Not pregnant," Willa rasped, shaking her head slightly. Then she reached for the oxygen tube and said, "Don't like this."

Dr. Nugent said, "It's fine, Ms. Camden. This was just to help your breathing for a while," and he removed the cannula. Turning to the men, he asked, "Is one of you the father?"

Casey smiled and announced, "Yes, and we have no idea which one of us it is. Willa! This is so great," he said with a happy chortle.

Jackson hadn't found his voice yet and just stared at Willa with his crooked grin firmly in place.

Scowling, Willa said tiredly, "Wrong, doctor. I have an IUD. Not pregnant." Then she asked, "Water?"

Casey grabbed for a glass and straw on a nearby table and held it to her lips.

The poor doctor looked from one man to the other confusedly until Jackson attempted to set him straight. "We're a triad. We all love each other, and we're as good as married to each other." He squeezed Willa's hand gently for reassurance.

Dr. Nugent blinked a couple of times and then continued on as professionally as possible, "Yes, well, as I said, we noticed the blood and right away performed an ultrasound. It's true, she had an IUD, but it was improperly situated in her cervix rather than fully up in her uterus, thus decreasing the effectiveness of the birth control by at least thirty percent. We immediately removed the device so it wouldn't cause harm to the mother or fetus. Should she choose to terminate..."

Willa managed to look at the doctor with a horrified expression.

"No!" snapped Jackson at the same time Casey gasped, "No way!"

"Well, I guess that settles that question." He finally smiled at all of them. "She's going to have to take it easy. The pregnancy is in its early stages, but losing a lot of blood under the circumstances isn't as scary as it sounds. She'll need to stay off her ankle, and crutches won't be an option due to her shoulder injury, so I guess you gentlemen will just have to wait on her hand and foot until she can get around."

"No problem," Casey assured him.

"It will be our pleasure," Jackson stated firmly and then asked, "But do you think we ought to hire a nurse for her?"

The doctor looked at their worried faces and answered, "I doubt that will be necessary."

Chapter Thirty-Six

Jackson arranged for Willa to spend the night in one of the VIP suites in the hospital for the night, and they all made their way upstairs to stay with her. There was no way either Casey or Jackson would let her out of their sight.

Once she was settled, Miles told them all, "I think I'm going to try to find a flight back up north tonight. I'll just be in your way, and you all need your privacy now."

"I have a better idea," Jackson told him. "You look exhausted, and it's hard to get late flights out of San Diego. Go to my house, get some rest, and I'll have someone fly you home first thing in the morning." Jackson made a quick call and set up the charter flight and gave his brother the code to get into his house. "Make yourself comfortable."

♡♡♡

They all returned to Jackson's house the next day. The specially made, giant bed he'd ordered was now in place, and they were all ready to try it out—at least for sleeping. Willa certainly wasn't ready for anything else.

The story of Willa's accident was all over the news, so a few hours after they arrived home, a large, beautiful bouquet showed up for Willa from the book club ladies. They'd been horrified to hear why she hadn't shown up to their meeting. The flowers were accompanied by several hand-written cards wishing her a speedy recovery and exclaiming over how much they'd enjoyed her book. Willa vowed to make it up to them soon.

For the next several days they all tried to regroup and calm down. Once one goes through a hair-raising experience, however, it's tough to figure out normal again right away. But they also discussed their new situation and all three decided that having a baby on the horizon was the most exciting, wonderful news they could imagine for themselves. They also decided that figuring out the biological father wasn't a priority for them. Kids tend to look like their parents, and it would probably become apparent over time. But if it didn't—it didn't matter. Casey and Jackson promised they would love the child unconditionally, no matter whose swimmer did the deed. Genetic testing could always be done later if it became necessary for medical reasons.

About fifty times a day, Willa had to answer the question, "Do you feel alright?" Each time she assured her men that she did. Her aches and pains were receding, and she felt no nausea from her pregnancy. Her only symptom so far was evident when she complained, "My boobs hurt. Do they look bigger to you guys?"

Plenty of detailed inspections ensued, and the men declared her tits "Just perfect."

When the typical first-trimester sleepiness kicked in, she spent several hours a day sound asleep.

"This is probably the best way for her to heal anyway," announced Casey. He'd been researching everything he could about pregnancy and felt like an authority on the subject. He also spent an inordinate amount of time Googling babies and how to be a good parent. Often over dinner he would throw out amazing factoids such as, "Did you know that babies are born with three hundred bones, but as they grow up, ninety-four of them will fuse? And they don't have kneecaps. Amazing, yeah?"

Another day he demanded, "You plan to breastfeed, don't you, Willa? It's absolutely the best thing for babies, you know." Then he recounted all of the nutritional and developmental benefits he'd read about. After he lectured a while, he got a stricken look on his face and added, "But if you want to bottle feed instead, that's also fine. Baby formula is an excellent food for babies as well, and I don't mean to tell you how you have to do it."

Willa regarded Casey fondly and reassured him, "If it works out for me, I plan to breastfeed. Don't worry."

Jackson located the most highly regarded OB/GYN in the area and made an appointment for Willa. When they all three showed up for the appointment, the staff was polite and accommodating, but they did get some odd looks. One of the nurses put her foot in her mouth when she assumed that Jackson and Casey were a gay couple who'd hired Willa to have a baby for them. She was mortified to discover what a gross error she'd made and apologized profusely.

Also, remaining true to his vows about safety, Jackson hired a couple more chauffeurs and bought two new town cars to go along with the limo so that no one had to drive themselves around any longer. Then he purchased a helicopter and a small jet with an aircrew for their transportation needs.

Casey and Willa grinned and rolled their eyes at him—and loved him all the more for his concern.

Sex was off the table for Willa for a while, so she cheerfully ordered Jackson and Casey to have lots of sex together—in front of her, of course. She loved watching them bring each other to ecstasy. A couple of times she told them, "I'm getting some new ideas from this," or, "Oh! You like that?" And then she would make a happy "mmm" sound.

Finally, Willa announced that she was recovered and could get around on her own with a boot. Her ribs and shoulder weren't bothering her much at all. So, she grabbed her laptop and got back in touch with her co-screenwriter Janie. It felt good to be working again. She alternated her work on the screenplay with writing her newest novel.

And gently, the men began to include her in their bed games, but only very carefully at first. After a few sessions of this, however, Willa cried out in frustration, "Oh for crying out loud, you guys! Fuck me like you mean it; I'm not made of glass!" Jackson started to protest, but she stopped him cold. "I'm *fine!*" The guys laughed finally at her ferocious expression and got down to business. She sighed contentedly, "Much better."

The next day, Jackson disappeared for a while. When he got home, he looked a little nervous to Willa and Casey, who stole questioning glances at each other. They both would raise their eyebrows and shrug when Jackson obviously missed something one of them said because he was somewhere in his own head. Jackson seemed jumpy all the way through dinner, but when they were finished eating, he stood up from the table and went to kneel between the other two. Finally, his demeanor seemed calm.

"Willa," he said as he looked lovingly into her eyes. "Casey," he said as he turned his attention to his lifelong best friend. "You both fill my heart with more joy than I ever imagined. Will you do me the greatest honor of wearing these bands and being my partners forever? I know we can't all three marry legally, but you're it for me. I will love you to my dying day." He held up beautiful matching wedding bands to them.

"Of course," Willa answered with tears in her eyes as Jackson slid a ring onto her finger.

"Yes, absolutely," Casey replied as he accepted his ring, and then he added, "Jackson, with you illegally marry me? And you, Willa? We're perfect together... as three." That got a smile from them, but none of this felt illegal to anyone, and they both answered yes to Casey's question.

Willa's attention went to Casey and she looked between the two men. "I love you both so much, and equally. I can't imagine being married to one of you without the other. Do you have a band for yourself too, Jackson?" When he produced it, she and Casey slipped it onto his hand together.

Lots of kissing happened for a while, punctuated with plenty of happy laughter and declarations of, "I love you."

"And now we're all each other's. Always," Jackson said with a catch in his voice. He smiled contentedly, but then regarded Willa with a pensive expression. "Do you feel in any way like you're missing out on the big white dress experience?"

Willa cocked her head in thought for a moment and then answered, "Not really. If my parents were still around, then maybe I'd feel differently." Her voice choked up suddenly. "My dad was such a softy, he always cried at weddings, and my mom used to dream about planning for mine." She shook off the sad face and went on, "But I honestly never had that big princess-for-a-day fantasy going for myself." She smiled at Jackson and then Casey lovingly and said, "Besides, I feel like that every day I'm with the both of you. I'm absolutely the luckiest woman alive. I'm sure of it. And a fancy white dress and a bunch of flowers won't add anything to that. We're us. That's what's important. We've all just made our promises, and that's enough."

♡♡♡

Often when they were done making love to each other, the two men would lie on either side of Willa and talk to the baby as they caressed her tummy. It was another one of Casey's research findings. "Babies can hear in the womb, and it's good for them to become accustomed to different voices and noises." Willa's favorite times were when the two men tried to outdo each other by telling the baby stories about one another. She laughed so hard, she routinely leaked tears.

Casey told the baby, "Your daddy Jackson used to go to school in his flannel pajama pants until the school made a rule against it. A lot of the other kids copied him because he looked so comfortable, but the administrators thought it 'set a bad example.'"

"I never got in trouble for it, though," laughed Jackson. Addressing Willa's womb, he said, "Your daddy Casey used to threaten anyone who tried to tease me. He scared the sh... the stuff out of Billy Waite, the school bully. Billy tried to harass me about my pajamas until the fad caught on. They really were comfortable," he added with a sigh.

Sometimes the men would strike up a song and sing it to the baby, and Willa thought she could just die on the spot. They both had smooth, deep voices that harmonized perfectly. Their choice of songs ranged from classic rock to country to nursery rhymes they'd probably learned as kids—and one or two Christmas carols—but each one was memorable. She ran her hands through their hair and tried not to cry as they sang. She failed.

Chapter Thirty-Seven

At the same time that Willa's pregnancy was beginning to show prominently, it was time for Ryker and Deb's trials.

When the jury saw Willa, an ethereally beautiful pregnant woman, glowing with the promise of a new life, and they heard how Ryker had almost killed her, they didn't give one single shit that he hadn't "meant to" do anything other than torment Jackson with his car antics.

He'd sealed his fate when Willa's lawyer Mckenna had him on the witness stand. She asked politely, "Did you try to kill someone with Mr. Mitchell's car?"

Looking shifty, Ryker replied, "Hell no! I was just messing around!"

The judge reprimanded him immediately for cursing in the courtroom and told Ryker to watch himself.

Without batting an eyelash, Mckenna continued, "Did you know you were controlling the car that was being driven by Ms. Camden, who was pregnant?"

"No," Ryker muttered. Then he had the bad sense to say, "Her boyfriend is an asshole and I wanted to pay him back."

The judge told him any more outbursts like that would result in some stiff fines.

Mckenna then asked Ryker, "Did you send the car over a cliff with the intent of killing Mr. Mitchell?"

"I made a mistake! But that fucker needs to be paid back for messing with me!"

"So," Mckenna continued, "Because Mr. Mitchell out-smarted you at a hacking competition, which is the entire point of the competition, I might add, you thought it was appropriate to endanger his life, but in doing so, you nearly killed his girlfriend and her unborn child. Is that about the size of it?"

Ryker glared at Mckenna while the judge imposed a fine and had him removed from the courtroom. Ryker hollered obscenities about Jackson the whole way out.

After finding him guilty, the jury recommended the maximum punishment for Ryker. The general consensus was that he was lower than scum.

The FBI had a team of hackers at their disposal. They had uncovered all of the nasty shenanigans he'd been up to over the years, and Ryker was not going to get out of prison for the rest of his life.

♡♡♡

The lawyers for Willa did some extremely fine sleuthing and located the original ghost screenwriter Deb Abbey had used when she stole Willa's first book. Under oath, the woman swore that the manuscript had said the name Willa Camden on it. She explained that when she asked Deb about it, Deb claimed it was one of her pen names. She also said that Deb introduced herself as Delia Abbott. Willa Camden was unpublished at that time, so her name meant nothing to her.

It turned out, as they'd suspected, that Deb Abbey had chosen the name Deborah Abrams because it sounded more professional and literary than the name she'd been given by her parents. They'd saddled her with Debbie Abbey, and she'd never liked it.

All of the proceeds from the more recent book Deb had stolen from Willa were awarded to her, and the unedited copies of the book were ordered to be destroyed. Willa donated the money to a literacy foundation. The jury also awarded Willa a million dollars in damages, but she was informed soon after the trial that she shouldn't hold her breath for a payout; Deb didn't have a penny left.

The Baxter Brothers studio that made a movie from her stolen story, however, was also ordered to pay damages, and it nearly bankrupted them. The jury reasoned that it should have looked suspicious to the Baxters when Deb was unfamiliar with the particulars of the story. That money went to the literacy foundation as well because Willa didn't want a cent of it for herself.

For her complicity in making a video of Willa, Jackson, and Casey, and for using the internet to threaten Willa and her men with harm, Deb was sentenced to spend time in prison as well. She would not be out for many years.

Deb also received a hefty fine for slapping her lawyer's face when the verdict was delivered. She left the courtroom bawling after she glared one last time at Willa. It just wasn't fair. Why should Willa have all the talent and beauty?

The Academy of Motion Picture Arts and Sciences stripped Deb of her Oscar. Deb bawled about that too. Her cellmate was unimpressed.

Chapter Thirty-Eight

The three parents-to-be ended up making several trips north to Castroville to see Jackson and Casey's families—now that they could pop up there easily in their fancy new jet. The novelty of having the plane was going to take a long time to wear off, and they all felt a giddy thrill each time they made a trip. And, just as the men predicted, the families in Castroville fell head over heels in love with Willa. Not one person raised an eyebrow at their triad, and everyone commented on how happy the three of them seemed. Their union was a beautiful thing, and who could begrudge such devotion?

Willa especially loved seeing where the guys had grown up, and the massive artichoke farm fascinated her. The fields spread out forever, it seemed, and there was a lovely café and a fancy gift shop on the property that sold artichoke-related products like cooking utensils, cookbooks, and jars of many varieties of preserved artichokes. A seasonal farm stand offered fresh artichokes to local shoppers and tourists when the buds were harvested. They also offered cooking classes that sounded interesting, but Willa was secretly happy she could rely on Phillipe rather than learning to cook more things herself.

She was happy to get to know Miles finally, and he was thrilled to see her looking better than the last time he'd seen her. Willa had to admit, "I'm sorry, I don't even remember that you were at the hospital, but I'm so glad you could help

Jackson out that day. I'm sure he was terrified, and having his big brother there probably helped tremendously. I can't imagine how he'd have been if he'd had to drive himself home during that fiasco."

Willa discovered that both sets of parents were thrilled to become grandparents. She felt as if the baby would be lucky to have two sets of them since her own parents would not be around. She often thought wistfully of her own parents, but it helped that Casey and Jackson's families welcomed her so eagerly. She knew now that if she needed a mother's advice, she had two lovely women she could turn to.

Another trip Jackson insisted they make once the trial ended was to see his newly completed estate in Aspen. It was past ski season—not that Willa could have skied anyway—but the views from the floor to ceiling windows were breathtaking, and the house was beyond magnificent.

When they got to Aspen, Casey had a surprise for them. He'd selected frames of their GoPro video of each of them skiing in the Cariboos and had the still photos blown up and framed as a large tryptic. He'd made sure to have it hung over the mantle of the enormous stone fireplace in the great room.

On the right side, Willa looked graceful and determined with her movements all precise and collected, but the viewer got the sense that she was traveling through the sparkling powder at breakneck speed. The pattern she made in the snow behind her showed a series of perfectly executed parallel turns. Her blonde hair was loose that day and created a shining golden aura around her. She looked like a snow goddess.

The left panel was filled with Casey, snow-covered with his hands held high, his body in a semi-tucked position and looking right on the verge of being out of control. Because his hair and eyes were concealed by his hat and goggles, the most distinguishable characteristic of the photo was his ear-to-ear grin. It was classic Casey.

The center panel contained Jackson. Rather than being in the sparkling snow, he was several feet above it, soaring through the air. His arms were raised in victory, and his legs were spread, making him into a giant flying X. His mouth was open and gave the impression that he was shouting with glee. As Casey put it, "You can almost hear him whooping it up."

Willa and Jackson were speechless for a moment as they took in the wonderful gift Casey had made for them. It wasn't fine art, but it was personal and recorded one of the best days of their lives. It was also beautiful with the clear blue sky, the pristine snow, and their colorful ski outfits. The triptych was a masterpiece to them. They both turned and showered Casey with kisses.

"It's amazing," cried Willa. "You're a genius to make this for the house and for us. Thank you so much."

"I love it, Case. Thank you. And you did a great job keeping this a secret. We'll all treasure this forever."

Chapter Thirty-Nine

As Willa's due date approached, they spent all their time in La Jolla, reasoning that they were close to the hospital and Willa's doctor that way. Willa also enjoyed taking long walks on the beach with her men, and the constant rumble of the surf grounded her.

Willa's labor became intense in the middle of the night while the men were sleeping. She scared Jackson half to death when she gripped his arm and started to moan in pain. He sat up in bed and said in alarm, "Do you need an ambulance? What's happening?"

Casey grabbed for his phone and announced, "We're going to time your contractions. Just remember the breathing exercises. He turned on the timer and patiently waited for Willa's current contraction to end.

Grabbing his hair, Jackson asked wildly, "Why are you just sitting there?"

"Don't worry, Jax. We'll just see how far apart they are. It might be hours before we need to go to the hospital," Casey said in a soothing, businesslike voice. He held his phone in one hand and came around to sit next to Willa so he could massage her back with the other.

Willa choked out, "I need to get to the bathroom *now!*" She scooted to the edge of the huge bed and moaned again, doubling over.

Jackson hopped out of bed and reached for Willa, scooping her up in his arms. He carried her to the bathroom and was just about to set her down when a flood of liquid poured down his body.

"Oh! My water just broke," Willa pointed out.

Casey followed them into the bathroom and asked, "How long have the pains been going on?"

"Um, they started at around lunchtime, but I thought I just had an upset stomach. Now I don't think that was it." She doubled over again.

"Willa! These aren't even a minute apart!" Casey cried, not nearly as calm and collected as before.

Jackson set Willa down and, with a rather green face, turned on the shower. He was in and out of it before the water heated up and immediately called the doctor—whom he had on speed dial, of course.

After a rushed conversation, it was determined that driving to the hospital would be faster than dispatching an ambulance, so they summoned their driver who said he would be there in less than five minutes. They cleaned Willa up as quickly as possible and wrapped her in a soft robe. The two guys threw on whatever clothes they could grab quickly, and Casey carried her out to the waiting limo.

Jackson's shirt was inside out, and Casey's shoes didn't match. One of them belonged to Jackson.

Willa kept insisting, "I can walk." Casey was not impressed by this assertion in the least, and Jackson was giving the driver instructions to break the sound barrier getting to the hospital.

Once they were in the car and relatively calmed down, Jackson asked, "Why didn't you wake us up, sweetheart?"

"You both looked so tired and I didn't want to worry you. It wasn't so bad at first, but nnnnggggghhhhhh!" She clutched her belly and began to pant. "The contractions kind of sped up all of a sudden in the past hour or so. Ohhhhh... a *lot*."

The streets were nearly deserted, since it was three in the morning, and the car moved swiftly toward the hospital. With each quarter of a mile they got closer to the hospital, Jackson breathed a little more easily. That was—until Willa scrunched up her face and hollered, "I need to push!"

"*What?*" cried Casey. "Willa, you can't! Wait until we get to the hospital, for the love of God! We're almost there! See? We're on Genesee, and it's just up ahead. Hang on, please!" The hospital was visible in the distance, but they weren't exactly close to it yet.

Unimpressed with their location or how quickly they'd be there, Willa cried, "I can't wait. I have to push *now! Owwwwwww!*"

At that point, everything went into slow motion for Jackson. He slipped to his knees on the floor in front of Willa. He'd done a fair amount of research on having babies too, and while Casey switched his hollering to spewing instructions about breathing, Jackson calmly delivered their daughter into the world. He sobbed for joy as she let out a lusty cry. "She's so beautiful, Willa. Meet our daughter." He raised the precious bundle so Willa could see. "Meet Matilda."

Just then, the limo came to a stop in front of the hospital and Casey threw himself out of the car in a panic, shouting as he ran through the automatic doors, "Help! We just had a baby in the car! We need a doctor!"

While admiring the incredible, brand-new, squirmy little person who protested her new surroundings loudly in Jackson's arms, Willa grimaced. Another colossal contraction grabbed her as she expelled the placenta. "We made an awful mess of the limo," she pointed out sheepishly.

Jackson chuckled, "I'll buy a new one." He kissed their daughter's head.

Casey returned almost immediately with the medical team who took over. He watched with tears streaking his face as one of the nurses said, "You all did a great job here. The baby looks healthy. Congratulations." She didn't really know who to look at, so she smiled at all three of them.

In a hushed tone, Casey finally sounded more relaxed. "We have a daughter. I've never seen anything more beautiful in my whole life." And he'd seen some pretty incredible stuff.

Epilogue

As expected, the three of them made excellent parents. Casey had created a masterpiece of a nursery, but Matilda was rarely in it. She spent most of her early days attached either to Willa's breast or to one of her daddies who adored her to the moon and back. As she grew, it was apparent that she would be a curly blond and seemed to be settling on having bright blue eyes. She didn't particularly look like anyone yet, but she had a beautiful smile, they all thought.

Shortly before Matilda's birth, production began on the movie made from Willa's book *Lost and Found*. The actual filming took the better part of a year to accomplish, and then it was another year in post-production. Willa was thrilled with the actors the studio chose. The leading lady was a former child actress just chomping at the bit to have a grown-up role. She'd been passed over by other studios who couldn't see how she'd matured, but Cyril's nephew and his partner saw her potential immediately. The leading man was a relative newcomer to acting who was handsome in an all-American way and self-deprecating enough to make him come across as charming and approachable on film. The pair of them together was electric.

Once the film was released, it became an instant hit. The video of Willa and her men somehow surfaced again amidst the hype about the movie, and it made even more people want to see *Lost and Found*. Willa Camden became a household name, and it was a huge status symbol among the rich and famous to have worked with Casey Melrose on a house or yacht. Willa's book sales quadrupled, and Casey had a waiting list of potential clients that would take at least two years to get through.

Jackson became a legend around Silicon Valley. He was often called "The Sex Nerd." Being a billionaire on top of that didn't hurt his rep any either.

All three of them got so much fan mail, they had to hire someone just to take on the task of handling it.

And, in perfect poetic justice, *Lost and Found* was nominated for an Academy Award in four different categories—one of which was Best Adapted Screenplay. Another was Best Picture.

When they got the news, Casey whooped and laughed, "We bought you the perfect dress in Monte Carlo to wear to the Oscars, so you'll be noticed on the red carpet. God, you look so sexy in that dress."

"Very funny," Willa replied.

Jackson snorted quietly and then put his arm around her. "You'll be the sexiest and most beautiful woman there, no matter what you wear. Just don't have *this* baby before the awards are all passed out, please?"

"You two are a couple of real comedians. I'm going to be around all of those gorgeous, skinny women, and I'll look like a beach ball with legs."

"Oh, forget them. You're much more beautiful and you're also brilliant and a wonderful mother," Casey assured her. "They'll all be jealous of you."

♡♡♡

Partially due to their notoriety and partly because of their talents, when Willa and her two gorgeous, tuxedoed men stepped out of their limo and walked the red carpet arm in arm, they were showered with as much or more adulation and paparazzi attention than most of the A-listers there. Willa's protruding belly gave her a "real person" vibe that the crowd ate up. Everyone loved her.

And so did the Academy. Willa Camden and Janie Arden won their screenwriting category, and then the movie won Best Picture. As producers of the movie, Jackson, Casey, and Cyril joined Twenty-First Century Wolves onstage to accept the award.

It was an amazing night, and they celebrated afterward at one of the most exclusive Oscar after-parties. People flocked around to congratulate them and bask in their glow of joy and success. Some of them were bad enough actors, however, that they failed to completely disguise their jealousy. That's Hollywood.

♡♡♡

Eventually Willa and Jackson decided to tear down the two houses in La Jolla. The houses didn't work for the needs of their growing family, so they planned to build one incredibly beautiful home in their place. This was fairly common practice in La Jolla where true beachfront property was scarce, but most re-builders had to manage with just one lot, whereas now they had the benefit of two that adjoined.

Jackson and Casey accompanied Willa on her final tour through her house before its demolition. She showed them the place where her dad used to hold her in his lap and read to her by the window in his favorite chair. "That's probably when

I decided I had to be a writer," she explained. "Sometimes I'd talk him into telling me one of his own Hunky Monkey stories, even though they were usually meant for long road trips. Hunky Monkey got up to some crazy antics, that's for sure." She smiled sadly. "Eventually he insisted that I help him out with the story and we'd trade off, trying to outdo each other. When I got older, he'd ask me to read him one of the stories I'd written." She sighed. "He was a great dad. And, boy, did he ever love my mom."

Then she showed them a tiny chip in the kitchen tile where she'd dropped the electric mixer. "My mother was trying to show me how to make a cake, but it freaked me out when the mixer went on in my hands. I jumped back and dropped it and managed to spray cake batter all over the kitchen. My mom just laughed instead of scolding me. That's when I knew I'd never make much of a cook," she admitted ruefully.

They moved out to Rancho Santa Fe while the houses were torn down and the new one built. And they also spent part of that time in Aspen when they wanted a change of scenery or they felt like skiing. It was good to have options, and they knew how lucky they were.

Architectural Digest and *Vanity Fair* both asked to do stories about them and to show off the new La Jolla estate once it was completed and decorated. They would have declined the offers for privacy's sake, but Willa and Jackson were so proud of what Casey had done to the new house, they decided to go along with the idea.

All of their careers continued to flourish, and Jackson made another billion with his new protective anti-hacking software. Banks and credit card companies around the world sang his praises.

He decided to buy a couple of mountains so they could ski the fresh powder whenever they felt like it.

Casey cut way back on business traveling and sent his assistant to do a lot of the footwork. He relied on shopping via the internet so he could spend more time with their children. When people asked him about it, he often swore, "I don't miss the travel in the least because I have heaven on earth right here at home."

Willa had three babies. Matilda was named for the spunky, eponymous character in Roald Dahl's book. Samuel got his name because they all shared a love for Samuel Clemens. Then they decided it would be fun to find something musical for their third—another little girl—and looked and looked for just the right name.

"How about Rhonda? Then if you ever need her to pitch in, you can say, 'Help me, Rhonda.'"

"Casey! Be serious," Willa laughed.

"Then how about Dreamboat Annie, or—I know... Eleanor Rigby? It's catchy, yeah?"

Cracking up, Jackson cautioned, "We'll let her know every day of her life that you were the one who named her that."

"Okay, I have it!" Casey beamed. He waited for them to stop laughing and made sure he had their full attention when he pronounced, "Rhiannon."

"*Yes*," Willa cried. "I love that one."

"And I love Fleetwood Mac, so that one's brilliant," Jackson added.

With his signature face-splitting grin, Casey told them, "Then you can both remind her regularly that her beautiful name was *my* suggestion."

They stopped after Rhiannon's birth because three was their favorite number.

The children were all talented, smart, open-minded, and had beautiful hearts—just like their parents.

The End

Ready for more MMF fun?

Please take a look at my next book *Compelling Urges.* Willa, Jackson, and Casey will show up again in this one about Ivy, Cooper and Bodhi. It's available from Amazon and free with Kindle Unlimited.

And in case you missed it, there is also *The Rule of 3*. A small-town, second chance, billionaire MMF love story that is also available from Amazon and free with Kindle Unlimited. Meet Tanner, Zoë, and Eli... who will melt your heart.

A Modern Love Story
The Rule of
3
"The heart wants
what the heart wants."
ARIELLA TALIX
Bestselling Author of the Lovers in Louisville series

Acknowledgments

First of all, my sincere apologies to the Tesla Company. While it's true that some models of self-driven cars are susceptible to being hacked the way I described, shortly before I wrote this book, Tesla issued a software update to prevent such attacks. I tried to make it clear, however, that Ryker was beyond the garden variety hacker, so I maintain that almost no program is completely impervious to hacking, and this scenario may be improbable, but is still possible.

The lithium batteries, however, can be a danger. The car is engineered with a crash-prevention app that should prevent an explosion or fire, but in certain circumstances, the batteries have been known to ignite or explode. Tesla is investigating the claims of some of these instances. All in all, a Tesla is a beautifully designed electric vehicle that is far safer than a gas-powered car, and the chance of the batteries igniting is actually way less than the chance of a gas tank explosion.

I don't mean to pick on the Tesla Company, but the reason I used that car is because of its tremendous popularity with the successful Silicon Valley people. It seemed like just the car that a guy like Jackson Mitchell would buy as soon as he earned a fortune.

With that all in mind, I would like to thank my technology advisor for this book. He clued me in about DEF CON, hacking, several computer-related issues, and just so happens to also be a proud Tesla owner. Obviously, I couldn't have done this without his input. He accepts the thanks graciously and prefers to remain anonymous. I respect that.

I also need to thank my lovely beta reader Susan who seems like my conscience sometimes while I'm writing. I'm so flattered that with her terribly busy life, she takes the time to read multiple versions of my books and tell me where I've messed up. She is kind-hearted and wise. So, thank you, Susan.

Thanks also to my husband who, the more and more I write, seems to be getting a bigger kick out of each book. He doesn't read them, but he's the best person in the world to bounce ideas around with. I know he'll never sugar-coat, and he has this wonderful, crazy imagination. Like minds, I guess...

Thank you to the other authors who converse with me regularly on Facebook. You keep me laughing, offer great advice, help with promoting books, listen to bellyaching and commiserate about the tough parts of writing and publishing, and are just a wonderful group of brilliant, imaginative people.

A *huge* thank you to the readers who keep downloading and buying my books. 2020 was a year of challenges for everyone, and I'm glad I'm able to provide entertainment for people who crave it during the dark times. I've felt blessed to watch my books succeed, so my year could have been a lot worse, had it not been for all of you.

Thank you to all of the people I've skied with over the years and all over the world. Those times have been some of the best events of my life. I hope that feeling comes through in my books where I've drawn on personal experience.

And finally, thanks to my editorial team. Amy Maranville, we're just getting to know each other, but so far, I'm impressed. The editing process was as painless as can be with your wonderful input. And Mattie Davenport, you're the coolest proofreader ever.

Usually, I make up names for restaurants, hotels, and even towns, but since all of the areas mentioned in this book are so near and dear to my heart, I remained authentic (except for the Pasadena motel). La Jolla isn't the sleepy little beach town I grew up in any longer, but it's still lovely. And Rancho Santa Fe is where I rode my horses for many years. It's beautiful there.

I may have to "stick around" in the area and write more stories. There are so many places I've left unmentioned and unexplored.

On a final note, obviously I have a fondness for artichokes. They are delicious and fun to eat, but I chose the theme because I wanted to demonstrate that California is more than Hollywood and a long coastline of beaches. It's an enormous state with fascinating deserts and mountains so high they're snow-covered all year. There are tiny, rural towns as well as beautiful cities. When people find out I was raised there, I often get asked if I ever met any movie stars. The answer is yes, but they weren't any more interesting or important than the millions of other wonderful residents whose careers span the gamut of, well... everything.

And in case anyone is skeptical that a person raised at the beach can become an avid skier, the answer to that is also a resounding yes, they can. I was far from alone.

Thank you for taking the time to read this book. I hope it made you smile a lot and warmed your heart.

Please stay tuned for information on deals and releases by signing up for my newsletter. https://landing.mailerlite.com/webforms/landing/m6f3i7

And please, leave a review when you finish a book. All authors will thank you.

Books by Ariella Talix

Porter the Importer: Prequel to The Drummonds Series
The story of the Drummond family begins with Molly Drummond and Porter Delaney in this prequel novella. Find out how Porter became the Importer and how Molly started her naughty boutique. Fall in love with Porter and the Drummonds.

Make Believe: The Drummonds- Book One
Lily Drummond's emotional love story with Finn Reilly is romantic suspense with plenty of humor and cute dogs. A page-turner! It's a Canterbury Tales-like saga with a host of interesting characters. It's a little bit like "Fatal Attraction" meets "Lassie."

The Artist: The Drummonds- Book Two
This is David Drummond's story with Amelia Hernandez. It takes place mostly in Paris, and it will pull at your heartstrings. Imagination and beauty from page to page. A sizzling, sexy love story and much, much more.

Save Her: Lovers in Louisville- Book One
This series is a spin-off from The Drummonds. Your favorite characters appear again in supporting roles. *Save Her* is full of suspense and a couple you will adore. Åse Halvorsen is a beautiful jewelry designer, and Gunnar Dahl is a famous mystery writer with a secret.

Saving Him: Lovers in Louisville- Book Two

Sibylla Eliana Xenopoulos (Sibley) was Åse's roommate and best friend in college. She returns to Louisville for a great opportunity and finds love with Gunnar's buddy Leo Spanos. Their chemistry is off the charts, but danger lurks in the shadows.

Savor This: Lovers in Louisville- Book Three

In this passionate and unpredictable story, Halden Dahl, Gunnar's younger brother, is a successful glass artist and total ladies' man. Handsome and talented with an ego as big as all outdoors, has he finally met his match? The answer is yes when he sets his sights on Madison Lassiter—beautiful, passionate, and extremely focused.

The Rule of 3

Since no one actually lives in Louisville in this book, it became a standalone spin-off from the popular "Lovers in Louisville" series. Tanner Lassiter, Zoë Deliban, and a new character, Eli Whittaker, all make for a delightful book about ambition, loyalty, and the deepest, most enduring kind of love. It's a second-chance, billionaire, small-town, MMF love story.

Just Curious

This standalone MMF story is about Willa, a gorgeous and highly successful writer who falls for her billionaire neighbor Jackson and his life-long friend Casey. An old acquaintance causes them trouble, and the seriousness of it escalates to a dangerous level. The setting is mostly in southern California, but they do some globe-trotting as well.

Compelling Urges

This is a very loose spin-off from *Just Curious*, but you don't need to have read *Just Curious* first. Bodhi, Ivy, and Cooper learn how to love despite some serious obstacles thrown in their way. It's another MMF love story set in So. California. How far will they be compelled by their urges?

The Golden Rush *Hearts of Gold- Book One*
This is an MMF romance set during the 1849 California Gold Rush. Six men travel across the country, creating an unbreakable bond of friendship, and find themselves in the right place at the right time. Jasper Langley and Royal Dawson eventually meet Adeline Hart, and both fall head over heels for her. It is a moving tale of perseverance, compassion, and sheer grit.

Fiddle and Fire *Hearts of Gold- Book Two*
The sequel to *The Golden Rush* will be out in 2022.

Info@AriellaTalix.com
https://www.ariellatalix.com/

www.ingramcontent.com/pod-product-compliance
Lightning Source LLC
Chambersburg PA
CBHW060344310726
48976CB00003B/710